THE
SONGWEAVER'S
VOW

LAURA VANARENDONK BAUGH

Æclipse Press
Indianapolis, IN

ISBN 978-1-63165-004-8
www.Aeclipse-Press.com

DEDICATION

To borrow a phrase: No writer is an island, and I am grateful for all the fantastic books I read growing up and as an adult which both inspired and taught me, and for my cadre of writing friends who critique and encourage and critique again.

My monthly writing group, the Indy Scribes, is something I've looked forward to each and every month since our inception nearly five years ago. High fives all around to my valuable critique partners.

And bonus shout-outs to my A-team readers, upon whom I can call to read a scene—or many—on short notice and occasionally at any hour. For this book, these were Stephanie Cain and K.T. Ivanrest, who boldly gave up hours of their lives to read and assist me with this story. Thanks, guys. I owe you a magnificent amount of sushi or chocolate or mead, whichever you prefer.

ACKNOWLEDGMENTS

I must express my gratitude to all the many academics, historians, curators, authors, and enthusiasts who made information available and accessible for research onsite, in books, and online. A complete list would be impractical, but I must especially acknowledge that being able to move among artifacts and recreations was a hugely different experience from my usual virtual research, and I found visiting the recreated villages at Trelleborg and Bork Vikingehavn extremely helpful; I took so many photos for reference! Museet Ribes Vikinger (the Ribes Viking Museum), Nationalmuseet (the National Museum of Denmark), and Vikingeskibs Museet (the Viking Ship Museum) in Roskilde provided a great deal of information into historic customs, travel, tools, and daily life, in a way I could not experience purely through reading or looking at photographs. Thank you to all the historians, curators and docents, and reenactors who obliged my questions and photography.

Thank you also to Annitha Faurholt, who stayed late to welcome us into Den Gemle Arrest, a charming jail-turned-bed-and-breakfast in Ribe (the oldest extant town in Scandinavia and fiercely proud of their Viking heritage).

And finally, an enormous and personal thank you to my enormously patient husband, who allowed me to drag him to "just one more" historic site or museum after another and waited uncomplainingly for Legoland. His generosity is much appreciated.

CHAPTER 1

The attack came at dawn.

Euthalia woke to the terse, worried voices of men, and she crawled into the dawn light. "What is it?" she asked, only half-expecting an answer.

But Miloslav stopped mid-sentence to turn toward her. "Get back!" he snapped. "Hide yourself!"

Euthalia swept her eyes across the camp, seeing men picking up weapons, and looked up the river, where she saw a dragon.

Its head rose from the water and curled upward, glaring down upon the surface in disdain. The river barely rippled around its sinuous neck. Its body was long and narrow, and she saw now oars protruded from either side, launching it across the river. Behind it came other boats, also bearing beast heads, but somehow—because she had seen it first, or because it was the nearest, or because for just a moment it had been a real sea serpent in her mind—the first one seemed the most frightening.

Pirates, she realized. Terrifying, horrific men who went a-viking to prey on traders.

Traders like them.

She shrank backward. "Do we run? Hide?"

"Get out of sight," repeated Miloslav. "They may wish to trade, not fight. They are traders themselves as often as pirates. They may wish only for news of Byzantium, or trade in southern goods."

But Euthalia, who had never been a warrior, yet looked at the ships and knew this was not the approach of a trading party. And the men with Miloslav knew it, by the way they gripped their weapons, and Miloslav knew it too, by the way his mouth stayed tight at the corners as he spoke. Her father knew it by the way he came to join Miloslav, weapon in hand and looking more worried than ever she had seen him, even on this trip when he had failed to marry her to a Byzantine merchant.

Euthalia turned and scanned for a place to hide. She settled for a bundle of fabric, bright with southern dyes, and wriggled beneath it. Any part of her which remained exposed would look like spilled fabric and would not betray her.

She could see nothing now. She curled up, trying to disappear beneath the pile, and listened through the muting of the fabric.

Her father's voice came first, calling down the river. "What do you carry to trade?"

For a moment there was no answer, and she tried to imagine the dragon-boat sailing by, eyes forward and passing unseeing over their camp, the sea-serpent leaving them all untouched. But a moment later, there was the unmistakable scrape of a hull running aground, like massive claws against sandy rock, and she knew the dragon had landed.

"What do you carry?" The voice was gruff, huge, the voice of a sea serpent or a man who rode a dragon. It wrapped about the words as if familiar with them but not quite comfortable, a second language.

"Good sailing to you, and safe travels to you as to ourselves," called her father Tikhomir. His voice held a note she had never heard before, not only the unexpected deference she had heard in Byzantium but an additional undertone of fear. Her father, a chief and a chief of warriors, feared these Northmen come down the river.

Come down the river, she realized, through her father's lands, or near enough to them. For it was impossible to reach the south and east from the north and west without passing through the middle, and certainly these boats had sailed this river down from their North home. She wavered between fierce indignation at the effrontery of sailing through her father's lands without permission and horror that they might have sailed past her home, might have stopped, might have killed or taken her mother and her brothers and all the people she knew there.

The man with the dragon voice did not return her father's greeting. "You come from the city, I see. Tell us what you bring away."

"Spices," said Tikhomir, "and silks, and dyes for fabrics. And iron ore, to be smelted into steel. It will make fine weapons."

"Hm." The voice seemed to consider. "Their ore is better, no argument. It will make better weapons, that is true." There was a slight sound of steps, and the voice faded and rose as it spoke; Euthalia guessed he was turning to take in all their men, Miloslav and the others. "We will take the ore and the dyes, and half the spices."

Tikhomir hesitated only just noticeably. "And will you pay in coin or barter?"

A laugh arose from the dragon's throat, and then from many, many more throats. Euthalia did not know how many men rode the dragon-ship and the other boats, but she knew she had seen many oars. How many? Twenty at a side? That was a fair guess, making forty per boat. And there had been three boats. That made one hundred twenty hostile men, warriors who rode dragons and spoke like sea serpents.

One hundred twenty, to oppose her father's band of sixteen.

Euthalia could stand it no longer. She pressed herself against the ground, the weight of the fabric over her, and peered out with one eye from beneath the bales of cloth. Now she could see, though it was hardly enough to be helpful. She knew her father's boots, and those were Miloslav's beside him, and the big set of leather-wrapped feet facing them, visible between their ankles, must belong to the man with the dragon's voice.

The laughter slowed, and the man with the dragon voice spoke again, a trace of levity still coloring his tone. "The ore, and the dyes, and half the spices, or all and as many slaves as survive the fight."

Her father did not answer immediately, and that was his mistake. There was a nearly-imperceptible movement in the third set of feet, simultaneous with a rub of oiled leather and a soft sound like a punch into a cow's flank. Miloslav's right foot took a step back, hesitated, and then he folded to his knees, clutching somewhere on the front of his torso.

"He will not be one of the slaves," said the dragon voice.

Miloslav tipped forward into the sandy dirt, one arm splayed and the other trapped beneath him. He had not even struck a blow in his defense or his chieftain's, a sad and pitiful death.

"Now," said the dragon voice, "will you fight, and die? Or will you surrender, and live as slaves?"

"Wait," urged her father. "I have another prize to offer. We are traders, and we would do business as men of trade."

"Oh?" The dragon voice was only faintly curious. "What can you offer that is worth your lives?"

Her father's feet turned away from Miloslav, bleeding his last on the sand, and came directly toward the pile of goods where Euthalia hid. She only just had time to wonder for one horrific instant if he meant *her* when he flung back the fabrics and seized her by the upper arm.

"Here!" he said, pulling her upward. "Here, what do you think of this?"

Euthalia stared at him, unable to look even to the river pirate standing just beyond Miloslav's fallen body. He could not—he would not—

But her father was not looking at her. "She will certainly be a prettier prize to bring home," he said, and he was using his merchant's voice. "A woman is useful in ways a man is not."

"Father!" she gasped, pulling weakly away from him. "You can't do this!"

Now he turned on her. "I said I would get you a husband on this trip," he snarled. "You knew it would not be one of your choosing."

"Father?" repeated the dragon voice. Euthalia looked at the raider, tall and armored in mail and carrying an axe worn with experience. His helmet wrapped about his eyes, shielding them and hiding half his expression. What was visible, however, showed a curious blend of emotions: pride, at having driven a chieftain to offer his own daughter in payment for his life, and disgust, that such a man could be so driven.

"It is not a husband you ask for her, I think," said the man with the dragon voice. "Nor is she, even a pretty and, as you say, useful girl, worth the price of sixteen male slaves." He glanced down. "Fifteen."

Now her father straightened. "You will not have fifteen slaves, not from us. I will die before I am taken, and I have other fine fighters who will not be taken easily, and you will need to kill them. You have enough men to overrun us, but not without losses of your own."

"My men are not afraid to die in battle. They would be pleased, in fact, and would consider it honorable." The helmeted man frowned as he looked over the remaining warriors of Tikhomir's party. "Though perhaps it would be less of an honor to die facing so few, and so disreputable, it is true."

"Whether they are pleased to die or not, it leaves you with fewer men to make your next raid," pressed Euthalia's father. "You may take our goods without risk by accepting the

11

girl, to your profit, or you may fight us and take only what remains." He put a knife to Euthalia's throat. "To your loss."

What was he saying? Euthalia reeled. He was bartering her like an ingot of ore or a bag of spice!

The helmeted man quirked one corner of his mouth upward in a smile. "We will take the girl," he said, "and I will go one better for you, since you are such a reasonable man of trade. I will make her a dragon's bride, a sacrifice to purchase your life." He shook his head. "But even so fine a bride is not worth fifteen male slaves, and not after an insult to my men's valor. You will send thralls as her dowry."

And then everything happened at once. The men behind the man with the dragon's voice rushed forward, raising axes and hammers and swords, and Tikhomir's band clustered together about their chief, or at least some of them. Tikhomir flung her down and stepped back.

Euthalia hit the ground hard and saw, between the ankles of the surrounding men, that a half-dozen had run for the woods, leaving their chieftain and their comrades. Leather-armored warriors followed hard after, disappearing with them into the trees. On the beach, a warrior called Daniil charged the pirates, shouting for others to follow, and was cut down mid-cry.

Tikhomir's voice barked out orders. "Stand down, men! Those who fled are given as slaves. A man who lacks faith in his chieftain deserves none. And those who remain—take Kazimir, and hold him for the ropes. He defied me thrice last year, and I'll not fight for him now."

Kazimir blinked once at his treacherous chief and then lunged desperately with his axe, swinging at both pirate and tribal comrade. But he could not face all directions at once, and the men from the beast-headed boats seized him from behind, dragging him backward and down and disarming him. Euthalia saw several men taking his sword and knife and other gear, but none of Kazimir's comrades protested. They were glad to be rid of him, as her father was, or glad he had been chosen rather than them, or simply afraid to upset the fragile equilibrium by challenging the pirates' assumption.

Kazimir was bound and held on his knees in the sand, heavy hands on his shoulders to keep him in place. His hands were bound behind his back, but his mouth was unhindered, and he cursed Tikhomir freely and fiercely, swearing to return and wreak his vengeance upon Tikhomir and his family and all their village. He had threats for his former brothers-in-arms, too, and vile words for their treachery in allowing him to be taken, listening to such an untrustworthy lord. "It will come!" he warned. "Your turn will come, when he will toss you like a half-gnawed bone to a stray dog! And pray that day of betrayal comes before I return to avenge myself, for no treachery can stand against the weight of the revenge I will take upon you all!"

The man in the helmet was utterly unimpressed by these continuous threats, and he turned his back on Kazimir and spoke, his dragon's voice carrying easily over Kazimir's insistent invective. "Let us wait here a short time, to see how many of your men have been brought back to their new fate."

And so they waited, uneasy in the knowledge that if not enough tribesmen were brought back to thralldom, the number would be made up from those standing upon the sandy bar. Euthalia looked up at the familiar faces around her, reading their conflict as they hoped for their friends to escape and yet hoped they would be caught.

No one spoke.

Warriors are not accustomed to fleeing, and these woods were not familiar to Tikhomir's men. Within fifteen minutes, the first captive emerged, bound and pushed ahead by three river pirates. A few moments later, another appeared, and then another. With each appearance, a painful throb of unhappy relief went through the little band about Euthalia, surrounded by countless mailed and leather-clad men.

Someone had gone to the beast-headed boats and brought back iron shackles, which were fitted upon Kazimir and the new captives.

"And now," said the man with the dragon's voice, "the girl."

Euthalia couldn't move. She couldn't speak. She looked up, and her father grasped her roughly under the arm and hauled her to her feet. "Don't be difficult now," he warned. "Be a good bride. You knew you'd take a husband on this trip."

Euthalia stared at the men on their knees, their shackled hands hanging before them. She was not going as a wife, no matter what her father might say.

Her throat seized, and she could not decide what to say even if she could speak. Should she plead for mercy from her father? Useless. Threaten vengeance, like Kazimir? Her revenge was even less likely than his, and threats were unbecoming in a woman. Should she weep, as she saw one young captive doing quietly on his knees? That would only please her captors, she thought, for they were vicious and cruel men. Quietly and stoically accept her fate, as other captives were doing? It seemed unthinkable.

But one of the beast-boat men was reaching for her, and she had to say something, had to act now or she would forever lose the opportunity. She gulped, choked on the first word, and then spat at her father, "I hope the sale of your daughter and your warriors' respect was worth your cowardly life."

A laugh and a whoop went up from a few of the beast-boat men who understood her, or at least her tone, and the dragon's-voice laugh boomed over them all. It surprised her. Euthalia had not meant to amuse them, had only meant to shame the father exposed as a lying and weak man despite his position, and she was a little afraid of their response.

She did not have the opportunity to see her father's reaction, for she was already being drawn away, but she imagined—she hoped—he flushed hot with shame, and she hoped his remaining warriors turned baleful eyes on him. Perhaps, when they reached home again, her father's stories would not be the only ones told. Perhaps others would explain that they had not lost comrades in a fearful and honorable battle, but that husbands and sons and fathers had been traded away for the life of a chieftain who would not fight, who hid behind the sale of his eldest child and daughter.

She could hope that would be how it ended.

Euthalia was guided into the boat with the dragon's head. She was not bound, not like the men, but she knew that was a mere formality. She was just as much a prisoner—more, because she did not know how to fight as they did. She could not fight, she could not flee; she was a thrall, just as they were. Helpless, just as they were.

Afraid, just like they were.

The other captives were shared out among the boats, two or three each. The crying boy went to another boat, which pained Euthalia for some reason. Maybe she wanted someone who expressed what she could not yet. Kazimir came to her boat, still snarling between his teeth, and was pushed into the belly of the boat. The trade goods, already sorted as they waited for the captives to be brought, were loaded onto the boats.

Euthalia would not—would *not*—look back as the boats were pushed again into the river. She did not want to see her father standing upon the shore, safe with his remaining men. He would not see her afraid and miserable in the slavery into which he had sold her. He would see her sailing into her new life with the fearsome Vikings as boldly as he should have faced them himself.

And if the brisk wind drew slow, hot tears to her eyes as she turned into it, he was too far to see them, and so it did not matter.

CHAPTER 2

There were many more men than forty in each boat; nearly twice that many, Euthalia observed when she came to herself enough to start looking around her. Not all rowed at once, and alternating benches were left empty. As she watched the rowers at work she saw that the benches were very close to one another, so that if each had been manned, the rowers would have had to curtail their strokes to avoid bumping one another. The extra benches then were for urgent work, maybe, or some situation other than cruising down an easily-navigable river.

She had been placed at the center of the boat, where warriors surrounded her on all sides and made escape, by either flight or suicide into the river, difficult. Below the planking upon which she sat, water swished with the boat's movement, the inevitable bilge which crept always into any vessel. Several men were bailing with casual efficiency, handing buckets up and tossing water over the side.

There was an exchange among a couple of these men standing ankle-deep in the belly of the boat, and then with a couple of the men on the decking itself. Euthalia could not understand their speech, but she followed their meaning well enough when one of the warriors turned to the two new slaves and gestured them down into the sloshing water.

One of the men had remained grim-faced and silent since his first reappearance as a captive. Euthalia had seen him of course, but she hardly knew the man. Now, he seemed both resigned and pragmatic; he rose and went to the hold, stepping with hardly a flinch into the cold water, taking the bucket with his shackled hands and starting to bail and pass up the bucket.

Kazimir was not so willing to bow under his new obligations. He got to his feet and spat on the decking. "Down there? I am no catfish to mildew in the belly of a ship. I am a warrior, and if you want my service, you'll take me as a fighter. I am a fighting man, and I'm meant to hold a sword or an axe, not a bucket. You can take your bucket and—"

The sailors did not understand Kazimir's words any more than he understood theirs, but they followed his meaning and defiance well enough, and at this point one bent and snatched his ankles as another shoved him hard backwards. Kazimir went down on the decking like felled timber, and before he could even roll or sit up, the two had lifted him and heaved his shoulders overboard between the working oars.

His feet they kept, braced against the shield-rail. Euthalia leapt to her feet and rushed to the edge. Another sailor caught her shoulder, but he did not pull her back. Perhaps he wanted her to see.

Kazimir hung with his head below the water, his bound arms working frantically to snatch at the shifting oars. He was trying to lift himself by the strength of his torso, but the continuous stroke of the oars kept pushing him down. His movements grew more frenzied as he jerked upward, twice striking his head against an oar, and then his movements weakened.

At this, the two warriors hauled him up by his ankles, dragging him none too gently over the edge and dropping him beside an empty rowing bench. Kazimir was alive and awake, and he choked and coughed for a moment, wiping his face on his dripping sleeve, and then he began to curse his captors once more.

A sailor pointed to the water in the hold, where the other new slave was bailing steadily, his eyes well away from Kazimir. Kazimir looked at the pointing sailor and spat in his face.

As quick as a bird, they heaved him over once more, as the rowers laughed and pulled steadily. On another boat, other captives had been pushed to the rail to watch Kazimir hang and struggle and choke.

Euthalia squeezed her fingers into the worn wood. Surely this was too long—surely they would kill him. Would they kill him for mere defiance? But of course they might. Her father had never suffered a recalcitrant slave, either. Kazimir was no use to them as he was, and already his punishment was encouraging obedience in the others newly taken.

At last Kazimir's struggles slowed again, and after a moment without any writhing or clawing at the oars, the two warriors hauled him up again. This time Kazimir did not respond. One bent to slap him awake. Kazimir choked and jerked as if astounded to find himself alive, and his eyes were white-rimmed as he stretched to feel the decking beneath him.

They pushed him toward the hold and kicked him over the edge, and he splashed heavily into the swill as the others dodged. Kazimir took the bucket someone shoved at him, and he began to bail, still coughing up water.

Euthalia drew a shuddering breath. What cruel madmen these were. All that she had ever heard of them was true. And she had been given to them, a sacrifice to their monstrous cruelty.

She was half-surprised, if grateful, that none of them had yet simply forced her right there on the deck, in full view of the others. She had heard of such things. Such things were probably yet to come. She wondered if she should hope for escape or for death, and wondered which might be less difficult.

She had no idea of how far they traveled before twilight, but with the regular rotation of rowers, she guessed it was much further than her father's party had ever traveled in a day, and well beyond his reach to follow and reclaim his daughter and warriors even had he dared to try. They beached the boats and made several small fires, where cooking was begun. The slaves were tethered by their shackles to several saplings, near enough to see one another but not so near that they could reach one another.

Euthalia was led to a fire and pointed to a place to sit, where she did so. She was given food, like the warriors and the new slaves. Then a helmeted figure came out of the deepening twilight, and she realized she had not seen the man with the dragon voice—how could she have forgotten him?—since the first hour of her captivity.

"You will stay on the boat tonight," he said in his deep, enormous voice, and her stomach coiled painfully about the food she had just eaten. *This—this is it. Father offered me to this man, and he's come to claim his prize. On the boat, out of the view of his men—he'll take me first, and then leave me to them.*

When he gestured for her to rise, her legs had turned to porridge and she could not obey. He reached down, and she flinched, and he took her forearm in a warrior's clasp and pulled her upright. He led her toward the dragon-headed boat.

He took her to the stern, farthest from the land, and pointed her toward the deck. Every fiber in her screamed at her not to go down upon that planking, even as some other part of her warned her to obey him lest he hurt her worse. And if they had half-drowned Kazimir for refusing to bail water, what would they not do to a mere woman who refused a woman's duty to the man who claimed her?

He handed her a heavy fur—bearskin, she thought without looking, for she could not take her eyes from him, though the helmet and the shadows hid his face entirely. "Sleep here," he said. "If you slip over the side, the night guards will hear you in the water. If you come down the boat, you will wake the warriors sleeping on the deck. If you get into the woods, you will die of hunger or be caught by the local tribes, a fate far worse than yours here. Stay, and you will be an offering."

Offering. The words made her shiver with thoughts of the ancient sacrifices to the spirits of the land. But her head nodded once, as if she understood or agreed, and he turned and left her standing on the upward sloping decking.

At last, after several minutes of staring toward the fires, as if she could pick him out, she sat with her back against the rising beam which formed the stern, and she wrapped herself in the bearskin. It was warm, and the most comfort she had known all the day, and against all expectation she fell asleep.

She woke in the night, disturbed by something—a snore or fart from the sleeping warriors scattered across the boat, maybe. She could just make out their sleeping forms gently outlined by the moonlight.

Her captor had been right; she could not have picked her way through them without waking at least one. They lay close together, with hardly space for a girl's foot to slip between, and even with the moon it was difficult to distinguish men from boat.

She stood, slowly, keeping the bearskin wrapped about her, and looked over either side of the boat. Due to the upward curve of the stern, it was a fair drop to the river below, and it would be impossible to enter the water silently. The man with the dragon voice had chosen his prison well; it was open and spacious and inescapable.

She let her eyes wander along the shore and picked out more men sleeping near the remnants of the cookfires. Beyond them, dark shapes moved, barely discernible against the trees: sentries to guard the men and the boats by night, and to prevent any of the new captives from escaping as well.

Euthalia slid back to her place on the deck. Even if she could escape, she had nowhere to go. She could find her way home only by following the river, the same water-road her captors would be taking. She did not have the woodcraft, much less the tools she would need, to survive alone in the deep woods, even if she did not meet any of the tribes hostile to her father's people. And if she did meet them, she would hardly be in a better position than she was here.

She settled the bearskin over herself, tucking in the edges. No, she was not surrendering, not entirely. She was simply awaiting her more opportune moment. The foolish warrior acted with no chance of success, and if she were not a warrior, she was also not a fool.

They would grow careless, if she appeared quiet and compliant. Already they did not bind her like they did the men. Eventually they would forget to guard her, and she could make her way out of their camp, perhaps even freeing one of her father's warriors to guide and protect her on the journey home. Yes, she would wait, and she would succeed.

CHAPTER 3

They traveled north for days, following the winding of the rivers. Four times they stopped and traded for goods with small towns or at sandy bars where other merchants—sometimes in boats like their own, sometimes with wagons—waited. They traded in silver, in beads, in slaves. Two of her father's warriors were sold, including the boy who had cried. Euthalia wished she could recall his name, so she had some other way to remember him and could name him when she would eventually tell of her father's treachery. Though perhaps it would be no favor to describe his tears to his family.

The silver coins they received looked much like the coins she had seen in Byzantium, and she marveled at their ubiquitous value. The warrior-traders also took or gave gold and silver arm rings, or silver chains. She watched one man cut links from a silver chain to pay for a worked copper brooch. She found a silver coin in the mud, nearly lost in a footprint, and she tucked it into her boot. She would need money, to bribe aid or to buy supplies on her flight. This was a start.

Thrice she saw the river pirates take gold, spices, ivory, and fine fabrics from merchants who were not quick enough to flee the beast-headed boats. Twice the merchants were left alive and mostly unharmed; once the pirates killed the men who offered resistance and then took all their goods.

She began to learn their language, too. She tried not to let on how many words she had picked up—best if they underestimated her and believed her stupid and ignorant—but gradually she began to learn the more common names of things and the daily actions on the boat.

And then, after three weeks of rowing northward, they veered from the river into a tributary, and then into a stream which fed it, and so on upstream. At last the crews cheered as they drew within sight of a village on the water, full of low earthen houses with grass-growing roofs or low-hanging thatch. Women, children, and a smaller number of men appeared to wave and welcome. With a sinking stomach, Euthalia realized that this was the raiders' home. She had missed her chance for escaping along the route; this was where they would stay.

Rough planking provided docks along the marshy edges, and each of the boats—without their beast heads, now—were guided expertly into place. There was much noise and embracing and calling back and forth, and twice someone was crowded off the dock and into the water by the joyful greeters. But there was much laughter each time as they were rescued, and it was apparent that no harm was done and no offense was taken.

Then the unloading of the cargo began, and this included the captives. The new slaves were set to work carrying coffers of precious metals or iron ore or other heavy goods, and Euthalia was pointed toward a woman older than her mother. Words were exchanged, none of them any she knew, and the woman gestured for Euthalia to follow her. Clutching her bearskin, Euthalia did.

Perhaps this was her fate, and this was her new mistress. She had a lined face, from smiles or scowls or weathering, and no hair visible beneath her white hood. Euthalia wondered if she were a reasonable owner or a harridan who would make her miserable.

The woman led Euthalia past a dark longhouse to a smaller, square house set into a mound of earth, with grass from the roof overhanging the door, and took her hand to tug her inside. The house was small and simply furnished, but it was as complete a home as Euthalia had seen, with a raised sleeping area and a table and chairs and shelves of utensils and a few stored pots of food. The woman guided Euthalia into a chair, saying something which must mean *sit down*, and opened a trunk. She withdrew several articles of clothing and spread them on the table for Euthalia's perusal.

The clothing looked lovely, even in its strangeness. Anything would have looked good to Euthalia—her own clothing was stiff and stinking after weeks in the boat—but this was appealing on its own. It was made of wool and flax, and the pinafore to hang over the shift was dyed a dark blue, making it a fine and expensive piece. Euthalia's father had paid a premium price for such a dye. The shift was a pale natural color and pleated, another luxury.

The woman fingered the material and offered it to Euthalia. She asked a question and waited with eyebrows raised. Euthalia fingered the material just as she had done and nodded obligingly.

The woman picked up the clothing and gestured for Euthalia to rise and follow. They went toward the stream again, but upward of the docks, where they came to a small wooden house set on the shore. It was, Euthalia was delighted to find, a bathhouse. The woman took off her white hood, revealing short-cropped hair, and indicated for Euthalia to strip off her filthy clothing.

She had never been so grateful for a bath in her life. The woman even produced a comb, finely carved of antler or horn, and helped Euthalia pick apart the weeks' worth of tangles which had taken over her hair. When they had finished, Euthalia put on the shift and pinafore, fastening the latter with two small domed brooches. Euthalia ran her hands down the pinafore, reveling in the feeling of being clean.

"Good, good," praised the woman, using one of the first words Euthalia had grasped.

They returned to the house, the woman continuing with a stream of words Euthalia could not catch. This time she noticed the door latch, an ingenious device entirely of wood to both latch and bar the door. They were clever craftsmen here.

Once inside, the woman went back to the chest and this time drew out a red cape. It was a full half-circle and hung to Euthalia's ankles, and with it over her shoulders Euthalia felt herself a great lady. The cape was trimmed in fox fur, and she stroked the fur as she looked down at herself. For the first time, she wondered if she might not find herself in total despair in this new place. Surely they would not treat their whores in such fine fashion. Perhaps she was not to be a thrall after all.

The woman pointed to herself. "Birna," she said. "Birna. I am Birna." She pointed to Euthalia and made a questioning face, eyebrows raised.

Euthalia realized this was the first time anyone had asked her about herself, even just her name. "Euthalia," she said. There was no need to specify her family; she was her father's daughter no more.

Birna nodded. "Euthalia." And she pointed for Euthalia to sit in the chair again.

This was not so bad. Birna had combed out Euthalia's hair, though her own was cropped short like the other thralls Euthalia had noticed. That might imply that Euthalia was not to be a slave, at least not yet. She hoped that was the case, anyway.

But of course, the man in the dragon helmet. The man who had taken her from her father. He had said she would be a dragon's bride; of course he referred to himself. It seemed he really meant to marry her, not just take her as a thrall.

Euthalia took a breath. It was not what she would have wanted, but it was not after all so different from what she had expected, a husband unknown to her in a strange land. Instead of rich Byzantium, she was in a Northland village, but in the end it was not so different. She was prepared for this.

Birna gestured with an open, flat palm toward Euthalia—Stop? Stay?—and went out, leaving the door open. Euthalia watched as she crossed a short distance to an open shelter with an earthen oven, where she collected several pieces. She returned and offered a flatbread to Euthalia.

It was fresher than the boat's provisions, at least, as they had saved the spices and treats to bring back to the village. And Euthalia, no longer surrounded by dozens of strange male warriors, found herself relaxing enough to feel real hunger. She devoured the bread.

"Good, good," praised Birna. She nodded. "Eat. Tomorrow, *blóta*."

Euthalia did not know the word. "Blo—what?"

Birna smiled, a little tightly, and drew her hand across her throat.

Euthalia stared at her, the bread going tasteless in her mouth.

CHAPTER 4

The entire village had turned out, and to Euthalia's unskilled eye, they seemed to be dressed in finer array than before. Everywhere the clothing was bright with color and trimmed with embroidery or fur. The men's cheeks were freshly shaved, and slightly reddened skin around the eyebrows showed where both men and women had subjected themselves to the same plucking Euthalia had undergone that morning.

They cheered when they saw her, whooping and clapping, and she felt very self-conscious. What did they expect of her? Had Birna meant her death?

The crowd surrounded her loosely and walked toward the edge of the village, where a newly-built house waited, conspicuous with its raw unweathered wood and the younger, greener grass on its roof. A shallow pit, long and wide like the base of another house which had not been built, lay to one side. Two men were leading a brown horse across the field toward them.

An old man came toward her, bent with years and work, and she saw by his close-cropped hair and the rounded iron collar about his neck that he was a thrall, kept for light work or charity in his old age. He nodded toward her several times and worked his mouth around a language rusty with disuse. "Wife," he said in her own tongue, his voice high with age. "Wife. Bride. You are the bride."

She remembered the words of the helmeted man, the man with the dragon's voice, accepting her father's offer of her. Her father had argued he had promised her a husband, and the helmeted man had agreed to fulfill his promise despite Tikhomir's cowardly bargain. Euthalia had not believed him then nor at any time during the journey. But had he spoken the truth? Was she to be properly wed, instead of given as a slave?

"A bride to whom?" she asked the old man. "Where is my husband?"

"Bride," he repeated, obviously pleased that he remembered the word. "To the dragon."

She started at him, certain she had not heard him correctly. Or perhaps he had not remembered the word, as it was obviously long years since he had spoken his native tongue. "No, who is my husband? The man with the helmet, where is he?"

He nodded. "The dragon," he repeated. "You are the bride. A sacrifice bride, to the dragon."

An agonized bellow interrupted him, and she looked up as a man finished drawing a knife across the throat of the horse in the shallow pit. Two other men held it by the ears as it bled, eyes wide, until it went to its knees. The crowd cheered.

Euthalia's heart froze and her breath stopped in her throat. *A sacrifice bride.*

The horse dropped to the ground and rolled partly to one side, tongue lolling. Several men stepped forward and began to butcher it, blood running freely over the ground.

Euthalia bent and vomited onto the grass.

The old man took her shoulder, leaning upon her as much as steadying her. "No, no," he said, "you go in. Sacrifice, big honor. He comes tonight. Not man. Dragon's bride."

Euthalia pushed at him, her heart racing. "No, stop," she breathed. "Not me. Not that. I will be a slave, but don't do that."

The villagers closed about her, speaking rapidly in excited tones, and they pressed her toward the house. She saw several of them carried torches, and she realized they would burn her within the new wooden house. "No!" she screamed. "No!"

But she could not escape them, for in each direction she turned she was pushed back, and as she grabbed at the edges of the door to hold herself back they pressed together against her, still cheerily arguing in words she could not understand, and she shouted protest as she fell through the doorway. The wooden door, with the clever wooden latch she had admired, closed solidly behind her.

There were no windows. Some light crept through the high parts of the roof, where the woven wattle abutted the thatching, but the interior was only dimly visible. She could make out a table, and two chairs, and a long chest, and two shelves upon the wall lined with objects she could not quite see. Along one wall was a raised sleeping surface, with painted sliding panels to enclose it for warmth in the winter. Now the door stood open, and she could see a pile of sheepskins.

It was a very lifelike grave, if it were a grave. But she had heard that the great men of the North were sent to death with all the possessions they might need in the next life, and so the completeness only frightened her further.

The torches were not set to the house. Instead she heard singing, and then the crackling of fire, but at a safe distance. They were roasting the horse, she decided, feasting upon her death.

Or maybe, if they had not killed her yet, maybe she was not to die. Maybe she really was a bride, and she had been put here to await her new husband, a man so dangerous and so respected in battle that he was called the Dragon, and the old slave had not had the words to explain a sobriquet.

She tried the door, hoping they had gone far enough and were distracted enough, but it was barred from without. She was trapped within the little house, helpless. She could only wait.

The dragon came at night.

Euthalia had sat long in the dark, her knees hugged close to her chest, wrapped in the bearskin the helmeted man had given her on the boat. She sat on the trunk pushed against the wall; she could not bear to sit upon the bed. Once in a while she looked at it and then looked away.

Was the dragon a figurative name for a dreadful man, a warrior feared above all others? Or was it a literal monster she awaited? Would she be raped or devoured? It was hard, not speaking a language. She could not even know what she should fear.

Birna had not seemed to worry for her, and she had even seemed happy as she prepared Euthalia for her bridal day. But that did not mean safety; Euthalia had seen people happily sacrifice animals, even precious ones, without grief or reservation. How much more should a dragon's prize be offered willingly?

And then there was a sound outside, a subtle sound which could have meant nothing on its own, but Euthalia knew, she *knew*, that he had come and now stood outside the door.

Warrior or beast? Man or monster?

She was seized with the sudden terror that she would scream when the door opened, and if it were a monster a scream would incite it, and if it were a man a scream would infuriate him, and so she pressed a handful of the fox-edged cape into her mouth as the wooden latch lifted.

The door swung open.

Euthalia made a tiny whimpering sound into the cape and squeezed her eyes shut. Instantly she could not stand her helplessness and opened her eyes again. But it did her no more good to look than to not—the moonless night offered no aid to her eyes, and as the door swung shut she could only get a sense of a bulk before it. He was tall and broad, if a man.

She could hear breathing. It was not her own; she was holding her breath, she realized. She swallowed and forced herself to speak. Her voice was unsteady. "Welcome, husband. I am the dragon's bride." If a man, would he even understand her?

"What are you called?"

Relief ran through her like water at hearing words so plainly spoken. For a moment she could hardly answer. "My name is Euthalia."

"Euthalia." He tested the foreign word, trying it, tasting it. After a moment, he seemed to approve it. "Euthalia. My bride."

She was so grateful to find he was human that she thought suddenly she might be able to bear what would come next. They said it was not unpleasant, if not done by force, and could even be agreeable, if the man took care to please his woman as well. She giggled a little with nervous confusion and embarrassment at her own inconsistency.

"Why do you laugh?" came the voice. It was a deep voice, and powerful, as if even the helmeted man had been only a child and had grown at last to full manhood.

She shook her head, embarrassed further. She had the uncomfortable impression that he could see her despite the darkness. "I do not laugh at you, of course, I only—I was so afraid, and now I am so relieved you are human."

There was a shifting in the darkness, and the pressure of the air about her changed as he leaned closer, lowering his head near hers. "Why do you think I am human?"

Euthalia froze, unable to speak, unable to move, unable to think of anything but the powerful voice and all her terrors of the dragon. Arms—or claws, or *something*—grasped her about the bearskin, cocooning her like a child, and then there was a brilliant prismatic burst of light, just for an instant, and she screamed without hesitation or shame.

CHAPTER 5

The light faded, so quickly that she might have imagined it but for the aftermarks in her eyes, and the man—not a man—set her down again on the trunk. "Euthalia," he said again, still working his mouth about the name. "I will come to you this day's night."

Then he turned again to the door and went out into the starlight too pale to illuminate him.

For a long moment Euthalia sat still, clutching herself beneath the bearskin, shivering beyond any cold in the mild night. He had come. He had done—something. There had been a bright light, no, a collision of many bright lights of all colors, and then nothing.

What if it had not been nothing? It felt as if only an instant had passed, but what if she had been dazed or unaware?

But no, she felt nothing in her relevant parts, and she had always heard it was painful at first even if the man were not a monster. And her fine wool and linen clothing was unshifted, and the bearskin undisturbed, and there was no reason he would rewrap her so carefully. No, she had not been touched. Not yet.

For a long time she sat on the chest, and at last the pounding of her heart slowed and her muscles ceased quivering and she began to feel exhausted from her fear. Whatever was to have happened this night, it seemed to have happened. She looked at the sleeping niche, thick with sheepskins and sheltered by the sliding door. He had said he would come the next night, which meant she had nothing to fear from the bed this night.

She uncurled herself from her place on the trunk, limbs stiff and protesting, and went to the bed. The sheepskins were delightfully soft and comforting after her terror. She nestled into them and slept.

She woke as the sunlight slipped into the sleeping niche via a chink in the external wall, where a knot had worked loose of its board. She had not closed the sliding door, not ready yet to be closed in, and she could see sunlight slanting through the main room of the house, dust motes dancing in its light. It was morning, and she was alive and whole.

She rose and straightened her clothing. Who would be waiting for her outside? What would they want of her? The dragon or whatever he might be had not seemed particularly displeased with her, but he had not taken her as a husband took his bride, and perhaps that would upset the people who had needed her as a sacrifice. What would she say to them, if the old thrall could translate?

But she needed to find a privy, and she was thirsty after her long vigil in the night, and there was nothing to be gained by delay. So she opened the door—unlocked—shaded her eyes against the light, and went out into the day.

Everything was the same, and yet everything was different. She hesitated on the threshold, frowning uncertainly. Her house was where it had been, yes, and there was the stream where it had been. It was not far to the dark longhouse. But the other houses were larger, slightly taller it seemed, though she had nothing but memory for comparison.

There should be people active and visible, even so early in the morning. No hours of daylight were to be wasted, especially not in the north. But she saw no one.

She went a few steps out on to the packed grass, worn with traffic, and turned in a circle. Had the village emptied overnight? Why would they abandon their homes, and where had they gone?

"Euthalia!" called a voice, and she spun toward it. "Good morning, Euthalia! Have you had your breakfast yet?"

It was Birna, smiling and coming toward her with a large basket. Euthalia realized she had spoken fluently, rather than the choppy, awkward speech of people trying to work around a very few shared words, and in Euthalia's own language, and without a trace of accent. "Birna! You have deceived me!"

"What?" Birna looked surprised and faintly hurt.

"You speak my language perfectly! Why did you pretend you did not?"

Birna blinked and then shook her head with a chuckle. "No, my dear, not I. It is rather you who speaks my language perfectly. Or perhaps both of us are speaking another language not our own. In any case, you are in a place where language is the least of the barriers among men."

Euthalia hesitated, considered. No, she was speaking just as she had all her life, without the weight of recalling and mimicking unfamiliar words. Birna was speaking nonsense. Or rather, she was speaking perfectly well, which had to be nonsense.

"Where is everyone?" she asked.

"You will see them later," Birna answered. "They will be interested to see you."

Euthalia was puzzled by this. "But they have all seen me already, at the feast and the ceremony."

"No, those were the villagers in Aros. You have not met those who live here."

Euthalia gestured at the houses around them. "Aros is the village? Then this is Aros. Who else lives here, but the villagers?"

Birna laughed again, and it was infuriating. "No, this is not Aros."

Euthalia wanted to fly at her and throttle her. "What do you mean? Speak sense! How can this not be Aros? I stayed in this house and this village and—"

"Not this village," interrupted Birna. "And not this house, not exactly. You were carried here last night."

The burst of multi-colored light—the instant of prismatic disorientation—had that been it? What had happened?

"He carried you here last night," Birna was saying. "The house was made for you in Aros, so that he would know where to find you among all the others of Aros and he would take the right woman. You are his bride now. And I have been sent to serve you here."

"Been sent?" Euthalia repeated. "You were not carried?"

Birna tipped her chin up and pulled upward on the skin of her neck, separating a broad gash which ran dark across her throat. Euthalia gasped and recoiled.

Birna dropped the skin and shook her head. "No worries, my dear, the pain is past now. Mere men and women cannot leave Midgard without death. You, on the other hand, you are different now. You are the bride of a god."

Euthalia's knees slipped from beneath her and she sat down hard on the packed grass. "The bride of a...."

Birna bent and smiled, her flesh slipping forward to conceal the line on her throat. "Come, my dear. It will all become easier when you've had breakfast and walked about a bit." She uncovered the basket and withdrew a smaller container with berries and a few nuts. "Eat these."

Epli. It was one of the few words Euthalia had acquired, a word for small fruits and nuts. It had seemed odd to her, a single word to refer to what she had always called different things, but now when she tried consciously to think of the raiders' word, it felt perfectly natural, as if she had used it all her life.

"Eat," Birna prompted, and she did.

Euthalia sat on the trunk, the bearskin wrapped about her again. She stared at the door and watched it fade into darkness as the last of the twilight left the sky. He would come, and soon, and she did not know what she thought of that.

It was easier, a little, to believe that her new husband was not a man, was not a human, was not an ordinary husband. That is, it was not a simple thing to believe, but if she could convince herself of that, then believing that Birna had died to follow her out of Midgard, or whatever it was she had called the human world, the *real* world, and believing that the village of Aros had not been emptied but had been left behind, and believing that her father had sold her and his warriors to the river pirates, all became just a little bit easier.

But it did not give her more confidence to face the night and her strange husband's coming. She was not sure that being opened and taken by a god should be more pleasant or less frightening than by a man. She had still never seen this husband, and that did not inspire an ease of mind. If he cared for her, if he were not monstrous, why would he come only by night?

But what choice did she have? If Birna told the truth, and as bizarre as it sounded Euthalia could find no evidence to dispute it, then she could not flee. She had left the world of men behind, and even if she fled the empty village she could not go home or to any other refuge. But she was no worse off than most women, and better than many others, so she would wait for her new husband to arrive and she would make the best of this unanticipated union.

When the wooden latch on the door rose, Euthalia turned to face the entrance, eyes straining in the dark. But she could see nothing, and again she had only a sense of a large figure entering.

"Good evening, Euthalia," he said in his powerful, dark voice.

She swallowed. "Good evening, husband," she said.

"May I sit beside you?"

It was his house, and his trunk, and his sacrifice of a bride, but it was kind of him to ask. "Yes, of course."

He sat beside her, not quite touching the hair of the bearskin about her, and she wondered whether the trunk were large enough to accommodate him, for it was not an enormous trunk and he seemed a big man. But he sat without appearing unbalanced or awkward, and she worried that sliding to the end of the trunk would appear more rude avoidance than politely making space.

"Euthalia," he said. "What sort of name is that?"

"It is a Greek name," she said. "I am a Greek, or my mother is. My father is Slavic. Though it seems I have learned your own language since coming here last night."

His voice gained the warm hint of a smile. "There are no languages where love or gods are concerned," he said. "Love should not be limited by nations' boundaries or tribal tongues, and gods know all that humans mean to say, no matter how they say it."

"That seems very profound," she said. "The great philosophers would have loved to debate that."

"Great philosophers?" he repeated. "Who are they?"

"Philosophers, lovers of wisdom," she said. "We had many renowned philosophers in our land, long ago. They are famed for speaking great words."

"Great words." He sounded amused. "I have heard of great deeds, of great works, of great leaders, of great battles, of great victories, of great peace. I have not heard of any man made great merely by his words."

She considered. "I believe it is that the great words can make possible the great works."

"If they have made the great works possible, then why not perform them instead of merely speaking about them?" He snorted gently. "No wonder your land has produced such weak men, who would sell their daughters to save themselves."

The words struck her hard, and yet she could not argue their truth. Perhaps the wisdom she had been taught to revere was not as profound as she had been told. No sophistry had come to her aid when the beast-headed ships carried her away up the river.

"But that is no reflection upon you," he continued. "Your land is full of weak men, but that is not your doing. You were, by all the accounts I have heard, a brave and tearless sacrifice."

She did not know how to answer this. "We have warriors in our blood, too," she said. "And not cowardly men like my father, men who hide behind the title and then do nothing themselves, but mighty warriors whose deeds have been told for centuries."

"Oh?" He sounded skeptical. "Tell me, Euthalia, what mighty warriors you once had."

She considered what might impress a god of the fierce Northmen, who loved battle and honor and courage. Not the story of the horse at Troy, no; that would smell to him of trickery rather than valor. But she knew another tale. "I could tell you of three hundred men who stood alone against one hundred thousand and held them off for days."

He half-turned on the trunk. "But no, that is a story for children. Even the songs of our most valiant are not so bold in their claims, and we speak not of mild Greeks but of the renowned Danes, greatest of warriors."

She had his interest now, she knew it; his denial proved it. "Let me tell you of Sparta's valiant defense against the invading army of Xerxes the Persian."

He shifted, setting his back to the wall, and she thought he crossed his arms. "Tell me, then."

"It was more than a thousand years ago, and three hundred years more," she began. "Xerxes the king of Persia grew hungry for Greek lands. He was a greedy man, for his empire stretched already over three continents, and yet he was not satisfied with what he had. And so he raised an army of one hundred thousand men, for he knew he would need every spear of them to take the lands of the Thespians, of the Thebes, of the Spartans."

"You speak as if they were warriors to be feared," rumbled her unseen husband, skeptical.

"The Spartans were the most brutal warriors ever to walk this earth," she said, "and I believe even your precious Northmen would be hard put to fight them. A Spartan boy could not become a man until he had killed."

"Hm. Continue."

"Sparta was, as I said, one of the strongest of the states, with the fiercest fighters. They agreed to defend the pass of Thermopylae, where the land forced a narrow passage and the Persians would not be able to sweep over them in broad ranks, but must come in narrow bands of men."

He grunted approval.

"But the Persian army was slow to come, and they arrived at a time when Sparta owed obeisance to their gods, and the Spartans did not wish to put off the rituals and not give the gods their due." She hoped this part would please him. "And so, in place of sending their entire army, as they had intended, their king Leonidas took three hundred veteran warriors and three hundred Helots, or slave warriors."

This intrigued him. "They armed their slaves? To fight?"

Euthalia tried to remember her history. "These were slaves to war. Their purpose was to fight for their Spartan masters."

He considered this. "So then they were not three hundred only, as you said."

In truth, they were not three hundred alone, but three hundred Spartans along with at least four thousand men more, from the various city-states threatened by the Persian advance, but while that was still an impressively disparate number to counter the hundred thousand Persians, it was not quite so eloquent off the tongue as three hundred. She countered, "Does my lord husband consider a slave worthy of claiming victory?"

He chuckled. "A thrall who fights well should be recognized and honored—but if a man were a worthy warrior, he would not become a thrall, so I will grant your point. So what came of these three hundred warriors and their three hundred fighting slaves?"

"The Persians came to Thermopylae, where the Spartans had made their defense, and offered free passage to those who wished to surrender or retreat. Leonidas refused. The Persians then pointed out their superior numbers and called for the defenders to put down their weapons. The Spartans replied, 'Come and take them.'"

He made a sound of grudging approval.

"On the fifth day, the Persians attacked. For two full days and nights, Xerxes sent first his common soldiers and then his elite Immortals against the Spartan defense, and for two days and nights they were turned back and destroyed. While the Persians sent fresh wave after fresh wave—"

"The Spartans held their shield wall and defended one another and their land." His voice was pleased. "And they endured. Excellent. I am impressed, I will confess." He shifted against the wall. "But after the two days?"

"It was not weakness which undid them, but treachery." She had him now, like a fish on a hook, and she had to play him in carefully. "There was a secret, small path over the pass at Thermopylae, and one weak-hearted man sold this secret to the Persians. The Immortals, the greatest of Xerxes' warriors, wound through this passage—by night, because they so feared the Spartans—and prepared to flank Leonidas and crush the defenders in a pincer."

"Curse the traitor-coward!" growled the unseen figure. "Who would do such a thing?"

Euthalia could not remember the man's name, nor the reason for his betrayal, and she did not want to lose the thread of his interest in the Spartan warriors. "King Leonidas sent away the bulk of the defending soldiers, and he remained himself with his own warriors and fighting slaves, and some of the men from the other city-states. Leonidas and the Spartans were ultimately killed in the final battle, but a year later, the Persians were defeated and driven out of Greece."

"A good death in battle, and ultimate victory," her husband observed. "Yes, you are right, these men were not cowards or weaklings. There is good blood in your land, even if it has been diluted."

She took that for the best compliment her people were likely to receive at this time.

"Do you have other stories of your people's brave fighting?"

"I have many stories. We delight in stories, and we keep them in poems and in plays."

"Plays?"

"Staged performances where trained men reenact events and comment upon them. Like storytelling, but with many people working together to tell the story."

"That sounds curious. Will you tell me another story tomorrow night?"

"Of course."

"Good. I shall look forward to it." He leaned toward her. "Now—" he took her head in his hands, and her heart leapt into her throat—"I will bid you goodnight." And his breath brushed her forehead, nearly a kiss but without contact, and he withdrew and stood.

She looked up at him, as if she could see him in the dark instead of merely feel his presence. She felt she should say something, but surprise stole her words.

"I will come to you again tomorrow night," he said. And he went past her to the door and out into the dark night.

Euthalia sat for a moment, trying to decide if she were relieved that he had left her untouched or worried that she had offended or displeased him. But he did not seem offended or displeased; she thought he had enjoyed the story. Better to be grateful, even if she did not understand.

It was late, for she had waited a long while before he had come, and she was tired with the past days' worries. She went to the bed of soft sheepskins and wrapped herself in their woolly comfort, and she slept.

CHAPTER 6

He came again the next night.

Again he sat on the chest beside her. "I have thought about the story you told last night. It is a Greek story?"

She nodded. "My father is a Serb, but I was named after the way of my mother, and she told me the old Greek stories."

"Then my statement remains, that his people are weak. He is not a descendant of those valiant three hundred." He sniffed. "Your father is a disgrace to whatever people might have spawned him. I would call him a dog, but that would be unkind to the worthy creatures who protect farm and flock."

Euthalia wasn't sure how to respond to this. "He... he is my father."

"He is the man who bartered you away."

That was true. And yet—he was her father. Even if he had intended to sell her into matrimony for profit, had in fact sold her for his own safety, he was still her father. He was the giant figure in her limited world.

Perhaps that was it. She had left home only once, to go with him to Byzantium to be found a merchant husband to enhance Tikhomir's trade network, and the entire experience had been one long disillusionment regarding her father's position and power and character. Perhaps—

"What is it?" her strange husband asked.

She swallowed. "I was just thinking... perhaps this was why he kept me always at home, so that I could never judge for myself and find him wanting."

He nodded slowly, considering. "You don't think it was for your protection?"

"Protection is one thing," she said. "But ignorance is not protection. Ignorance protects only him."

He chuckled. "That may be so." He leaned back against the wall. "Do you have a story for me tonight?"

"What kind of story?"

"Another tale of your people as warriors? Or one of your legends?"

Euthalia had spent much of the day sifting stories from her memory, trying to guess what would be fantastic enough and valiant enough to please him. "Shall I tell you how Odysseus escaped the dread one-eyed Cyclops which daily devoured his ship's men?"

She told him the story, and the bloodthirsty tale intrigued him as she had thought it might. But when Odysseus bound the sheep into woolly rafts and escaped the blinded Cyclops, she sensed her strange husband's disapproval. "So then he did not fight the monster," he protested. "He did not test his strength against him, did not avenge his fallen men. What sort of hero is this?"

"Odysseus had not come to kill the Cyclops," she said. "He led his surviving men to freedom and to continue their voyage; that was his purpose. To stay and fight would have further endangered his men."

"Still, it does not seem right that he should flee by trickery."

"I am sorry the story does not please you. I will think of another for you the next time."

"I did not say the story did not please me." He reached for her hands and turned them over, and she felt two large cool objects pressed into her palms. They were metal, and engraved by the feel of them. "A gift," he said. "For you to think of me by day."

"Oh, but I do think of you," she said. "How could I not?"

"Nonetheless, take them," he answered. He leaned close and kissed her forehead. "And I will come again tomorrow night."

"Will you—" Euthalia caught herself. She had almost asked if he would stay, but she realized what that would mean to him.

He was still a moment, as if waiting for her to complete the question, and then he rose as if she had said nothing. "Good night, Euthalia."

When he had gone, she wondered if she should have asked him to stay. She could not guess her own mind, and that frightened her a little.

She slept with the two metal objects lying beside her. In the morning, she took them out and examined them in the sunlight. They were gold brooches, each the size of her palm, engraved with figures and what she supposed were runes. She could not guess the meaning of the runes or the figures, but the brooches were a gift from her husband, a raft of hope in her sea of displacement, and that gave them value beyond their precious metal.

Birna did most of the heavy chores, and Euthalia occupied herself with others, picking vegetables and shaping candles from honeycomb taken from the hives and spinning flax and wondering after her peculiar situation.

The candles fit well in the lantern she found in the house, a wooden holder with shades of rawhide to soften the light and protect the flame. The flax she stored in a chest, and Birna promised to show her how to weave during the long winter. Each day Birna brought a small quantity of berries and nuts, carried in their own tiny basket. The storage boxes were always full of vegetables and grain, despite the lack of a grain field within sight, and Euthalia wondered if Birna were producing it from some secret place or if the box supplied itself.

By night, he came, and they talked. Euthalia told him stories, histories of her mother's people and tales of their gods and the little fables to teach lessons. Each night he listened, he laughed, he debated or acknowledged a point, and then left before the dawn.

One afternoon Birna started fussing with Euthalia's clothing, twitching at it and straightening where it was not crooked. "We must dress you well, lady," she said. "This evening you will feast with the gods in Odin's hall."

Euthalia was not yet fully accustomed to thinking of her nominal husband, as yet a husband in name only and not in deed, as a god. She had gleaned a few facts about this place and its gods, from Birna's chatter or her husband's conversation or stories she had once heard among Slavic traders of the fearsome Northmen and their ways, but she was still fitting them into a full picture of her new life. To hear that she would be greeting other gods and dining with them, and in particular such a famous one as Odin himself, gave her a moment of pause. "I—to the hall? With Odin?"

"Your husband has told them of your beauty and your stories," Birna said, "and they are anxious to judge for themselves."

"My beauty?" repeated Euthalia. "But how can he know anything of my appearance, for he comes only by night?"

"Oh, lady, you see him only at night," Birna said with a knowing smile. "But he saw you before you left Midgard, of course. That is how the people of Aros knew you would be an acceptable sacrifice."

Euthalia frowned at this. "He chose me to be sacrificed?!"

"No, no, lady, it was your people who did that. He named you as acceptable. There is a difference."

Euthalia couldn't see the difference just yet, but Birna seemed to understand more of all this than Euthalia did thus far. And it made no difference how she had come, if she had found herself here now, and Birna did not seem to say anything which reflected poorly upon Euthalia's unseen husband. She would not have told Euthalia of the sacrifice if she thought it would offend.

Euthalia dressed herself in the freshly-washed linen shift and the pinafore of wool expensively dyed with indigo. The two brooches of gold he had given her held the pinafore in place, and she found herself hoping he would notice that she wore them. The scarlet cape with fox-fur trim came next, again bright with expensive dye. Euthalia felt extremely wealthy as she dressed, and then she recalled that she was the wife of a god. She wondered if she had dressed well enough to do him honor before his friends and fellow gods.

She combed and combed her hair with the carved antler, running her hands over it to make sure it was clean and smooth. At last Birna looked on her with an air of accomplishment. "You're ready."

Euthalia thought differently, but she did not argue.

She left her house and looked out upon the empty village. It was less empty now, though; she could hear the sounds of activity nearby, the carrying of water or the thump of crates and the swish of cloth being hung. Had she returned to Aros? Had someone else come to the village?

The sound was loudest from the longhouse, the great building like an enormous overturned ship. She looked at it, trying to summon her courage to cross the village toward it.

"Are you Euthalia, then?"

She turned and saw a woman a dozen paces away. A woman, at least, in that she was not a man, but beyond that she was unlike any woman Euthalia had ever seen. She stood fully a head and more over Euthalia, and she was muscled in a way that showed through her man's tunic. She held a spear like a tall pine, thick like a young tree and trimmed with barbed points.

Euthalia swallowed. Was this a goddess? "I am Euthalia," she said. "I have been invited to the hall tonight."

"So I have heard." The enormous woman planted the butt of the spear into the ground and twisted it in her great hand. "I am to bring you." She nodded toward the hall. "It is not so far that you cannot find it, but it can be a dangerous place. I am to bring you safely inside."

"Would a guest be in danger during the dinner?" Euthalia was curious and a bit scandalized. Even the most barbarous understood and respected the sacred duties of hospitality. A guest's safety was inviolate during a meal.

"In deliberate danger? No. But when a human dines with gods, there is danger, even if the gods mean no harm."

Euthalia nodded. "And you are a goddess, I presume? I must apologize, for I do not know you."

The woman laughed. "I, a goddess? I am no Æsir, nor even Vanir, though I will forgive your insult because of your ignorance. I am a Jötunn, and I am called Skathi."

Euthalia nodded, though she had no idea what any of this meant. "I am sorry if I gave offense, Skathi. My husband has given me little instruction yet."

Skathi sniffed. "It is typical of the Æsir to think only of themselves."

This Skathi might consider herself slighted by the others, then, Euthalia noted. It would be good to remember these things, if she had to make her way among immortal politics.

"Come," said Skathi. "Let us go to the hall of Odin."

CHAPTER 1

Euthalia could not have explained it, but when Skathi pulled open the door of the longhouse, the rest of the village seemed to fall away along with the day itself. Inside, it was night, or at least the long twilight of the North, and those feasting within had no need or thought of the next day's morn.

Men and women lined the longhouse walls and sat at tables in its center. A few were taller like Skathi and noticeable even from the door, but most were of a height. Most were fair-skinned, but a few were like the darker men she had seen in Byzantium, and a few folk were nearly hidden in the unlit corners with their skin like night and their short statures.

Some hailed Skathi as she entered, others ignored her. None called to Euthalia, though she felt eyes upon her as she followed Skathi along the tables.

These were the many gods of the North, and there were others, too—for surely the night-skinned ones clinging to the dark were dwarfs, and there were long rows of men along the walls, raising joints of meat and horns of mead, stretching too far to see against walls much too long to belong to a single longhouse. This longhouse was Valhöll, the Hall of the Slain, and these were the dead, the warriors who had earned their place here with a good death and now awaited Odin's order.

Women and men, all humans to her eye, moved among the men and served out more meat and mead. They were dressed more humbly, without armor or knives, and she recognized they were thralls. Probably dead thralls, sacrificed like Birna to serve in the afterlife.

At the head of the longhouse, overlooking all the tables of feasting gods and the long rows of dead warriors, sat Odin. Euthalia missed a step as her eyes found him. He sat in a huge chair carved with beasts like the prows of ships, and where one of his eyes should have been gaped a dark hole of half-healed scarring. Two large ravens perched on the back of his chair, flapping occasionally to keep their balance as he moved or lifted bits of gristle to their waiting beaks.

"Odin, father of all," called Skathi. "I have brought her."

Odin turned from the conversation he was having with a tall man and set his single eye on Euthalia. "So this is the girl of whom we have heard," he said slowly, his expression detached and appraising. "The sacrificed bride."

Euthalia did not know whether to curtsy or kneel or prostrate herself or stand erect. There were two wolves crouching at Odin's feet, and so she elected to remain standing. "I am Euthalia, Lord Odin."

"And you are a storyteller, or so we hear," Odin said.

"A songweaver," said another, a man in brightly-colored clothing and a full beard. "So we have heard."

She had not expected this. "I have a few tales of my people's history," she said. Humility or braggadocio? Which would a god prefer? No, she knew which a Greek god would prefer—but what about a Norse god?

Braggadocio, of course, but she had already spoken.

"History?" Odin sniffed. "Who could bear to listen to a recounting of history? Traders bickering over last year's prices? A good story tells of great deeds, of obstacles overcome, of valiant achievement despite fierce opposition. Do you have any proper tales of the mighty, or only pitiful stories of years passing?"

Euthalia reached for the boldest daring she could recall. "I could tell you of Prometheus, who defied the gods themselves to steal fire for mankind."

Immediately she regretted her choice. What gods would want to hear of defiance? She had doomed herself.

But these were not Greek gods, concerned with keeping their ranks and defending their superiority from grasping men. These were Norse gods, who valued bold action even above reverence. Odin leaned forward, resting an elbow on his knee, and ordered, "Tell me of such a man."

Euthalia swallowed. The cheerful commotion of the longhouse did not quite still, but it did seem to slow, as if some of the nearer gods and goddesses and others were listening.

"Well, Prometheus was not a man," she began unevenly. "He was a Titan, one of those who came before the gods, and he helped the gods to overthrow the Titans."

"A traitor?" asked Odin, and his lip curled in disgust.

Euthalia shook her head. "He was a giant who saw the benefit in alliance with the gods, who recognized their rule as more right and more profitable to all," she tried. "And with this view, he allied himself with Zeus, the greatest of the gods."

Odin raised an eyebrow. "He was a Jötunn," he declared. He looked at the dark-haired man on his left. "A Jötunn who swore alliance with the All-Father."

A cheer went up at this, and the dark-haired Jötunn made a smile, though Euthalia was not sure if the smile were true pleasure or false agreement.

"When it came time to make humankind," she continued, "all the best gifts had been distributed to the animals—speed, flight, fur, feathers, claws. Humans had nothing to use for hunting or protection, because they did not yet have tools or towns. Prometheus took pity upon them, and he decided to bring them fire from the mountain."

Odin grunted. "What mountain?"

"Olympus, the mountain of the gods, where they dwell. It is both a physical mountain upon the earth and a place beyond human reach." Euthalia was nervous, and she could tell she did not have Odin's attention as she had held her husband's. And she did not know the stakes if she failed to entertain Odin. "So Prometheus went up to Olympus, and he took fire, and he brought it down to give to the race of humans, so that they might warm themselves, and protect themselves from beasts, and make tools of iron and steel to hunt, and make fine objects of other metals for all purposes."

Odin frowned. "So it was an easy thing, to steal fire? Even Loki can thieve with impunity." He gestured to the Jötunn beside him, who grinned, this time with pleasure and pride.

Euthalia shook her head. "The theft may have been easy, but the punishment was not. Zeus seized Prometheus, though he owed him much for his service, and bound him to a high rock with unbreakable chains. He swore Prometheus would remain there for eons, for ever, without sleep or respite. When Prometheus refused still to repent, Zeus set an eagle to come each day and rend Prometheus' body to rags, tearing out his liver and eating it upon his own chest, only to return the next day and the next."

This had caught Odin's ear. He looked at her, fully attentive for the first time. "And he hung on that rock, picked apart by birds?"

She did not quite follow his question, but it seemed important to agree. "Yes."

He nodded approvingly. "A good story. But," he continued, "not told so well as I had been led to believe you could." He sat back and turned away to speak to a blonde woman, forgetting her instantly.

Euthalia hesitated, uncertain of how to retreat, and she glanced to the side in the hope that Skathi was near. But the Jötunn had already turned away and was joining a crowded table, her back to Euthalia.

The second Jötunn, the one Odin had called Loki, rose from his place beside the All-Father and came toward

Euthalia. "Little bride," he said quietly, "if you stand here with your face hanging like a sheep's, they will mistake you for a thrall or a cut of meat." He nodded toward the wall where one long row of dead warriors sat. "Go and take a seat, and eat and drink if it suits you. There is no prestige in standing silently in a hall of great men and women."

Euthalia nodded, feeling stupid, and went where he directed. But a woman seated there looked up at her and said, "You have earned no place here."

Euthalia resisted the impulse to look behind her for Loki's guidance or permission. "My place in this hall is mine by right, for I am the bride of a god."

The woman sniffed. "Let the years pass, and see what that means to you then. No one will recall your name or your deeds, not human skald nor gods themselves. Do you know me?"

Euthalia had no choice but to be honest. "No, I'm afraid I don't."

The woman nodded. "I am Sigyn, and I too am the wife of an immortal. But no one can speak or write my name without his. I am nothing of myself, because they know only him. Whatever worth I had has been lost."

Euthalia did not think it helpful to point out that she knew almost no one here, being a newcomer both to Asgard and to the North lands themselves. She would not know Sigyn nor even any of the gods who had not yet been introduced to her. She sat down beside the woman and said, "But is it not a wife's duty to bring honor to her husband's name? Is she not an ornament to his house and a mother to his children?"

Sigyn laughed without amusement. "What a little sheep you are. A name is not so much to ask. Is a man so much more worthy of one than a woman, simply because he has a soft sack of fragile stones dangling between his legs?"

Euthalia blinked and found she had no answer.

Sigyn smiled. "There, now you are beginning to think. That is good, for you will be less of a sheep. Sheep are sacrificed."

I was sacrificed, thought Euthalia.

A thrall brought her mead, and she drank. It was good wine, sweet and tart, and she drank it all.

She had so many questions, and she thought she might ask Sigyn, but she did not wish to appear more foolish than she already had. She wished she had been a woman of a North family, that she might have heard of their gods and known something of their politics. "Who exactly are the Jötunn?" she asked at last. "Skathi said she was not a goddess, but a Jötunn."

Sigyn's eyes widened. "Oh, did you think her one of the Æsir? That must have been quite the blow to her ego."

Euthalia clenched her fists, ashamed and embarrassed. "I was not raised in the North. I do not know the tribes and ranks, and I cannot help but give offense."

Sigyn pointed discreetly toward Odin. "That one above all you must not offend. He is Odin, the All-Father, and he is always aloof and withdrawn and does not make merry like most of the others. He sacrificed his eye for wisdom, they say, but I say it was his eye and his sense of humanity. He is not human, of course, none of them are, but most of the others understand some of what it is to be human. Not Odin.

"But to answer your question, he is Æsir, a god of Asgard, where you are now. The Vanir are of Vanaheim, but many of them stay here and treat with the Æsir as if they were of them. Like Freyr and Freyja, those two over there, the obvious siblings." Sigyn's voice held a dripping note of distaste. "Siblings, I say, but they are close—*very* close, if you take my meaning."

"Oh. *Oh.*" Euthalia needed a moment to follow her. Incest was something known only in tragic tales, always held as the most horrific of acts. Oedipus had been ignorant of his unintentional transgression and still had put out his own eyes upon learning the truth, and his mother-wife had killed herself. That two siblings might knowingly fornicate together was incomprehensible. "Do they know?"

Sigyn gave her a sidelong look. "Do the others know they are lovers, do you mean? Some do. Some may choose to be ignorant, which is not to say that they don't know." Sigyn raised and lowered a single shoulder in a dismissive shrug. "Some might say I have no ground to think ill of others' habits and predilections, not with the songs they could sing of my own husband, but accusation is a poor defense."

Euthalia had meant to ask who Sigyn's husband might be, but now she felt it would be in poor taste, and she did not want to alienate the woman. "I meant to ask if the couple knows they are siblings. I know a story where a husband did not know his wife was his mother, and it brought great tragedy upon their whole city."

"Oh, they know," Sigyn assured her. "Only they do not care. But they are Vanir, as I was saying, who live among the Æsir. The Jötnar are the devourers, those from beyond." She looked at Euthalia and screwed up her mouth. "Let me think how to say this. The Æsir are those who hold together, while the Jötnar are those who pull apart."

"Harmony and chaos," Euthalia supplied, glad to grasp her meaning.

But the words did not seem familiar to Sigyn. "Hm. But the Jötnar are not evil; one cannot have saplings without the decay of fallen trees, or spring without winter. They are essential for the greater cycle." She held Euthalia's eyes. "Not evil."

Euthalia sensed this was an important distinction, and particularly important to Sigyn. "Right. They are chaos, but without chaos, there can be no civilization."

Sigyn nodded. "Their land is called Jotunheim. Some of the Jötnar, like some of the Vanir, choose to live among the Æsir." She nodded toward Skathi. "That one was persuaded by Loki, and she married Njord, though it could not last. It was Baldr she wanted in the first place." She pointed at a handsome blond man smiling as his shoulders were slapped in appreciation of some joke.

Euthalia surreptitiously ticked these points off on her fingers, committing them to memory. *The Jötnar oppose the Æsir, but not all of them just now. Skathi is a Jötunn who sought to marry Baldr but took Njord instead, and their marriage failed. Freyr and Freyja are brother and sister and lovers. Loki is a Jötunn.* This last reminded her, "Odin called Loki a thief."

Sigyn frowned. "They call each other many names. They are sworn brothers, though Æsir and Jötunn. No one can say why, not even I."

Euthalia was curious. "Why should someone expect you to say?"

Sigyn smiled and nodded toward the carved chairs where the great gods sat. "Loki is my husband."

Euthalia nodded, doubly glad she had not asked about the sexual deviancies at which Sigyn had hinted.

"And which is yours?" Sigyn asked.

Euthalia's throat tightened. "I—don't know his name," she said. "I did not speak the language well enough to understand the ritual by which I became his bride. And he has not told me his name in the nights when he comes."

"Too busy doing other things," snorted Sigyn.

Euthalia said nothing. She looked across the longhouse, scanning the gods laughing and eating. He could be here, she realized. He could be here, and she would not know him. She might have embarrassed him here before his comrades with her poor telling of the tale of Prometheus.

Or, perhaps, he might have failed her by not standing with her before the harsh scrutiny of Odin.

She drank the mead the thralls brought.

After a time, Odin called upon a skald in brightly-colored clothing, who rose and began to sing a tale of warriors hunting a man hiding in the house of his mother. "And she instructed him to sit before her, unmoving, and she began to comb out his hair. And when Arnkel and his men came to look for him, they saw only Katya brushing out the coat of her goat, and they ransacked the house and did not find him."

Euthalia should have listened, should have watched the hall to see what they liked in their stories, but the mead was swimming in her head and the constant noise of the hall was echoing in her skull.

"And again they came, and again Katya used her seidr and spun *sjónhverfing*, the magical seeing, so they sought him inside and outside the house and saw nothing of him, only a boar asleep in the ash heap. And so they went away again, and this time they returned with another *seið-kona* to counter Katya's magic."

"Now it comes," called Freyja, and her twin brother laughed.

But Euthalia did not catch what came, though she roused enough when the audience cheered to hear that the second seidr-worker had put a bag over the head of the first, blinding her and ending her spell. But then again the story blurred and droned and her eyelids drooped.

"Go," said Sigyn quietly in her ear. "I will go with you. We will not be missed."

Euthalia glanced at her, a bit embarrassed to have been caught drowsing, and nodded. "Thank you."

They rose and picked their way to a door, and those they passed took no more notice of them than of the thralls who carried yet more food and drink. When they reached the door, Sigyn hesitated, her hand on the wooden latch. "It is good to have another here," she said at last. "They can be so taken with themselves and their own affairs... I am sorry I said you had no place."

Euthalia felt a smile break over her face. "And I am so glad to find a friend here," she agreed. She would have continued, but Sigyn only nodded and smiled and stepped through the door.

Euthalia followed, but Sigyn was nowhere to be seen. She could not have run quickly enough to get out of sight around a corner—but Euthalia was beginning to guess at the treachery of appearances. She turned, and indeed, there was her little house in the little village that was not a village, though she could hear the distant clamor of Valhöll from the longhouse behind her, as if echoing over a distance.

Euthalia set off to her little house, grateful for its cozy privacy after the crowded hall.

CHAPTER 8

Some days, Euthalia walked her empty village, imagining who might live there in its mirror-village of Aros. On the outskirts was an irregular circle of poles set into the ground about several large, mostly-flat rocks. Euthalia came upon it only as she followed the stream one day, for it was sheltered by tall obscuring grass.

A cow's skull, half-decayed of skin and hair, hung from the top of one pole. On the largest stone lay a scattering of fruits and grains and colorful beads. Euthalia looked about the circle and found more poles, set at an angle, from which several sheepskins hung, discolored by exposure.

This was a place of sacrifice, she realized. Most of Aros was only mirrored here, but this place was like her house, built to span both Asgard and Midgard. This was a place where humans could leave gifts in the world of the gods.

She looked down at the offerings on the rock. She was a sacrifice, like the beads or the meat.

Now you are beginning to think. That is good, for you will be less of a sheep. Sheep are sacrificed.

She pushed away from the offering place and went to her little house. She would not stay home, waiting passively, she decided. Tonight she would go to the longhouse again, and she would present herself well.

This time, Euthalia had no escort, but took herself to the longhouse. The noise of the carousing warriors and gods and Jötnar grew steadily louder as she drew nearer, and at last she put her hand upon the latch, took a breath, and stepped into Valhöll.

Inside it was twilight again, and she wondered if it would always be. She looked across the room to where Sigyn had sat and she saw the woman sitting comfortably, looking down the long room away from Euthalia's entrance. Euthalia started toward her, picking her way through the crowded carousal.

A hand reached out to her from one of the tables, and a woman—a goddess—spoke to her. "Euthalia?"

She stopped and nodded, pleased beyond speech that someone knew her and showed interest in her. "Yes?"

"I am Gefjon," said the goddess. "Euthalia, are you yet a maid?"

The blunt question surprised her, and in her astonishment she answered honestly. "Yes. My husband has not yet lain with me."

Gefjon nodded. "I thought so. But that is not a bad thing, though some here would certainly think poorly of it. All my attendants are virgins, and I have been robbed of many fine maids by overeager men. Your husband is cautious and wise."

Euthalia's cheeks were growing hot; she had not thought to discuss her marital bed with anyone, certainly not a stranger and a goddess, but Gefjon at least did not seem to think ill of her for having her marriage yet unconsummated. "I thought him kind," she admitted. "I was a sacrifice in a strange land, and I thought I was going to be killed by a dragon. I was much relieved when he proved to be something other than a monster, and when he did not take me by force."

Gefjon laughed. "Vidar is no monster, whatever else he might be."

Euthalia's stomach leapt. Was this his name? Had she learned his name?

Gefjon was still speaking. "Many of us thought him unwise, but his choice has been borne out. You are a good woman, Euthalia. Do not let him corrupt you."

Euthalia was surprised by this. "Is he likely to? Would he?"

Gefjon snorted. "All men would," she said simply, and turned back to her plate with an air of dismissal for either Euthalia or the subject, Euthalia was not sure which.

She turned away and started again up the long row of tables, and another hand stretched to interrupt her passage. She glanced from the hand to the man who had extended it.

Not man. One of the gods, dressed in bright colors and beaming beneath his beard. She stared at him, knowing she should greet him and utterly helpless to recall his name or position.

"Bragi," he said, and the skin about his eyes crinkled in a nearly invisible smile. "I am Bragi, skald of the Æsir."

She nodded gratefully. "You sing the epic tales."

"Yes," he said. "I am a storyteller, like you."

"Oh, not like me," she corrected him quickly, looking down. "I cannot sing the epics and sagas as you do. I only tell stories."

"All stories are songs," Bragi said. "Only some have music."

"Now you mock me," she said. "I am no... skald. You are a master of story—of song. A god of poetry."

"I, as you say, am a god," he answered. "And I entertain gods. And you have the power to entertain gods even as a mere mortal. Which of us then has reached farther, which deserves more praise for our efforts?"

She hesitated, and he laughed aloud. "And now I am teasing you," he admitted. "You would not answer that, of course. But what I said before—you are a songweaver, the same as I."

"Songweaver," she repeated. It was a good word, and one she realized was familiar to her—in her own Greek, an ancient *rhapsode* was a stitcher of poems.

She had never thought of herself as anything so grand. But Bragi was a god of wisdom and poetry, and she could not argue with him, no matter how it made her flush.

"You must come to me sometime and tell me your stories," Bragi said.

"Oh, I couldn't! They are poor things, not fit for the halls of gods."

Bragi held up a finger. "Do not sell great fish for the price of small ones," he said warningly. "Your stories are of such a quality that I have heard of them, and Odin as well. Learn to weave them properly, and you will entertain here as well as I."

She fumbled for an answer. "But, they are only stories...."

"Nothing is only a story," said Bragi, "and nothing is so mighty as a story." He held up a finger again, smiled once more, and waved her on her way.

She went on to where Sigyn waited, waving her into an open space. The other woman welcomed her with a smile. "Hello! I was hoping you would return."

Euthalia was grateful for the warm greeting. It seemed she had won Sigyn's respect after all. "A chance to humiliate myself before gods and goddesses and great warriors? I would not miss it." She smiled and took the seat. "And as much as I am growing fond of Birna, her conversation is fixed upon chores and she circles that subject like a tethered goat, wearing out a path."

Sigyn laughed. "And who is Birna?"

"She's a thrall, who was—" Euthalia hesitated. "Sent with me."

Sigyn nodded, understanding. There was only one way a thrall followed to serve outside of Midgard.

Euthalia regretted her lightly mocking words. "I shouldn't have criticized her, not when she died because of me."

"She did not die because of you," Sigyn said. "Well, she did, in a way, but you had no part in it."

"She's always been kind to me, even before we could speak together, and she tried her best to gentle my fears before the sacrifice. She's very sweet."

"Then it seems she does not blame you, either," Sigyn said. "And in truth, she might have had quite another end altogether."

Euthalia did not wish to speak of this. "And where do you live? Do you have a house like mine? That is, my house seems to be in another place entirely, though I can walk from there to here."

Sigyn nodded. "Distances and places can be deceiving. We are all in Asgard, but this longhouse can be reached from all parts of Asgard. My house is set apart from the rest; my husband is not fond of neighbors."

Loki, Euthalia recalled. She looked toward Odin's great chair, and Loki beside it. "Was it long ago that you came here?"

Sigyn made a tiny sound of false laughter. "Long enough." She looked at Euthalia. "The years do not matter. It is enough to say that my family has been long forgotten in Midgard."

Euthalia had not thought of that, that she might remain here unaging with the gods. "Do you have children?"

Sigyn's eyebrows drew together, and Euthalia thought it an expression of pain. Had she unwittingly probed a wound?

And then a roar went up from another table, and Baldr leapt to his feet, all handsome grin and smooth muscle, with another god—another Æsir—and they faced one another as the warriors began to shout and chant encouragement. Baldr's opponent was blond and heavy with muscle, grinning through his beard.

"Go ahead!" called Baldr. He slapped his chest, standing tall. "Come, Thor, try your best."

"I never tire of this game," growled the blond man, and he took up a drinking horn from the table beside him and drove it, point-first, into Baldr's chest. Euthalia's breath caught in her teeth.

But Baldr never flinched, and as Thor drew back the horn, Euthalia saw it had splintered, as if struck against stone.

The hall cheered, and Euthalia drew breath again. She leaned close to Sigyn, partly to conceal her question and partly to be heard in the tumult. "Can they not be killed?"

"Oh, they can," Sigyn assured her. "But not, it seems, Baldr. At least not by weaponry."

"Come again!" cried Baldr, slapping his chest, and this time Thor took up a knife from the table and cut across Baldr's breast. Again, the handsome god was unharmed.

"Loki!" called Thor. "Come down and game with us!"

Loki's mouth twitched before settling into a smile. "But of course." He came down from the little platform on which Odin's chair sat, stepping carefully around one of the wolves. "How good of you to ask."

But as Loki reached the table, Baldr chuckled and called, "No, first it is your turn to play the target!" and flung a platter toward Loki. The dark-haired Jötunn raised his arm, but not quickly enough, and several dozen gooseberries pelted him across the face and torso.

The hall roared with laughter. Sigyn went stiff beside Euthalia, and Euthalia reached for her hand. What could she say, what could she do, should Sigyn go to him or—

Loki wiped the back of his hand across his face, where one of the berries had burst and left a smear of juice. "Ah," he said, his voice dark and velvety, "who would not wish to play such games with a mother's favorite?"

The laughter slowed as the hall tried to catch Loki's words.

"Now, Loki," began Thor.

But Loki pressed on. "This warrior," he gestured at Baldr with barely concealed derision, "is made invincible only by his mother's begging, and to what great purpose does he dedicate himself? To flinging food in the hall of his father, for the amusement of his bastard half-brother."

The laughter slowed, as even the half-drunk warriors recognized the passing of the joke.

Baldr was visibly swelling with indignation, his arms swinging wide as he tried to puff up. "Watch your tongue, Lie-Smith. You will—"

"Do you say that I lie, Baldr? Or is it not true that fair Frigg, mother of the shining god, extracted an oath from each material thing never to harm her dear, dear son? Or do you mean to say that it is your own valor which withstands the renowned strength of the mighty Thor?"

And now Thor's face darkened. "My strength is not the question. If I used the full measure of my arm, even Baldr's protection must fail."

Loki looked at him with exaggerated surprise. "What? Surely that cannot be, for dear Frigg's protection could not be so flawed. Thor's great strength could not be confounded by a woman." He grinned suddenly. "Shall we test it?"

Thor started to pull back an arm, but Baldr acted first, lunging at Loki. Loki leapt backward, planting one hand on a table and vaulting it as men and thralls scattered. "Oh, but shining god, what valor is it to enter battle when you cannot be harmed? What honor could be found in that victory?"

Baldr hesitated, confused, and now Thor stepped forward, and there was a hammer in his hand which had not been there a moment before. He looked uncertainly from Loki to Baldr, as if trying to decide which of them to shout at or strike. He looked again at Baldr, and the hammer twitched in his hand.

"Enough!" Odin's commanding baritone cut across the hall, silencing all at once. One of the wolves at his feet snarled. "This petty brawling is unbecoming."

Baldr turned from Odin to Loki, and his gaze might have cut flesh.

"Loki, sit down. You've done enough mischief for now."

Loki started toward his seat again, letting his eyes shift just enough to Baldr that the handsome god saw. Thor turned away, taking again his seat at the quieted table.

"What was that about?" asked Euthalia, as conversation and eating slowly renewed.

Sigyn took a deep breath, her first since the argument started. "Loki is not fond of Baldr, and Baldr spares no love for him."

"They nearly fought!"

"It would not be the first time they came to blows," Sigyn said. "But Baldr is protected from every weapon, as you see, and so the fight is unequal in any case."

"From every weapon," repeated Euthalia, "even the fist?"

Sigyn gave her a small smile. "I like what you say. No, not the fist, I don't think, but that would matter little when he himself might bear an axe or a club."

Euthalia looked about the room. Most of the warriors had resumed their usual drinking and eating, and few were watching Loki as he sat beside Odin, his chin resting in his hand, one finger propped against his chin, watching Baldr accept a new horn of mead.

CHAPTER 9

When her husband came to her that night, she was ready for him. "Vidar!" she declared. "I know you! You are Vidar!"

He stopped in the doorway, faintly puzzled. "Yes, I know." He took another step and stopped again. "Did you not know?"

"How could I have known? You have never told me!"

He sat down in the wooden chair, his outline only faintly discernible in the dark. "You did not ask me, love. Vidar, a son of Odin. I thought you knew."

She shook her head, though she did not know if he could see it. "I knew nothing. I thought—I thought I was possibly being given to a dragon."

For just a moment he held his laughter in check, his heavy silence betraying him as surely as braying hilarity, and then his control failed and he laughed aloud. She clenched her fists. "Why do you find that amusing?"

"No, no," he laughed, shaking his head, "I am not laughing at you. Not at your confusion, anyway." He hesitated. "Well, a little at your confusion, I admit. But as valiant as I hope I am, I am no dragon."

"I was terrified!" she shot at him. Distantly she realized this was their first fight, and distantly she wondered how that mattered in an artificial marriage such as theirs. "I thought I would die that night!"

His laughter stopped. "And for that I am truly sorry. I did not know, or I would have done more to alleviate your worry." He hesitated. "But when I came, I was not so frightening, was I?"

She pressed her lips together. "You were frightening enough."

This seemed to hurt him. "I did not mean to be. I meant to be careful of you." He inhaled and exhaled, clearing the last of the gaiety from his voice. "Were you never told what the ceremony was?"

"I hardly spoke the language," she reminded him. "It wasn't like this place, where I can understand you and everyone else. There was an old thrall to tell me what was happening, only it must have been a lifetime since he spoke any Slavic, and he only told me I would be a bride of the dragon. A sacrifice. And then they killed a horse, and—" She stopped, because her voice was wavering, and she realized she was afraid again despite it having been long done and harmless in the end and why did her body betray her now?

But he reached out to her, his hand first brushing hers on the wooden chest and then settling over it. "I'm sorry," he said. "I shouldn't have laughed, at least not without making it plain that it was not because you were afraid. You are right, you had every reason to be alarmed."

"Not alarmed," she corrected. "Terrified."

"Terrified," he agreed. "You were a young woman sold into a strange land by a cowardly father not worth the price of his piss, and you were made a sacrifice and sent into the dark to await a dragon." His hand rose to caress her cheek. "And yet I found you unmarred by tears and facing the door, not weeping and clawing at the rear wall."

She relaxed a little and realized his voice was pleased. "And you thought well of that?"

"Thought well of it? I was proud of you. And I am more proud now, now that I know how great was your fear."

"Proud of me?" She had not expected this, and it was an odd piece of knowledge to be given.

"Of course." His fingers spread to cup her face, soft against her cheekbone and jaw. "As I was proud of you when you spoke to Odin and told him the tale of the fire-thief."

"You were there?!"

"Of course I was there," he said, surprised. "Why would I not be?"

"Because if you were there," she returned, "you would have stood with me, would have claimed me and introduced me, would have kept me from being a fool with my silly story and my ignorance."

She was being demanding, she realized, she was echoing her mother's tone when her mother spoke too far, and now he would respond as her father did, and she had lost—

But his voice returned steady and gentle. "Euthalia, my love, you were no fool. You answered Odin and gave him a bold story. You did not tell it quite so smoothly as you tell your tales to me, but it was your first story in a great longhouse. You would have been no less nervous if I had been beside you— more so, perhaps, if you were thinking of me instead of your audience."

That might be true, she reluctantly admitted. She would have been thinking of how her words reflected upon him, instead of thinking of how they played upon Odin. "But I was left standing alone!"

"Only for a moment, until Loki went to you and directed you to a seat."

Euthalia hesitated. "You were watching."

"Of course I was watching. But if I had intervened, you would have been my wife only. Now they have seen you for yourself."

No one can speak or write my name without his. I am nothing of myself, because they know only him. Whatever worth I had has been lost. Sigyn had warned her of being only a wife. But it seemed Vidar had steered her clear of that rocky trap before she even knew of it.

"As it went, you brought Loki down to give you aid. And Loki does not give his affection or assistance lightly. You presented yourself well, well enough that he respected you and thought to help you."

"That was not out of pity?"

Vidar laughed. "It may be possible Loki has the capacity for pity," he said, "but if he does, he would not spare it on the human bride of an Æsir. No, my love, you won those words from him, though you did not realize you had fought for them."

She frowned. "He called me a sheep."

"And that is a sure sign of his respect, for he did not call you much worse."

His hand was warm on her cheek, his fingers brushing her ear, and she was enjoying the feel of it. Was this the first time he had touched her this way? It was certainly the first time she had thought of it this way. "It is a sad thing that I cannot recognize my own husband at a feast."

He left the chair and came to the chest, sitting beside her. His hand did not leave her cheek. "I am sorry for that. I would have you know me, not by sight, but as a wife knows her husband."

Her pulse quickened, and she moved her face against his fingers. "You have been wisely careful of me, Gefjon says."

He chuckled, the sound deep in his throat. "Gefjon would. She prizes virgins. But it is true, I wished to be careful of you. You were not a prize to be wasted or lost with haste."

She was not afraid of him now—not now that he had heard her stories, had answered her questions, had spent his nights talking with her as a friend and not a husband. Or, she thought, as a husband who was a better man, a greater man, than her father. "Yes," she said simply.

He did not answer her with words, but leaned toward her and kissed her on the lips. And it was slow, and rich, and her body tightened and tingled at the feel of it. His other hand slid around her back and cradled her close, and she bent with him, her breath quickening before his mouth cut it off.

For a moment they kissed, and she marveled at the pleasure of it.

He put his arms about her and lifted her as if she weighed no more than a loaf of bread, and he settled them both in the carved chair, Euthalia resting on his legs. "This will be more comfortable than the chest," he said softly, cushioning her spine against the chair with his arm. "Let me help you prepare."

She had an idea of what he wanted, and she helped to draw her skirt high enough to accommodate his hand. But it was his hand alone which he slid beneath the fabric, letting in a brief chill which clashed delightfully with the heat of his torso against her. He brushed her secret places and she jumped, half with startlement, half with surprised enthusiasm.

She was a little afraid, yes, but not in the way she had thought she would be. But this was so new, and so unlike what she had imagined, and yet it was good. He shifted her so that he could kiss her neck and jaw, and she shivered with unexpected pleasure. Those kisses....

She and his hand were moving together now, and she couldn't tell which of them was leading, and she was feeling things she had not felt before, had not expected to feel, and she was still unsure of herself but she wanted to continue, to press on, to go further.

His lips worked up her jaw and he whispered near her ear, "Are you ready?"

She nodded. "Yes."

He gathered her into his arms, holding her tight so that the warmth of him was not lost to the cool air, and took her to the sleeping nook. He settled her upon the sheepskins and then drew the sliding door closed.

It did not take them long to warm the small space, and when he drew her dress over her head, she shivered only a little from the air and a little from his breath upon her breasts. She undressed him, moving carefully in the narrow nook, and he caught her hand and discarded the shirt and he was kissing her again, and they lay together on the sheepskins and became husband and wife in more than ceremony.

He was gone when the morning came.

Euthalia thought, before she had fully come awake, that he might have stayed with her. After all, they were truly wed now, fully husband and wife, and what reason would he have to leave her?

But as she woke, she realized the warmth against her back was a heavy woolen skin, not his torso, and she was alone in the sleeping nook. Light was creeping through the knot in the wall.

Perhaps he knows the knot is there, she thought, *and doesn't want to be seen even so dimly.*

Still, she had his name now, and the memory of his touch. And now there would be more to his night visits than stories.

CHAPTER 10

Odin called upon Euthalia to tell a story.

She was so surprised by his words that she bolted upright from her place beside Sigyn and then for a moment she could not respond. "What—I—a story, my lord?"

Cringing at her own poor words, she glanced about the hall for aid, and her eyes met Bragi's. He smiled at her.

Odin had one of his ravens on his fist, raised near his ear. "Have you no story for—"

"I shall tell you a story of hunting and vying for honor," Euthalia said quickly. "Of many brave men and one brave woman who competed for the trophy hide of a great monster."

This quick interruption did not displease Odin, but seemed rather to intrigue him. "What monster?"

"A great boar," Euthalia answered.

Heads swiveled toward Freyr, who laughed and raised his drinking horn in acknowledgment of the attention. "No boar is greater than Gullinbursti," he challenged Euthalia with a smile. When she hesitated, he explained for her benefit, "He is my own, forged living by the dwarfs as a gods-gift to me. On land or sea or air, he runs better than any horse. His tusks

77

plow the land for aid, and his very bristles glow golden with light for the darkness."

"The Calydonian boar did not plow the land, but destroyed it," rejoined Euthalia. "This monstrous boar was sent by a jealous goddess to punish a king, to ravage his land and starve the people. The king called upon all the heroes of his age to kill the monster. Would you like to hear how they fared?"

The hall rumbled with enthusiastic agreement.

Euthalia worked her way to the center of the tables, before Odin's great chair. "The king Oeneus forgot one year to honor Artemis, the goddess of the hunt, the bow-maiden and huntress-mother." She had heard Bragi's kennings and thought they would draw her audience into her foreign tale. "In her fury at having been forgotten, she sent an enormous boar to trample the kingdom's crops, to gore and terrify its people, to rake the ground and destroy all it came across."

She looked at Freyr. "I am sorry to say I have not yet seen Gullinbursti," she said, "but I can tell you this boar was enormous and fearsome. Where you might feel pride in your golden boar, only fear and loathing were felt for this boar of Calydon."

Freyr raised his drink to her deft assurance of Gullinbursti's prominence and nodded for her to continue.

"All the heroes answered the king's call for aid, great men of renowned deeds and the subjects of many songs and legends. The king's son Meleager invited also a woman called Atalanta, who had been suckled by a she-bear and carried fame as a huntress."

"A shield-maiden!" called a voice.

"A berserker-woman!" called another.

Euthalia had only a vague idea of what a berserker was, so she pressed on with her story without acknowledging the interjection. "Atalanta was the first to wound the mighty beast, striking it with an arrow."

Men and women cheered together, thumping the table and sloshing their drinks. "But the hunt!" protested Bragi. "Surely it was not ended so quickly?"

She took his meaning, and she supposed that this audience would like best all the parts her own mother had preferred to rush over. "Indeed, the hunt did not end quickly, nor did it start well. They tracked the boar to a marsh, following footprints the size of a large bull's. There the boar burst from concealment, scattering and killing their hunting hounds and charging directly into the hunters."

She looked about at the fixed eyes and the shortened breaths and she realized they *wanted* to like her story, they wanted to be entertained. She leaned forward, catching them with her eyes, and continued. "On its first charge, it tore into two young men, laying them bloody upon the marshy grass. It shattered the knees of another as it passed, dropping him helpless into the swamp. It charged a fourth man—Nestor, who would be hero of the Troy battles one day, only because he fled the boar by vaulting with his spear into the air and taking refuge in a tall tree." She was gesturing now, demonstrating how Nestor planted his boar-spear and used it to leap to safety.

"The boar tore at the oak where he hid, ripping apart the trunk and sharpening its tusks. Then it turned on the next hunters. It raged through their line and disappeared into the woods, where the trees grew too closely for their horses to follow."

The hall voiced mingled cheers and disappointment.

"Atalanta drew an arrow and sent it speeding after the monstrous boar, where it skimmed over his back and stuck hard just behind the beast's ear. Blood streamed from the wound, and the hunters cheered—until they realized who it was who had loosed the arrow. Meleager praised her winning first blood, and the others grumbled against such an honor going to a female, and against Meleager's notice of her despite his own wife at home.

"A man called Ankaios—who had first refused to hunt alongside a woman, for his pride and disdain were so great— met the boar first. He drew his two-headed axe and set to meet the monster."

"What fool would refuse to fight alongside a woman?" interrupted Skathi. "If his skill is so much better than hers, then he has nothing to fear. If her skill should prove better, then the honor is due her, and he must acknowledge it."

Euthalia nodded at her. "But Ankaios was contemptuous of Atalanta, and when her arrow pierced the beast, he said he would end the boar before she could. He faced it and began to brag of how he would kill it. He pushed into the woods, wielding his axe, and shouted, *Learn how far the weapons of a man surpass a girl's and leave this task to me!*"

Skathi snorted. "That will not end well, tale or no."

Euthalia gave her a grin. "So Ankaios faced the boar, and he raised his axe overhead with both hands, rising up high on his feet, and he shouted his defiance." She stopped, balancing on her tiptoes with arms high overhead, and looked at Skathi.

"He looks dangerously open," Skathi observed.

"And the boar rushed at him and hooked its wicked tusks into his groin, cutting upward, and all his guts poured out upon the leafy ground, and he died."

Men and women cheered the braggart's demise.

"Then Meleager charged the boar and speared him in the back, and as the beast spun and raged at the stabbing wound, Meleager sank his sword into the animal's heart, and the monster died."

The hall cheered again.

"So Meleager presented the skin and the head with its massive tusks to Atalanta, who had struck first blood—and whom Meleager admired and hoped to bed. But some of the rest of the party resented his awarding of spoils to a woman, and they set to arguing among themselves over whether a woman could receive them or even whether Meleager could award them. Words grew heated, then became threats, and then at last swords were drawn and men were slain. As for Atalanta herself—"

"They took it from her."

The words caught Euthalia by surprise, and she turned to where Freyja sat beside her brother. The goddess was watching Euthalia coolly. "They took it from her," she repeated. "Didn't they?"

Euthalia nodded. "They did. Two men seized her and took the prize from her. The boar's hide and tusks remained in a temple for centuries, before they were carried away by the Romans."

Freyja nodded, her suspicion confirmed.

"How did it end?" asked her brother Freyr. "Was the matter of the spoils settled? Did Meleager consummate his love for Atalanta?"

"Many died in the strife," Euthalia said. "Meleager himself killed his two uncles. When his mother heard this, she drew out a piece of wood which she had taken from the Fates, the women who weave all destiny."

The hall stilled, and Euthalia noted she had brushed against something more than a story to them.

"This wood marked Meleager's life."

Around her, they nodded. "Each life has a length of wood," someone muttered.

Euthalia glanced around at them, looking for a clue to what they meant, and noted a blind man gazing emptily over the table. She thought for an instant of sightless prophets, but shook the thought from her mind and focused on her own story. "This piece of wood, according to the Fates, would end Meleager's life when it was burned. His mother drew this brand out from the chest where she had hidden it, and she threw it upon the fire herself in vengeance for her slain brothers. Meleager died in the same moment."

"Such a mother's love," sneered Loki. "To kill her son for quarreling with his uncles."

Euthalia considered trying to explain the lengthy voyage of the Argonauts and the intertwined families, but she decided

81

it would only complicate her story, which had found its audience and did not need muddying.

"And this is why a woman should not fight alongside men," Baldr said, turning to gauge the effect of his words. "Look at the strife they cause."

"Or, this is why men should not be so petty when they are shown up in fair sport," returned Skathi pointedly. "If they had given honor when it was due, there would have been no strife."

Baldr nodded in acknowledgment of her point. Euthalia turned and looked to Odin to see how he had taken her story. He was nodding, expressionless, in what she assumed was approval.

Beside him, a mature blonde woman straightened. "I don't know how it is among the Greeks, but here in the North, a mother's love is greater than any grievance," she said stiffly. "But I suppose a foreign woman might succumb as you say."

Odin's mouth curved in a faint smile. "I think the songweaver gave us a suitable story," he said.

Frigg frowned slightly but did not argue. Euthalia made a small nod of obeisance and then retreated to her previous seat.

Sigyn welcomed her with an excited squeeze of her arm. "That was wonderful!"

"Really?"

"Everyone enjoyed it. You got them talking about it after. They will argue about it for days." Sigyn smiled. "And your stories are new. Most everyone here has heard the same old stories again and again."

Euthalia was uncomfortable with the praise. She nodded toward the blind man, sitting at Baldr's table. "Who is that?"

"Who?"

"There." She pointed at the man, as someone pressed a horn of mead into his hand. He nodded and smiled.

"Oh, Hodr. He cannot see. He is brother to Baldr." Sigyn shifted and nodded toward the stately woman nearest Odin's carved chair. "If Frigg had spent half the effort in seeking a cure for his sight as she did in securing safety for Baldr, Hodr would have the eyes of an elf."

"Ah, so even her unbounded mother's love has limits?"

Sigyn sniggered. "Frigg is very taken with herself at times."

"You came again to the feast," Vidar said that night, cradling her close. "Does the company please you?"

They reclined together in the dark, warm in the closed sleeping compartment and sheepskins. He had come again only when all lights in the house were extinguished.

"I have a friend there," she said, "and fewer friends here. But I wonder if I belong there, for all that I am your wife."

His smile could be heard in his voice. "Valhöll can be rather monotonous after a time."

"Is there nothing else but the feast?"

"That is the promise of Valhöll. A warrior who dies bravely and honorably in battle will be taken by the valkyrjur to the Hall of the Slain, to feast until they fight at Ragnarok."

"And what is Ragnarok?"

"It is the end of all things, when chaos finally overwhelms order, and all the gods and humankind will be destroyed."

She blinked. "And the warriors will stop it?"

"No, it cannot be stopped."

"Then—what can be done? Why will Odin call them to fight?"

His voice changed as he tipped his head to regard her, perplexed by her confusion. "To fight, as I said. It is not to stop Fate; that cannot be done. It is to fight bravely and die courageously."

She could not quite decide whether this was admirable self-possession or futile madness.

Vidar sensed her hesitation. "The great end of a warrior's life is to be a hero. And no one can be a hero if his cause is easy and prevails without obstruction. Any man can pretend to be a hero while the fight is easy, or can even fight the difficult fight for a time in the hope that respite will come. But real heroism can only be proved by a lost cause. A man who fights to the death is a different man than the one who fights for a time and then surrenders or flees because he cannot see victory."

"But the tales of—"

"None of your Greek heroes are true heroes. Your Apollo, your Heracles, they are invincible. The wonder of their tale is in their unusual fiber, not in their valor. When was Heracles ever unsure of his victory? When did Bellerophon face the chimera without the miraculous aid of a flying horse to keep him well out of flame and danger? Did Perseus attack the two immortal Gorgons, or only the mortal Medusa—and did he not attack even her as she slept? No, the heroes of your tales are not heroes, they are bullies who use their strength against opponents who cannot hope to resist, cowards who attack only those they are certain to defeat without risk to themselves."

Euthalia started to protest, began to name all the dead heroes of Odysseus and the house of Oedipus, but she hesitated. Even these, she realized, did not purposefully go to meet their deaths. Even Jason had relied upon trickery and the treachery of Medea to win the Golden Fleece.

He shook his head and smiled at her. "Our bravery is not how you think, my love, but it is what we know. The end will come whether we fight or not, but we choose how we will meet it."

She nodded slowly. "I understand. Well, not entirely, but I think I understand what you are telling me."

"Good enough to start." He kissed her temple. "What question next, my love?"

She took a breath. "Why will you not come in the day?"

His voice was casual, but his answer came a heartbeat too slowly. "I have many duties by day, my love. I come to you when I am free."

His lie stung her. "Even by night, you will not come while a light is burning. Why—" she braced herself to say it—"why don't you want me to see you?"

For a long moment he was quiet, and she thought he was preparing to explain. But at last he said only, "It is my only command to you, that you do not look on me."

"But why? I know your body, I have touched you, there is no damage to your face, and—"

"Stop," he said, and his tone cut through her protest like a blade. "Euthalia, please—are we not happy? Don't I love you, and you me? Can we not continue this way?"

She hesitated. "I do love you." She had not said it before, and she was unhappy to have first said it now, in this conflicted conversation.

"Then let us be content with what we have. Do not light a lamp while I am here. Wait for the winter, when we will have more hours together. And let us be content with our happiness."

There was a strain to his voice, an urgency he tried to hide. "Vidar, what is it? What are you hiding?"

They still lay together, but there was a cool distance to him now. His voice grated. "Can you not grant me this single request, this one favor? For your love of me?"

"That's not fair," she returned. "It is for love of you that I ask."

They pulled apart, half-sitting in the low compartment, facing one another unseen. Cold air slapped at Euthalia's flesh where the sheepskins fell away.

His voice, always deep, rumbled now like an angry dragon's. "Do not look upon me. Ever. We will speak in the dark, we will eat in the dark, we will love in the dark, and we will be happy in the dark. That is my final word on the matter."

For just an instant Euthalia thought of her father, threatening his household in what she knew now was fear for his precious and precarious status, and her blood flooded hot through her. "Then if that is your word, you had better command also that the sun should not rise and the moon not shine, lest a beam come through this knot in the wall and illuminate whatever it is I am not to see. In fact, as a good wife,

I should go and patch it now." She pushed herself out of the bed and into the cooler main room.

"Euthalia!"

She drew on her clothing and seized the bearskin she'd been given on the boat. She shoved her feet into her shoes.

"Euthalia, stop."

She pushed out the door and went around the side of the house, snatching up a loose handful of crumbly dirt bound with grass roots. She found the knot by the light of the slivered moon and crammed the handful into it, sending showers of dirt down the wall.

His voice came through the wall. "Euthalia, stop."

But he did not come out of the house, fearful even of the thin moon.

Euthalia turned away from the house and went across to the baking oven, curling herself against the warm clay and wrapping the bearskin against the cold.

She woke in the morning light, stiff with huddling to the oven and her residual anger. The sun hung over the horizon, slanting beams beneath the baking hut's low roof to pierce her sleep. She rose, pulling the bearskin about her, and started back to the house.

She hesitated at the door, wondering for a moment if he might have stayed, and then pushed it back. But there was no one inside.

She went to the sleeping compartment, finding the sheepskins spread smooth and flat. He had gone. And when he had gone, he had passed by the oven, and he had not stopped for her.

She climbed into the skins with her bearskin, clenching her fists in the anger she needed to bury her fears. If she offended her husband in this place, what would become of her? Would she be returned to the human world to live as a thrall among the raiders, or would she live alone in the empty village with only Birna?

If he so feared being seen, even in the faint light of a crescent moon, what did he hide?

She fell asleep again and woke only when Birna entered. "Still abed, Euthalia? It must have been quite a night."

Euthalia did not have the humor to tolerate such jests. "Birna—you did not see my husband leave, did you?"

The thrall shook her head. "Oh, no. I sleep too far from here." There were plenty of empty houses in the village.

"Do you ever see him go?"

"Of course not—I would not watch you at night!"

"I didn't mean that you did. I only.... Have you ever seen him?"

"What?"

"Seen him! Have you ever just—seen him? With your own eyes?"

Birna tipped her head as if considering Euthalia's reason. "Yes. But I am not the bride. I have no place in the world of the gods, save to serve you here. What does it matter if I look upon a god?"

Euthalia's breath ran out of her in a stream. "Oh."

"What's the matter? Don't you believe he is real? Doesn't he come to you?"

"He does, but—why can't I see him?"

Birna's eyes went wide. "Has he no form when he is here? How is he husband to you?"

Euthalia shook her head. "No, he's real, he has a body, he is really here, but I cannot see him. He comes only by night, and he will not enter if there is a light. He forbade me to look at him. What is he hiding?"

Birna shrugged. "It seems to me you would have discovered any deformity or defect by now."

Euthalia felt herself blush. "His body is complete in every way, yes."

"Then why question? You are the wife of a god, Euthalia—you must expect it to be different than to be the wife of a man. And you have advantages over many unhappy women. It may be ingratitude to question them as you enjoy them."

Euthalia bit her lip. If nothing else, Birna was right that she could not expect marriage to a god to be without surprise. And perhaps she should not question.

If she offended her husband here, what would become of her?

She nodded. "If it is a quirk of his preference, then it is a far milder one than many wives must suffer. Show me how to weave the flax."

The sliver of moon was a bit thinner that night, edging toward complete darkness. Euthalia curled within the sleeping compartment, wrapped in comforting sheepskin, and waited for the sun to disappear below the horizon.

He knocked once and then entered, calling from the threshold. "Euthalia?"

"I'm here."

He stepped inside. "I thought you'd be near the fire. It's brisk tonight."

"It's darker in here."

He slid open the door, blocking the light so that he appeared as a black bulk. "I did not mean that you could not enjoy the fire."

She kept her eyes away from him. "I love you, Vidar. But I also know I cannot afford to anger you, and that can make it difficult to discern if an action is rooted in love or fear. On both counts, I wish to honor your request that I not look upon you." She laid a subtle emphasis on the word *request*.

He took a breath, waiting in the entrance. "I will endeavor to make my request in a reasonable and compassionate manner. And I will remember to appreciate your gracious accommodation of my particular oddity." He looked up, his face invisible against the faint firelight. "Is that acceptable?"

Euthalia rolled onto her knees and crawled to meet him. "I suppose it will be."

They kissed, gently, and then he crawled into the sleeping compartment. She wrapped him in the sheepskins with her, and they lay close together in the dark.

CHAPTER 12

"Tell me of Loki the Jötunn," Euthalia said one night.

"Loki?" Vidar repeated. "Why do you ask about Loki?"

"I know his wife," she said. "She is a friend to me here—and while I look forward to my talks with you, and while my days here with Birna are pleasant, I am lonely, too, and she is a comfort to me."

"Hm. I had forgotten Loki had taken a wife," he mused.

No one will recall your name or your deeds, not human bard nor gods themselves, Sigyn had warned. "Her name is Sigyn. I don't know if she might have been a sacrifice like myself."

He leaned over and kissed her forehead. "You are no sacrifice," he said, "though you were intended to be. But I love you for yourself." He sat back against the wall. "Loki is a sworn brother of Odin, but he is not trustworthy, not like one of us. He can be helpful, and we owe him much, but he can also be cruel in his tricks or pranks and yes, even malicious. Do not treat with him, not ever, for it is like bargaining with the sea, which rolls backward and forward at once without ever appearing to contradict itself."

She nodded, though he could not see her. "I will keep that in mind. Sigyn said the Jötnar are forces of chaos."

He laughed. "Loki is, certainly."

"What do you mean?"

"Loki has great power," he said, more thoughtfully, "but also great pride. He fancies himself put upon when things go against him, even if it was his own doing. His mind is clever, very clever, but he is as likely to spin a clever lie as to forge a clever solution." He hesitated. "And he has a furious temper, when it is roused, and a long memory."

There was an edge to his voice, and Euthalia wanted to ask for an example but shied away. "Do they have children?"

"Loki and Sigyn? Yes, though I have not thought of them for years. And Loki has other children as well. He fathered Hel and Jörmungandr and Fenrir, all with another Jötunn. And of course he is the mother of Sleipnir, Odin's horse."

Euthalia wondered if the magic of their shared language were slipping. "You mean father."

"Er, no, I mean mother. It is an awkward thing to explain, but when we were in danger of losing a wager which would have cost us dear, we tasked Loki with distracting a powerful stallion to keep him from his work. Loki accomplished this by becoming a mare—and quite a fetching one, to judge from the stallion's reaction. In due time, Loki gave birth to a grey colt, with eight legs, and that is the steed which Odin now rides up and down Yggdrasill to travel between the worlds."

Euthalia took a moment to try to fold this revelation into her comprehension. "He—then—and Odin rides him?"

"Sleipnir is a horse," he assured her. "Just a horse, although an unusual one, with more legs and more bravery than most. But he does not have a mind or speech like Fenrir."

"Who—what—is Fenrir?"

"Fenrir is a wolf, though that is the same as to say that Yggdrasill is a tree. He is a mighty beast, and fearsome, and one day he will kill Odin, in the time of Ragnarok. And then I will fight him."

He said this in such a matter-of-fact manner that she did not instantly recognize the awful meaning. "But if Loki is his father, then Odin is sworn family, and why should he kill him?"

"Ah, gentle Euthalia, Ragnarok is all about the destruction of the ties which bind the world. If Odin himself were his father, then Fenrir would hesitate not a heartbeat longer."

She thought a moment, but one thought occurred to her and pressed the others aside. If the children of such beings could be such dangerous beasts, what might she bear, if she were to conceive? "Are all the children of the gods so terrible?"

"What? Oh, no. No, Fenrir is not the child of a god, but the offspring of a Jötunn with another Jötunn. Hel and Jörmungandr are the same. And Sleipnir is the product of a Jötunn with a horse. No, none of them are the product of the gods." His voice warmed. "You need have no concern on that point."

She felt herself flush warm and was grateful he could not see her so plainly in the dark. "And his other sons?"

"Nari and Narfi? They are not like the others, but take after their mother, the woman you know. She came long ago, I cannot remember how."

"Was she a sacrifice like me?"

He shook his head. "I really can't say. There cannot be so many who would offer a gift to Loki, for he is a treacherous slope and few would petition him. He might have won her in a gamble, or taken her in a trick, or even wooed her himself somehow—though I cannot imagine that, to be honest."

She had to agree with his skepticism. "I don't see how a woman would be wooed by a husband who becomes a mare to bear children with a horse. But you said that was to save a wager. What bet was that?"

"Ah, Asgard needed strengthening after our war with the Vanir, and a wall was offered to us. The price for the wall was Freyja, who would marry the smith building the wall. We considered the price high, and Freyja flatly refused, but Loki suggested we accept the bargain with the condition that the wall must be completed within a single winter. This seemed safe enough, and so the pact was made.

"But three days before the equinox, the Jötunn builder had only to set the gate to complete his task. He was a far better smith and engineer than we had guessed, and his horse had such strength to haul boulders and set stones that the work had progressed much more quickly than we had supposed possible. And so we turned to Loki, who had suggested the intolerable agreement, and told him if the wall were completed and Freyja consigned to the builder, it would be his death."

She stared at him open-mouthed in the dark. "You cheated!" she cried. "When it seemed you would lose fairly, you cheated!"

"We did not cheat. Loki distracted the horse, but we did not interfere with his work directly."

"You did enough. And why threaten Loki?"

"It was Loki who recommended the terms."

"And did his oath bind you to them? Or was it your own?"

There was an uncomfortable silence.

"You agreed, and then you cheated. The lot of you."

"And would you have had us give Freyja away as a prize?"

"Oh, no." She pointed a finger at him. "If you felt it was an unfair thing to promise Freyja, then you should never have agreed in the first place. The time to debate terms is before a contract is signed, not when it is due."

"Spoken like a merchant's daughter," he answered with grudging tone. "But we needed the wall, and indeed it has served us well since then. Without the wall, Asgard might be lost."

"And wasn't it you who told me that there cannot be heroes without lost causes? That the thing was not to win in safety, but to strive past the point of hope? But here you tell me that when there was a chance to hide behind a wall, you took it at any price, even the price of one of your own, and then you betrayed your word to wriggle out of paying." She shook her head. "And I will venture that you did not even pay the builder for his work, did you, though he did all the work you asked."

He hesitated just a moment too long in answering. "No."

"What do you mean by that? There's more there, I can tell."

"The agreement had a penalty by each party," he said. "If the wall was completed, then we lost Freyja. If the wall was not completed... Thor killed him."

She opened her mouth, stopped and then closed it sharply.

"No, Euthalia, you are right. It was cruel, and more than a little treacherous. We... are not as great as we were."

"He must have felt so happy," she said. "He had done the impossible, pleased the gods, earned the wife of his dreams, an actual goddess, and then abruptly he was foresworn and he was killed."

"You sound as if you think he should have won Freyja."

"No," she said. "But men—many men—think to win women by deeds. No matter what Freyja might think, he would still be happy to think he had succeeded."

"And you think his happiness should have been fulfilled."

"I think he should not have been promised what was never possible—Freyja as a prize."

An owl hooted outside, and Euthalia jumped with the closeness of it. "It must be on the roof!"

"It is hunting close tonight," he agreed, grateful for the change of subject. "The new moon and the shortening days are giving it fine eating before the winter."

Euthalia did not bring up Loki or the wager again that night.

CHAPTER 13

It was a bright day, full of birdsong, and Euthalia had nothing else to demand her attention, and so she walked out upon the empty village.

She had already explored the other buildings, slightly larger than what she seemed to remember and eerily vacant of both people and tools, household objects, personal treasures, all that made them human dwellings. Still, she walked among them, imagining the purpose of each—this was a metalsmith's workshop, by the forge in the center, and this a weaver's—and savoring the crisp air.

She walked outside of the village, curious to see how Asgard stretched beyond it, but remembering Sigyn's description of deceptive distances, she kept within sight of the buildings.

She circled until she came to the stream, north of where the beast-ships had come into the village. She sat by it a while, tossing grass and leaves to be carried away by the current, and watched two rabbits foraging on the opposite bank. At last she stood and started back toward the village.

She parted the tall grass as she walked, hardly able to see her route but knowing she could not go wrong as long as she followed the water. The wind rustled the grass about her, muffling her steps, and she felt even more than usual that she was alone in this curious fragment of a world.

She was surprised when her next step took her into the offering circle, and more surprised to find a man sitting in its midst.

She pulled back a little, startled, and he whirled on the ground to face her. It was Loki, she recognized, and he was gravely wounded.

He relaxed upon seeing her, and she wondered very briefly whom he had feared to see. But then his expression shifted to embarrassment and resentment. He spoke before she could. "What are you doing here?"

"You're injured," she said, thinking that was more important. "What happened? How can I help?"

Loki rolled his eyes at her. "I tripped on a pebble."

Well, she probably shouldn't have asked. She stepped into the circle, looking him over. His nose was crooked, broken, with dried blood crusted beneath. One eye was swelling, and the opposite cheekbone seemed to sit lower than it should. By the way he cradled his side, leaning against the offering rock, he had cracked or broken ribs, and the sudden turn at her entrance had abused them freshly.

"It was Thor and Baldr," she said aloud. "They came for you."

He started to retort and stopped abruptly, curling an arm about his torso. He tried again, less forcefully and perhaps more truthfully. "It was."

"Why?"

He chuckled. "For all that I am known as a lie-smith, and not without reason, I will tell you this—nothing provokes like truth." He shook his head. "And I was a fingertip's grasp from setting Thor's full strength against Baldr's invincibility. Did Frigg secure a promise also from Mjollnir? It would have been grand to see."

"Who is Mjollnir?"

He seemed surprised at her ignorance. "Thor's hammer, of course." The corner of his mouth curled. "I brought it to him. I goaded the dwarfs into making it, the finest of god-gifts." He looked at her. "And when the dwarfs wanted my head and I fled, do you know who it was who brought me back to them? Thor. And he stood by, new gift in hand, as they pierced my lips with an awl and sewed my mouth shut."

Euthalia stared, horrified. "They...."

"And it was my cunning which won Mjollnir back when it was stolen. I am the reason we have a wall against Asgard's enemies. It was I who brought the ransom when Odin and Honir were held captive. And yet for all that, I am their plaything and scapegoat."

Euthalia swallowed. "Let me help you."

"Heh." He shook his head. "I have a wife of my own, you know. If I wanted tending, I would have gone home to her."

But he was ashamed to be seen beaten, and she doubted he would let even Sigyn see him in his defeat.

"You must tell Odin what has happened," Euthalia said. "He can put an end to this."

Loki raised his eyes to her, and she saw incredulity and laughter and disdain, all at once. He shook his head once, dismissing her amusingly foolish suggestion, and gingerly took a piece of fruit from the rock to eat.

Euthalia looked at Loki, at his broken face and his bleeding skin and his dry, untroubled eyes. "But how?" she asked. "How can you stand this? You are Odin's sworn brother, and you are one of them in all but blood—and they owe you for so many services. How can you take what they do to you without protest?"

One corner of his mouth curled upward, a sardonic smirk made more horrible by the trickle of crimson it brought from his broken lip. "Naive little butterfly," he said. "You forget the simplest of truths. I am not of the Æsir, no matter how much time I spend with them here in Asgard. I was born Jötunn, and I am still Jötunn, and Ragnarok is coming. And when Ragnarok descends, no matter how the Æsir and Vanir fight against the end, they will die, and the Jötunn will prevail and destroy all, Asgard and Midgard and everything above and below." He grinned. "And while they pick at me with their petty words, and when they beat me with their stones and staves, I know that it is only time which stands between this momentary pain and my complete victory, and that finite time is running like water down a hill." The grin widened, showing bloody teeth. "And sweeter yet, I know they know it, too."

Euthalia stared, her stomach hollow with horror.

Loki took another piece of fruit. "Leave me here to consume these offerings," he said, "and I will be well enough in time. And while I might ask your discretion, innocent little lamb, there would be little point; Baldr and Thor will be boasting enough tonight of their prowess in outnumbering me while armed with invulnerable skin and a belt of great strength." His voice dripped disdain. "And they will have the laughter of all."

Euthalia tried twice to speak. "What can I do?"

Loki's mouth curved. "Wait. Wait and watch." His teeth flashed red.

CHAPTER 14

Euthalia went to the longhouse that night, and she looked first for Sigyn—there, beckoning her to join—and then for Loki, in his usual place near Odin's carved chair.

She looked next for Vidar, though she did not know how she might know him. The hall stretched long and it was full of big men, and none of them seemed to watch her with more regard than the others.

Loki bore some recognizable bruising, if she looked for it, but he looked much better than she had expected. Most in the longhouse probably had no idea of the injuries he had suffered. Euthalia slipped beside Sigyn and asked, "How is he?"

"What?"

"Your husband—how is he?"

Sigyn's eyes dropped. "How did you know?"

"I found him after. He was at the offering circle near my house." Euthalia hesitated. "He was in poor condition, but he refused my help."

Sigyn nodded, smiling wanly. "That is typical of him. He cannot bear to be helpless or pitied by others, even if he pities himself at times."

"He seems nearly well now."

Sigyn nodded again. "That is one advantage they have. An offering, a magic nut or berry, and all the miseries of mortality can be discarded."

"A story!" someone shouted. "Give us a story!"

"A story!" the cry went up. "A tale!"

Bragi, the gods' own skald, stood, but the call continued. "No, a Greek tale! Tell us a new story, a story of the strange southern gods! Where is Euthalia?"

Euthalia felt her face grow warm, but she glanced at Sigyn and smiled. "I suppose they like me at least a little," she said, and she hoped it did not sound like bragging to the forgotten Sigyn. But Sigyn was smiling with real pleasure, she thought, and urging her up with the others.

Euthalia climbed atop a table so that all could see and hear her, and the long hall whooped with approval and anticipation. She lifted her hands. "And what kind of story would you hear tonight, friends?"

"Bravery!"

"Treachery!"

"Love!"

"Victory!"

She gestured for quiet again. "What about you, Lord Odin? What would you have us hear?"

Odin, detached as ever, grunted from his chair. "Your Greeks are fond of tragic stories, and those are different enough from our own. Give us a story of tragic death."

"A tragic death." Euthalia scanned her memory.

"A dear one's death," Odin added.

Euthalia wondered if she were missing something in the court politics of Asgard, if Odin were using her to deliver a message, but she could not think of anything which might be related. "I could tell you of Apollo and Hyakinthos," she said. "It is not a long story, but it is very sad."

"Very sad!" cheered the tables of gods and warriors.

"Apollo is the god of the sun," she began, "or so the Greeks say. They say he rides a chariot of fire across the sky, and that is what lights the world."

The Æsir jeered good-naturedly at this.

"Apollo is the handsomest of the Greek gods, forever a young man in the prime of life. And he has had many lovers, both mortal and immortal."

The hall cheered again at this. Sex was always a popular subject for a story.

"But he was especially fond of his dearest Hyakinthos."

They liked the strange names, which added to the exotic feel of the stories. "Was she human?" called one voice.

"Was she beautiful?" called another.

Euthalia hesitated. "Hyakinthos was very beautiful, and human, but—he was a man. A young man, handsome beyond all others, like Apollo himself."

The general enthusiasm faltered, and Euthalia regretted her error in judgment. Even among the more scandalous reports like Freyja and Freyr's incestuous union or the many unions with Jötnar or other outsiders, nothing she had heard here involved two men as lovers. She might have shocked the fierce warriors into disapproval.

But she had failed to recall the general proclivity for the prurient, and this new fact only underscored their general amusement in the Greek ways. "Man-lovers!" Baldr declared. "It is very Greek of them!"

Euthalia breathed a sigh of relief and went on. "But Apollo and Hyakinthos, while wholly infatuated with one another, were not alone unto themselves. Remember I said that Apollo had many bed-mates, willing and unwilling, mortal and immortal. He sired many children. And Hyakinthos was also greatly admired by Zephyrus, the god of the western wind."

This triangle of man-lovers was a new level of titillation for the more than half-drunk audience, and they laughed and cheered. The laughter grew suddenly louder, and Euthalia turned to see Loki the Jötunn standing beside the fire pit, fists grasping after an invisible and elusive lover as he drove his pelvis again and again into nothing at all. He stumbled about, seeking and always missing his unseen target. "It is hard to hump the wind!" he declared in mock frustration, and the listening hall roared with laughter.

This was supposed to be a tragic tale, Euthalia reflected with faint despair. It would be difficult to bring her rowdy listeners under the story's spell. Best to move past the sex and focus on the skills of training, something they would also appreciate but in a different way. "Apollo taught Hyakinthos to throw the discus—that is, it is a projectile, a flat disc to be thrown as far as possible. It is a contest of skill among the best athletes."

"It seemed they had other athletic skills that were in great demand," called Loki in an overloud whisper, and the hall burst into fresh laughter.

Euthalia gritted her teeth. "It is a weapon," she said. "Surely such skilled warriors who have earned a place in the Hall of the Slain can appreciate the deadly efficiency of a metal plate which strikes in the head at a hundred paces or more?"

They could, and they nodded and cheered, and she had them again for a moment at least. "So Apollo taught Hyakinthos this difficult skill, and they spent long hours together, and Zephyrus grew jealous to see that Hyakinthos preferred Apollo to him.

"And so one day, as Hyakinthos threw the discus with Apollo, Zephyrus observed them, In a sudden fit of jealousy, he determined that if he could not have Hyakinthos to himself, then no one should have him, and he blew hard upon the discus—"

"Blew hard," intoned Loki, and the listening gods and warriors snorted and laughed.

Euthalia pressed on. "And Zephyrus caught the discus with his wind and turned it back upon Hyakinthos. It struck him hard in the forehead and he dropped to the ground, bleeding."

The listeners quieted a little, caught off-guard by the sudden death though they had been warned it was a tragic tale.

"Apollo ran to his Hyakinthos and cradled him in his arms, sobbing, but there was nothing to be done. The pretty boy's head had been crushed, and bone and brain spilled onto the grass." This was a rather more lurid telling than any she had heard, but she thought her listeners would appreciate the detail, and she was not wrong. "And Apollo cried and wished aloud that it had been him to be struck instead of Hyakinthos, and he swore that Hades would not have his dearest companion. And so he took the broken body and the blood, and he transformed them into a flower, a beautiful purple flower, marked with characters to read, *Alas*, to express forever Apollo's mourning."

There was a moment of quiet, and then a voice called, "And then what?"

Euthalia shook her head. "And then the flower grew and spread, and they may be seen yet today. That is the end of the story."

"No, did Apollo go and kill Zephyrus to avenge Hyakinthos? Was there blood feud?"

"Er, no. No, the Greek gods do not war with one another. That is, they certainly have their disputes and their quarrels, and at times they are even petty in their politics, but they do not enter blood feud on—"

"Then this Apollo is no god!" declared one of the valkyrjur's chosen. "How can a man allow his lover to be murdered, even a man-lover, and do nothing?"

"Where is Zephyrus now?" demanded another.

"He—he is the west wind, he resides on Olympus with the others," she tried. "But this was long ago—"

"Murdered blood does not dry," they shouted. "Apollo should have acted!"

For a moment she thought they meant to assault Olympus itself, to drag Zephyrus from the mountain and demand justice for a death a millennium and more ago. But their contempt for Apollo's weakness kept them from taking his side, she realized, and thus from joining his cause.

"Certainly it was a lapse in Apollo's justice," she agreed. She tried to remember what had become of Zephyrus, to see if she could placate them with a satisfactory conclusion.

"It is a good story," said Odin, and that seemed to settle the question. The hall cheered.

"It paints a better picture of the Greeks," conceded Loki. "Even if they cannot avenge their dead, one has to admit the discus is an efficient weapon."

"Let us have our own contest tomorrow," called Baldr to the Æsir and Vanir and Jötnar about him. "We can throw our own weapons!"

"And you can be the target!" added Thor, and all laughed and agreed.

Sigyn leaned close as Euthalia returned to her seat. "A good story," she agreed. "They won't soon forget that one."

CHAPTER 15

They met for the game in a broad, flat field, lined with thorny bushes marked with bits of captured wool from browsing sheep. The gods and Jötnar gathered, joking and slapping one another's backs as they displayed their choice of weaponry to attack Baldr.

Euthalia divided her attention between their preparations and simply looking about the field and surroundings. Sigyn had instructed her on how to pass through Valhöll and into this separate part of Asgard, and she was delighted with her new ability to travel beyond her own tiny empty village. She would learn how to visit all of this strange country.

Baldr stepped out, arms raised overhead, and the group cheered. Blond, tall, powerful, he was every bit the shining god Loki had called him. He was clearly a favorite among the Æsir and Vanir.

"Bring your best!" he challenged.

Freyr went first, throwing a fist-sized rock with disturbing precision against Baldr's skull. It struck and bounced off him without harm.

The missiles began flying in earnest. Pebbles, rocks, a spear, even a throwing axe. Laughter and cheers rang around as Baldr withstood them all without so much as a flinch.

Frigg, Baldr's mother, watched with a tight expression varying between worry and pleased relief. Her arms were folded across her chest, daring anyone or anything to harm her favorite son.

"Could I try?" asked Sigyn, and Euthalia turned toward her in surprise.

But no one seemed to think anything of the woman stepping forward with a switch cut from a sapling. Baldr smiled at her, a bit distantly as if he were trying to place her face or recall her name. Sigyn did not introduce herself as she stepped forward and struck him full across the face with the switch .

A roar of surprise and hilarity rose from the spectators, and Baldr himself laughed with the ferociousness of the attack. It did not hurt him, of course. Sigyn lashed him with the switch a dozen times before dropping it with a little shrug and a smile. The onlookers cheered her attempt and turned their attention to the next assailant.

Euthalia caught Sigyn's arm as she returned. "He did not know you, I think. He didn't know why you did it."

"No," Sigyn concurred. "But I feel the better for it."

They looked across to where Loki stood a little apart, watching. His eye met Sigyn's, and for a moment Euthalia saw a tiny smile pass between them, a glimpse of something she thought she should not have been privileged to see.

A few paces from Loki stood Hodr, Baldr's blind brother. He was not participating in the sport, either. Loki closed the distance between them. "You will not challenge Baldr with the others?"

Hodr looked surprised to hear someone speaking to him. "Loki? No, of course not."

"It is one thing to shun me, a Jötunn and a thief and a liar. It is another to shun Baldr's own brother. They should let you join them."

Hodr smiled wanly. "I think it is obvious why I cannot."

"Oh, of course," said Loki. "It is because you did not bring a weapon." He produced a slender shaft of pale green wood. "Here, I will lend you one."

Hodr chuckled. "Even you, oh shifter of shape and of words, must know that it is not the lack of a weapon which keeps me from sporting with the others."

Loki snorted. "So you cannot see. What, are you afraid of accidentally hitting him?"

Now Hodr laughed aloud. "I suppose that would be a foolish fear, after all."

Euthalia, watching, smiled to herself. There was a tender side to Loki, after all. He loved Sigyn and appreciated her striking back for him in her own way, and he could show kindness to a blind man and bring him into a communal game.

Loki pressed the pale green wand into Hodr's hand. "Go ahead," he urged. "While he's standing alone, and there's no risk of hitting anyone but him."

Hodr started to speak, hesitated, and then grinned. "You know, I think I will."

Two dozen paces away, Skathi loosed an arrow into Baldr's chest. He slapped the place where it struck and grinned proudly.

"Now, he is standing alone," Loki said. "Go ahead."

Hodr raised the wand over his shoulder like a spear, point forward, and Loki gently adjusted his aim. Then Hodr stepped forward and threw the little green shaft. It sailed forward past the grinning group to pierce Baldr's throat, sticking partway through his neck.

Baldr stood frozen for an instant, eyes wide, and then he raised his hands to grasp at the protruding shaft. His mouth opened, but no sound came out.

"Did I strike him?" asked Hodr with a grin.

Frigg screamed.

Baldr's knees went from beneath him and he spilled onto the grass. The group surged toward him, all speaking or shouting at once, and Frigg clawed her way through them all to reach her son. "Baldr! Baldr!"

"What happened?" demanded Hodr, reaching a hand toward Loki. Panic edged his voice. "What happened?"

"It seems the shining god has fallen," drawled Loki.

Euthalia stared at him, sick horror crawling through her stomach and lungs and up her throat. He had done it, he had used the game—

Like Zephyrus.

Sigyn's fingers were digging hard into Euthalia's arm. "No," she whispered. "No, no—they will say it was Loki. They will say he did it."

"But...." Euthalia was having trouble forming words.

"But it was Hodr. Hodr cast it. Not Loki."

"He is dead," declared Freyr, rising from beside Baldr's sprawled body. "Baldr is dead."

Thor turned in place and roared, "Loki!"

Loki straightened. "What? I did not throw anything."

Hodr was working his mouth like a fish. "Dead? Dead? But I only—how could it have harmed him?"

"Perhaps it is because you are his brother," said Loki. "Perhaps that undid the protection."

"It is you, Loki!" snarled Thor. "We know it was you!"

Loki raised his hands. "Now wait one moment," he said. "This is a sacred field. We cannot shed blood here, not even mine."

"Blood has already been shed," snapped Bragi.

A number of the gods and goddesses about the fallen Baldr turned and started toward Loki. For a moment he looked at them worriedly, and then he sprang into the air and compressed into a smaller shape, unfolding two pointed wings and catching the air as a falcon. He climbed into the sky and sped away.

Thor roared a series of expletives after the disappearing form as Euthalia stared open-mouthed. Hodr began to sob, going to his knees.

Frigg rose beside Baldr's handsome corpse, and the crowd quieted, turning toward the grief-stricken mother. Frigg turned her dreadful pale expression upon them. "Who here would earn my love and favor?" she asked in a terrible, level voice.

A chorus of voices rose around Euthalia.

Frigg nodded once, a sharp movement like the drop of a blade. "Then *bring me Loki.*"

CHAPTER 16

Valhöll was Odin's greatest hall, but it was not his only hall. The einherjar, the dead warriors, were not invited to this function, but all connected to the Æsir and the Vanir were summoned. Euthalia could not have refused even if she wanted to. And she did not want to. Sigyn would need her.

They stood close together, clutching hands, as they waited.

Frigg sat rigid in her chair, weeping silently. Euthalia wanted to go to her, to put an arm around her and cry with her, but she could not leave Sigyn, and Frigg did not know Euthalia, to want comfort from her. But Frigg looked very alone as she sat there.

There was a sound of hoofbeats, and Odin sat upright in his great chair, his face a carved mask like the wooden beasts on either side of him. "They have come," he said simply.

Sigyn's fingers clawed into Euthalia's.

The doors at the rear of the hall opened, and a mounted party entered. At the front rode Kvasir, lent Odin's own eight-legged horse Sleipnir to speed the search. He led the others inside, hooves loud in the anxious silence, and they drew to a halt in the center of the hall before Odin's great chair.

"He had hidden himself as a salmon in a waterfall pool," reported Kvasir, "but we netted him out."

He hauled a bundle over Sleipnir's quarters and dumped it onto the ground. Loki landed hard, naked and tangled in the netting. Sigyn gasped and choked, but the sound was swallowed by the angry murmur which arose from the onlookers.

Euthalia looked around the assembled gods and Jötnar. *Vidar, where are you?*

Sleipnir turned his head to look at the sprawled Loki, his ears pricked. Euthalia wondered whether the horse could recognize its parent, or whether it was merely curious as to the proceedings.

Odin glared down at the dark-haired Jötunn, now kneeling within his tied-off net. "Why did you do it?" he demanded.

Loki worked his mouth a moment to answer. His face was swollen and dark with bruising. "I did not kill Baldr," he said, his voice thick. "I could not harm the shining god."

"Mistletoe."

All eyes shifted to Frigg. Her voice was quavering steel. "I sought an oath from all things, that they would not harm my son Baldr. All things, rock and wood and iron, but for the young mistletoe, which was too small and too weak to pose a threat."

"How was Hodr to know that?" asked Loki. "Or I?"

"I told only one person of that omission," said Frigg. "A bothersome old woman, who wanted to make chatter with me about every silly thing, even to the caretaking of my shining son."

"Then you have said yourself that there could be no way for Hodr to know—"

"That old woman was you!" snapped Frigg. "You change your shape as you change your mind, Lie-Smith. You were a horse when it suited you to receive a stallion's pleasure. You were a falcon when you needed to flee, and a salmon when you sought to hide. And you were an old woman when you wished to spy."

Loki raised his head to meet her gaze. "So your accusation is that I became an old woman in the hope that you would carelessly mention your favorite son's only weakness, and then I put that single, improbable weapon into the hand of a blind man, in the hope that he would somehow be fortunate enough to strike down an invincible god with a green twig?" He shook his head. "It seems you have far more to blame in yourself and in Hodr than in me."

Frigg seemed to swell with rage, her arms rising from her chair as she leaned forward and hissed like a snake. "It—was—you!"

"Enough!" Odin rose from his chair, and the room fell silent.

He had done it, Euthalia saw. Loki had manipulated Baldr into suggesting a throwing contest and Thor into inviting fresh challenge against Baldr's protection. He had set Hodr to throw the mistletoe at his otherwise-invulnerable brother. He had done it all.

Euthalia recognized his guilt, and she remembered him sitting in the little offering circle, bloody and broken. She wanted to speak against him, wanted to speak for him, and the conflicting words bound in her throat and she could say nothing.

Sigyn's breath sobbed close beside Euthalia's ear.

Odin took a step forward, and the two wolves backed out of his way. "Hodr will be dealt with for his part in this," Odin snarled. "But yours is the greater fault."

Loki looked up at Odin. "We are brothers, Odin. We are sworn brothers."

"That was before you killed my son." Odin pointed. "But fear not, I will not have you killed. We will not soil the ground with your blood. But you will be bound, so you can do no further harm." He raised a hand. "We will travel the Bifröst."

There was a gentle rumble and then light burst around them, breaking into a thousand prismatic points. Euthalia recognized the brilliance which had first brought her to Asgard from Aros. They were taking the rainbow road back to Midgard.

The trip was longer than her first, either with farther to go or so many traveling at once. Her eyes only just had time to adjust and recognize individual streams of colored light, like being inside a waterfall of rainbows, when they came to an abrupt halt. The light cleared, and Euthalia blinked away the sparkles, and they were at the mouth of a cave.

Two of Sigyn's hands were about one of Euthalia's, squeezing hard. Euthalia wrapped her remaining arm about her. She had no words for her.

"Follow," ordered Odin, and they did.

They made their way into the cave, wide and low and filled with stalactites and crystalline formations which reflected back the torchlight. They had to pick their way across the ground, treacherous with stalagmites small and large. Kvasir's men dragged Loki over them.

Two gods from the pursuit party came to Sigyn and detached her from Euthalia. Euthalia stared after them as they guided Sigyn nearer to Odin. They remembered her now; would they punish her with Loki?

"Euthalia!" barked Odin. "What was the name of the giant who stole fire?"

Euthalia blinked and struggled for her voice. "Pro—Prometheus, Lord Odin."

Odin nodded. "Prometheus," he repeated, shaping his mouth about the foreign word. "An outsider from before the time of the gods, who first allied himself with the gods and then betrayed the All-Father. Like you, Loki. But instead of stealing the shining fire, you stole the shining god." Odin looked back at Euthalia. "This Prometheus—tell us again what was done to him?"

Euthalia stared at him. "I—I don't—"

"Tell us!"

She swallowed. "He was bound to a rock with unbreakable chains, without sleep or respite as an eagle tore out his liver each day."

Odin nodded. "A fitting punishment for a traitor." He raised a hand. "Bring them."

There was a prismatic burst and then two of the search party appeared, each with his hands resting heavily on the shoulders of an adolescent boy.

"No!" gasped Sigyn. "No, they've done nothing! Leave them alone!"

"No, Odin," repeated Loki, his voice taut. "My sons have done nothing to offend you, not in all their lives."

"You have taken two of my sons," said Odin, "in killing Baldr and in making Hodr the murderer who must pay. Now I will take two of yours."

Loki surged to his feet within the net, and Kvasir and the others caught at it to restrain him. "No! Odin, don't do this!"

"Please," Sigyn urged, pulling against the men holding her, "please, they are only boys, they have done nothing, please—"

The boys were staring wide-eyed at Odin and at their restrained parents. They did not speak as they looked anxiously back and forth.

"Narfi?" asked Odin.

The older boy, tawny-haired, nodded. "Yes, lord?" His voice cracked with youth and nerves.

Odin raised a hand and pointed at him *"Ver vargr."*

Narfi stared for a heartbeat, confused, and then he abruptly convulsed in the grip of his captor, doubling over as he grasped his abdomen.

"No!" roared Loki, clawing forward through the net. "No! Narfi!"

Narfi looked to his father, his eyes wide and terrified, and then he folded to the floor, kicking and moaning.

Sigyn shrieked and fought the hands holding her, but she was one woman against two warrior gods, and she could not break free.

Narfi's moans turns to howls, and his skin began to darken as it rippled over his seizing body. Bones cracked as his muscles jerked them out of shape, and as they watched he reformed, longer, lower. His clothing tore as he wrenched and writhed and grew out of it, and then he struggled to his feet—four feet—and snarled through the muzzle of a tawny wolf.

"Nari," called Loki. His voice was ragged and afraid, a tone Euthalia could never have imagined in him. "Nari!"

The younger boy was staring at his brother, weaving on his new legs and growling in pain and terror. He tore his eyes away to look at his father, his eyes like twin moons.

"Nari," ordered Loki, "run. Now! Run!"

Nari did not immediately understand, but then he twisted hard against the Æsir holding him. The god had expected it, but he was not prepared for the vicious bite Nari sank into the back of his unprotected hand, and with his involuntary jerk Nari broke free. He bolted for the light, the cave opening far behind them, past the wolf-shaped Narfi.

The wolf jerked at the movement, reacted in pain-maddened terror, and struck Nari's leg just above the back of the knee. Nari went down, screaming, and rolled to kick reflexively at the wolf with his free leg. The wolf snarled and dove onto the prone boy.

Euthalia dropped to her knees, horrified and unable to react. What could she do, even if she could command her limbs to move?

Sigyn was screaming, striking at the men holding her and straining forward to reach her thrashing sons. Loki was half-suspended in his net, held back by four Æsir, snarling out incoherent words and stretching one hand desperately toward the fight.

It did not take long. The wolf severed the tendon so that Nari could not rise to run, and then it dove for the throat and bit hard. Nari was choked mercifully unconscious before the wolf turned to his abdomen and tore it open, dragging a mouthful of steaming intestine free.

Sigyn's shriek shook the cave.

Euthalia couldn't breathe. She could not speak, could not look away, could not blink for even an instant's relief.

Kvasir stepped forward, spear ready, and the wolf snarled and backed away. It looked down at its prey, and it froze, just for a few racing heartbeats, and Euthalia could not guess whether it was the wolf or Narfi who looked down. And then the wolf spun on its haunches and ran for the cave's mouth, fleeing the staring spectators, and it disappeared into the light.

Sigyn collapsed. Euthalia could not see whether she had fainted or merely lost the strength to hold herself upright to see more. Loki fell forward within the net, braced on hands and knees, his whole body shaking.

Odin walked to Nari, dying on the floor, and reached down for a handful of stinking entrails. "This will do," he said. "Bring him."

They dragged Loki's net forward, and he did not resist.

Odin kicked three grouped stalagmites, breaking them off to form three roughly even platforms. "A rock," he said. "Bind him."

They lay Loki backward over the three flattened stalagmites, his head and lower legs hanging loose at each end. They drew out the entrails into long ropey strands and used them to bind Loki to the three stones.

Loki did not resist.

Euthalia wanted him to. She wanted him to fight, to cry the names of his children, but he was utterly lost in his stunned grief. She looked to Sigyn, who was sitting upright, braced against one arm, watching them bind her husband.

"Bound," said Odin. "And as this cave is not convenient to an eagle, we must call upon another. Your first two sons, Loki, were a wolf and a serpent to plague us. We have had another wolf here, and so I have brought another serpent."

He gestured, and someone brought a large bowl, containing a shifting bag knotted at the top. Odin pulled his heavy cloak carefully over his arm and then loosened the knot. A snake's head emerged, tongue flicking. Odin caught it just behind the head and drew out the snake, long and lean. It opened its mouth, baring fangs, and venom dribbled onto Odin's arm. The cloak sizzled and burnt thin where the venom touched.

Loki shook his head. "Odin, please—"

Odin strode to the ridged column behind Loki's head, and he wound the angry snake about it and tied it into place by its own coils. The snake flexed and pulled but was unable to work free. Furious, it opened its mouth to threaten Odin, and venom spilled onto Loki's head below.

Loki gasped and wrenched against the entrails, but they had hardened into iron-like rigidity. The movement disturbed the enraged snake, which looked down and bared its fangs in open warning. More venom dripped, and Loki screamed.

Sigyn scrabbled to her feet and darted toward her stricken husband, snatching up the discarded bowl as she passed. She raced to Loki's head, pushing the bowl between the angry snake and his face. With one hand she dabbed at the spatters on his skin with her pinafore, which smoked faintly as it absorbed the venom. Loki's arched back came to rest again on the stone, and he panted raggedly.

"Then it seems we will leave you to your wife's tender care," said Odin. "Farewell, Loki. We will meet again."

"How long?" Loki gasped out the words. "How long will you leave me here?"

Odin looked back at him. "Until Ragnarok."

Odin started walking toward the mouth of the cave, the Æsir and Vanir following. Euthalia braced her hands against the cool, damp floor—Loki must be freezing on the rock, she thought stupidly, as if that mattered beside the intestine-ropes and the venom—and pushed herself shakily to her feet. She started toward the rocks where Loki was bound. "Sigyn, what can I—"

Sigyn looked up, and her eyes were murderous. Euthalia froze mid-step.

"Get away," Sigyn snarled, her teeth flashing like her new wolf-son's. "You and your Greek tales—this is your doing."

Euthalia gaped. "My—no! No, I wanted none of this! I only—"

"You gave Odin this punishment for my husband. You gave my husband the idea for the deed. All with your stories. And now my sons are dead, and my husband is tortured until the end of time, and it is all your doing."

Euthalia tried to shake her head. "No. No, that's not true." She licked her lips. "Loki had his reasons, but he acted on his own. He wasn't without cause, but he—"

"Shut up!" roared Sigyn.

Her hands moved with her fury, and the bowl slid from beneath the dripping venom. Loki cried out and arched against the rock, straining against the adamantine bindings. "Sigyn!"

She adjusted the bowl, shielding his face once more, whispering an apology. Then she looked back at Euthalia. "You're a monster," she snarled.

"Like your husband." Loki's words were strained and vicious. "What a pair you make, and the things you'll breed."

Fresh horror seized Euthalia. "What do you mean?"

"You have not even seen him," Sigyn said. "Why do you suppose that is?"

Euthalia could not answer.

"Little sheep," forced Loki. "What do you think you would see, if you saw him? Really saw him?"

Euthalia forced a breath. "My husband is kind, he's considerate, he's—"

His choked, rasping laugh interrupted her. Loki's head hung upside down against the broken stalagmite, and he laughed. "Listen to you," he said. "You already know, or you wouldn't rush to defend him to a grieving, tortured Jötunn." His eyes rolled to find hers, and he grinned horribly. "You know."

Euthalia stared at him for an eternal moment and then whirled away. She ran for the light, ran for the others, ran to reach them before they took the Bifröst back to Asgard and left her in this horrible place.

They were just assembling outside of the cave when she caught up to them, gasping and pushing tears from her eyes. *Vidar—why aren't you here? Vidar?*

The Bifröst was opened, and they rode the rainbow way back to Gladsheim in Asgard.

CHAPTER 11

Euthalia stumbled out through the longhouse door and found herself in her own empty village. She gasped with relief and ran for her house.

Birna was there and started to her feet as Euthalia tumbled through the door. "Oh, Euthalia! What's wrong?"

Euthalia shook her head. "Don't—I can't—"

But now that she was in her own home, away from the eyes of all the gods and goddesses and Jötnar, now her defenses finally collapsed, and she began to sob uncontrollably.

Birna rushed to her. "Oh, Euthalia, come and sit. Here, close, where it's warm. I'll bring you some sheepskins, your skin is frigid to the touch. You're pale as an álfr." She stirred up the fire and pushed a pot into it. "Here, I'll heat something for you."

Euthalia could not bear the thought of food, but protesting was more effort than she could manage. She sat in the chair and cried, and when Birna at last pushed a hot bowl of broth into her numb hands, she did not drop it, but she did not even look at it.

And then the door opened behind her, and Birna started up. "Master!"

"Go," rumbled Vidar's voice. "Leave us alone."

Euthalia started to shift in the chair, started to turn, but his hand caught her shoulder. "No," he said. "It is not dark enough yet. But I knew you would be upset, and I could not bear the thought of leaving you alone."

She choked on her tears. "I needed you earlier. Today. I needed you today."

His hand tightened on her shoulder. "I am sorry, my love. For all of it. I am truly sorry."

Fresh sobs broke out of her. "It was—the boys, they were only boys...."

He stooped and embraced her from behind, and she cried anew, spilling liquid from the slopping bowl onto the hearth. When the ragged sobs finally slowed, she sniffed and rubbed her arm across her nose. "Why weren't you there?"

"I saw it all," he said quietly.

"But were you there? Did you watch? Did you watch me, watching my best friend here watch her children die?"

He squeezed her tightly. "I am sorry. I am so, so sorry."

"Why didn't you do something?"

You're a monster, like your husband.

"What could I have done? Odin had made up his mind, had chosen his judgment. No one could gainsay him."

"No one tried!" Euthalia choked. "Not even me!"

He held her.

She shook her head. "Why Birna?"

"What?"

"Birna could see you, when you entered. But not me. Why is a thrall permitted to look at you, but not your wife?"

He did not answer.

"Why Birna?" she repeated.

"It is not Birna's love I want!" he burst, and he pressed his face into her neck as if he regretted the words.

Her heart spasmed in her chest, and she felt ill. "Why wouldn't I love you if I saw you?"

He shook his head into her neck.

Tentatively she reached upward, fingers out-splayed, until she found his half-exposed face. She spread her fingers across his cheek and jaw, feeling, as she had done before but now searching harder than ever for something else.

He caught her fingers in his own. "No," he said. "Just trust me. Love me. Please."

She could turn her head. She could turn, too fast for him to react, and she could see him in the dim light lingering in the house. She drew a breath.

His hand caught her cheek, gently blocking her. "No," he said. "Please."

There was pain in his voice, and fear, and she had heard too much of both this day and could not bear to hear more. She covered his hand with her own. "Later," she said. "We'll talk later."

He did not answer.

She looked down at the bowl, spilling broth across the cooking hearth. "Poor Sigyn. I don't—I don't know how she can...."

"We are strong in love," Vidar said. "And she—she has nothing to bring her back to Asgard, no sons now to raise. She can remain in Midgard with him."

"Until Ragnarok."

"Until then."

Euthalia sniffed. "I can't even imagine.... Why not just kill him? Wouldn't it be kinder?"

Vidar exhaled slowly. "It was not about being kind. Loki has long angered many; this was not a response only to the death of Baldr, though certainly that was a large part of it." He shook his head. "He should not have done that."

"Baldr had beaten him," Euthalia supplied. "Badly. With Thor."

"That does not surprise me," said Vidar. "But does that justify killing him?"

Euthalia supposed it did not.

"And why did they beat him?"

She started to answer, and then stopped. "I—I don't know. He may have...."

"He may have done something to provoke them? Like shaving Thor's wife's head as she slept as a jest, or delivering the magic *epli* which perpetuate the Æsir and Vanir into the hands of an enemy Jötunn? Yes, he has done these things and more. He has earned himself beatings time and again, though he will lick his wounds and tell himself he has been poorly used."

"But no one could deserve this," she protested.

He sighed. "That may be, or it may be that Odin has spared us something worse than fratricide."

"Those boys were not a danger."

"Remember that Loki's other children are anything but harmless. Odin is wise, and he sacrificed a great deal to gain vision and wisdom. If he let such monsters as Fenrir and Jörmungandr and Hel survive, but he chooses to kill Narfi and Nari, what might he see that they might become?"

"Or what might he think of killing two sons to avenge two sons? He said himself it was vengeance."

"Well, that is true."

Euthalia shivered. "I cannot stop hearing them. I had not even seen them before. She kept them at home. Maybe to protect them."

He slid his arms about her. "Let me take you to bed—just to hold you, to warm you."

She nodded numbly.

Euthalia lay awake beneath Vidar's arm, feeling the cold through the outside wall. Autumn was coming on.

You're a monster, like your husband.

They had at last made love, slowly, comfortingly, and then lay together until he had finally fallen asleep. Euthalia did not sleep. She saw again and again Loki's face—upside down, with venom burns running into his eyes, grinning.

What did he know?

She had needed Vidar today, needed him like never before, and he could not be with her because he would not allow her to see him. If she knew his face, he could be a truer husband to her, able to stand with her before Odin and the hall of einherjar or before such monstrous travesties as she had witnessed this day. If he were not afraid to show himself to her, he could have held her as she wept for the destroyed children.

His selfishness kept them apart. If she could but see him once, his excuse would be ended, and they could be closer than ever. Vidar was afraid; he needed her to act on his behalf. She had to look at him to bring them closer.

Outside, the moon was full. She had only to knock out that knot and let in a thin beam, and she would see him. She would know.

Vidar is no monster, whatever else he might be. Gefjon had said that, hadn't she? Wouldn't she know the truth? What had she meant by *whatever else*?

Her father had lied. He had pretended he was a great man, a respected trader, and then in Byzantium she had seen he was only a lowly peddler and a coward willing to barter his daughter. Men could hide what they were.

The things you'll breed.

Sigyn's husband had fathered the guardian of the death-realm and two world-destroying monsters. She must know what was possible.

Loki hung upside down, writhing in pain, laughing at her feeble defense.

Euthalia sat up, pulling a skin about her shoulders to stay warm. She drew her knees under her and knelt, looking down where she knew her sleeping husband to be.

She had only to press out the knot. She would see him, and then she would lie down again beside him, and he would wake in the early dawn and go, just as usual, and he would never know what she had done. Or she would see him, and she would never lie with him again, but then wouldn't it be better to know?

But of course there would be nothing, and she would lie down again, and it would be as if nothing had ever happened. No, it would be better, because he would realize there had been nothing to fear, and now he could stay with her through the day and always.

You know. You already know, or you wouldn't rush to defend him.

She placed her hand on the wall. Cold radiated through her palm and into her fingers as she slid her hand along the rough wood, seeking the knot.

The dragon's bride.

Her fingers found clumped dirt. She hesitated, breathed, hesitated again.

You already know.

She pressed open the knot to admit the moonlight.

CHAPTER 18

Moonlight slid through the knothole like a tangible thing and, as if precisely planned, fell upon Euthalia's abandoned place, leaving Vidar's face in shadow.

But there was enough to faintly edge his features, and if she leaned close she could begin to make him out.

He had dark hair and high cheekbones, and a gently angled chin covered by the short beard she already knew well. Aside from the color of his hair, none of this was new to her. She had imagined him attractive, of course, but this was no monster. What had Loki meant?

She looked down at him. He was very attractive. Beautiful. Like Apollo, or Adonis.

But the strong bones beneath the skin were very strong indeed, stretching the skin taut and looking almost... almost animal. For one stomach-churning heartbeat it seemed his bones and skin were shifting, like Narfi turning to wolf.

Euthalia jerked backward, fighting sudden nausea. But now in the stark moonlight his skin looked pasty and soft, like a corpse rotting. She blinked, trying to shake the horrific impression from her mind. Of course his skin was not moving, of course his bones were steady, she had touched his face a thousand times and—

His eye opened, and it glowed red.

Euthalia screamed. Vidar jerked upright and then immediately pulled a sheepskin to block her view of him, but she was already pushing back against the cold wall. He could not cover himself quickly enough, and now she saw a twisted, animalistic face like a half-melted ogre, fully revealed in the direct moonlight. How could he have appeared normal, even handsome? How could she have embraced him?

"How could you?" he demanded, backing toward the sliding panel. "How could you?"

She started to answer him—*how could you keep this from me?*—but the words stuck in her throat.

He tumbled off the platform, crawling away on the floor. "I loved you! I trusted you!"

She stretched across the bed. "What—what are you?"

"I'm your *husband*." His voice broke. "Or, I was."

Her heart caught between beats. "No—I'm sorry—"

But he was pushing out the door and fleeing into the night, trailing an anguished cry.

A monster.

I trusted you.

Euthalia scrabbled out of the sleeping compartment and snatched at the bearskin as she ran outside. "Vidar! Vidar!"

But he was nowhere in the empty village.

Euthalia wept until dawn. She cried for Narfi and Nari, for Sigyn, for Loki, and for herself and her lost love.

She sobbed until she was exhausted, and then she quietly sniffed and rubbed away tears as she thought on what she could do now.

There seemed few options.

She could wait in her house until Vidar returned, if ever he did, and then apologize and ask his forgiveness, as she forgave him for keeping such a secret from her. But it was possible he would not return, after she had so betrayed his trust—and anyway that course depended entirely upon his action, not hers.

She could go in search of Vidar, chasing him through Asgard. He might be more likely to believe her apology if she sought after him, and it was something she could do herself. This seemed the wiser course, acting instead of wishing. But she had few ideas on how to find him, and he might still refuse her apology.

But there were others who knew more than she did about where in Asgard Vidar might have gone, and one in particular who might be able to help her, who knew many things and saw many places. The question was whether Euthalia dared to approach Odin after yesterday's atrocities.

She washed her face clean of tears and dressed herself as well as she could, pinning Vidar's golden brooches with care. She left the house before Birna came—she could not bear to explain to the older woman what had happened—and started for the empty village's longhouse.

Valhöll had five hundred forty doors, Sigyn had once told her as they looked down the impossibly long hall. Euthalia had assumed, but was not certain, that each door led to a different part of Asgard, like her apparently-isolated village. But then, Sigyn had exited the same door and had apparently gone elsewhere, so perhaps that was not to be relied upon.

Regardless, five hundred forty doors were five hundred forty chances of finding Vidar or someone who could help her to find Vidar. She pulled open the longhouse door and stepped into the hall.

The feast was not ongoing, as she half-expected even at this early hour. There were still einherjar on some of the benches, but most were drowsy or sleeping. Many were sprawled or splayed on the platforms along the walls.

She had not really expected to see Odin himself still in his chair, but he was there. Perhaps after the previous day's events he had wanted to be in a place of laughter and feasting and people who revered him, rather than alone with his blood brother's pleas ringing in his ears alongside the cries of murdered children.

Euthalia hoped that was why he was here.

One of the wolves raised its head as she started toward the massive carved chair. She balled her fists, determined to fear nothing. She had already seen Odin at his worst, and now she came with a petition to find and help his son, and surely Odin could find no fault in that?

His son, whom she had disobeyed and driven away from his own bed. No, Odin might find fault in that.

"What brings you here so early in the morning?"

Odin's voice startled her. She had been so caught in her own worried thoughts that she'd failed to recognize when he saw her.

"My lord," she began, her voice unsteady, "I have a petition of you."

He grunted. "I thought you might. I know you are friends with his wife."

For a moment Euthalia was confused, and then she realized. *Loki.* Odin thought she'd come to beg mercy for Loki.

For a moment the idea took her. Even Prometheus had been freed, eventually, and perhaps she could convince Odin to be merciful. And maybe, maybe, if Vidar saw how she treated Loki, maybe he would think she could love a monster.

She did not know what Vidar was, not really, but she knew he was kind to her. He was not a man like Loki, who might indeed be kind to Sigyn, she didn't know, but who had arranged Baldr's death and was responsible for other misadventures. Not Vidar. She could love him.

Odin shook his head. "Do not waste your breath. Loki has well earned his place there."

Euthalia swallowed. "Loki is not the reason I have come to you, my lord. I have come because of Vidar."

He looked at her, and whether it was because of his vast knowledge or the way her voice had caught on Vidar's name, he sighed a great sigh and looked suddenly sorrowful. "Ah," he said. "You have seen him."

Euthalia nodded.

Odin took another deep breath. "It is ended, then. Go on, little butterfly, and flit away from here. Here is little to be done."

Euthalia's breath caught in her throat. "But—"

"Faithlessness is poison to love. All know that."

"But what now? He has left me, and I am alone in this place."

"By your own doing," Odin reminded her with a growl. "Go and do what you will. There are einherjar who might have you, or perhaps you can find a place with another Æsir or Vanir."

Euthalia stared at him. "You cannot leave me to—"

"The woman who abandoned and betrayed my son, I can leave without further aid, yes, and without acquiring dishonor or shame. Find your own way, fickle little butterfly. It is your doing that has brought you to this."

The worst of it was, she could not refute him. She swallowed hard against the mounting pressure in her throat. "I will go," she said, her voice thick. "But I will come again, and I will ask you again where to find him. For I wish to find him."

Odin's mouth curved upward in something the very opposite of a smile. "I doubt that," he said in a low tone. "You only wish to protect yourself."

Euthalia drove her fingernails into the flesh of her hands, concentrating on that pain to keep the hurt of his words far enough that she could speak. "I will find my husband," she said. "He was afraid of my reaction, and indeed I justified his fear. But I never loved him for his face, and I will not now for his face abandon my love. I mean to find him. I would have your help if I may, but if I cannot, I will find him another way."

She turned her back to the god, heedless of wolf and raven, and stalked to the door. There was a sound behind her, but tears were already blurring her vision and she dared not stop to argue further. Weeping before a god like Odin would not win his pity, only his derision.

She made it out the nearest door just as she choked out the first suppressed sob. She pushed to the side of the timber wall and cried.

Not Odin, then. But someone would help her, surely. Someone would tell her where to find Vidar. And she would tell him that his twisted face did not matter, or if he insisted then they would go to live in the dwarfs' black home of Nildavellir where she would never look upon him again, and they would be happy.

Someone would help her.

CHAPTER 19

"Good morning, Greek," said Freyja as Euthalia entered. She was reclining in a tall chair at the head of the hall, and she held a drinking horn. "What brings you to my hall Sessrúmnir, and so early?"

Euthalia had judged the beautiful Freyja as the next to approach, after Odin's dismissal. Freyja had not spoken to Euthalia as say, Gefjon had, but then Gefjon and Skathi had shown little further interest in Euthalia herself, and Freyja seemed to reside at the heart of Asgard. She might have Odin's ear, as much as anyone might, and Euthalia had to choose a powerful ally.

Euthalia approached the chair. "Good morning, Freyja. My name is Euthalia."

"I know your name." Freyja took a drink.

Euthalia hesitated. Had Freyja meant to insult her? Was she misinterpreting the goddess? "I have come to ask for aid."

"Whatever could you need aid for?" Freyja asked. "You are the wife of a powerful immortal. No mortal woman could complain in such a match. You have much luxury and privilege with little responsibility or care."

Euthalia stiffened. "Sigyn might not agree with you."

"Sigyn?" Freyja thought. "Oh, Loki's woman?"

Euthalia nodded. "His wife. The mother of the boys killed yesterday."

Freyja raised an eyebrow. "And what aid do you wish for her? I cannot return her sons." She raised the horn to drink.

"No. But we could return her husband."

"Free Loki?" Freyja nearly spit her mead. "Are you drunk or mad? Or only stupid, like the sheep you resemble?"

"He must be punished, certainly," Euthalia said quickly, raising her chin and ignoring the insult, "but not tortured, not for hundreds of years."

"No," agreed Freyja. "Thousands." She frowned. "You are a newcomer here, little Greek. Do you know what this Loki is?"

"I know he is sworn brother to Odin," said Euthalia. "I know he brought Mjöllnir from the dwarfs for Thor and made the Asgard wall possible."

Freyja sniffed. "I know he is the one who stood in Odin's hall and declared to all that I had slept with every Æsir and álfr present at Odin's great feast."

Euthalia did not know how to counter this. "All know Loki as the Lie-Smith," she said. "Surely no one would believe such an accusation. I at least know it cannot be true."

"Of course it is true," snapped Freyja. "Only he didn't have to speak it so plainly."

Euthalia tried to recover. "It is not for Loki," she said, "but for his wife Sigyn, who has offended no one." She had meant to ask after Vidar, not to speak of Loki, but now the thought returned to her: maybe, maybe, if Vidar saw her help Loki, maybe he would think she could love a monster.

Euthalia straightened. "I mean to petition Odin on her behalf. Surely you can find sympathy for her losing both her children and seeing her husband bound and tortured?"

"If I had been so ill-fated as to bear Loki's sons," drawled Freyja, "I would now be celebrating my having been relieved both of them and of him." She took a drink.

There was no sympathy for Sigyn to be won here. Euthalia swallowed. "I will not trouble you further on this. But may I ask, if you see Vidar, will you tell him I am looking for him?"

Freyja lifted an eyebrow. "Ah, have you lost your husband? And so soon? I thought your eyes looked swollen."

Euthalia tightened her jaw and immediately tried to loosen it, lest Freyja read her expression too easily. "I have not lost him. I am only looking for him."

Freyja's mouth curved. "Well, now so am I."

Euthalia's shoulders stiffened. "He is my husband." She laid a subtle emphasis on the final word.

"And I am a goddess."

Euthalia stared at her, trying to invent something suitably cutting, but she could think of nothing believable. In fact, there was no reason for Vidar not to welcome Freyja if she approached him now. The knowledge settled heavy in her stomach.

"There's not much to be said for husbands, anyway," said Freyja, and her careless tone was frosted malice over something else.

Euthalia lifted her chin and turned toward the door of Sessrúmnir. She had done this all wrong, she realized. She should have come not begging a favor, but offering a benefit. But what could she offer a goddess?

"Wait," called Freyja. "Do you want my help to convince Odin, or not?"

Euthalia hesitated. "I thought you had no interest in helping Loki."

"In helping Loki? None at all. But telling Loki I had the power to free him? Oh, that particular pleasure might interest me." Freyja smiled, catlike and pleased. "Now, tell me how you plan to petition Odin."

"I, er, don't have a formal petition, not yet. I have only just thought to act." Freyja had stopped her from leaving, so there was a bargain to be made, if only Euthalia could think fast enough to find it. She wished she had seen her father's trading more than the single ill-fated trip to Byzantium. She needed bartering skill and the merchant's knack of reading a customer's true desire, maybe the one he himself didn't know he had.

"I can advise you," Freyja said, "or I can sway his opinion myself." She smiled meaningfully.

Euthalia regarded her. All the Æsir, her own brother, and now Odin... *Is there no other way you know to discourse than to open your legs?* "What would that have to do with me?" She made her mouth a firm line, hoping she looked resolute and dignified. "Do you want me to step aside while you petition my husband as well?"

Freyja laughed aloud. "Oh, no! No, silly girl, if I want Vidar I shouldn't need you to let him go. If I can't sway a man, then he can't be swayed." She shook her head. "No, I require a handmaid. And you are, unless I am very much mistaken, presently without a husband and therefore available to serve me."

Euthalia did not answer, caught between the sting of the accurate assessment and the surprise of the request. "Your handmaid?"

"Yes."

"For how long?"

"So you anticipate a quick reconciliation, then?" Freyja smiled. "Because otherwise, you will have no place in Asgard and you'll be grateful for my patronage. Gods don't keep discarded wives."

Euthalia felt ill, hearing all her fears spoken aloud. "Until Vidar and I are reconciled," she answered more bravely than she felt. "And if I am your handmaid, then you will... use your influence with Odin to negotiate Loki's release, for the sake of Sigyn. And you will help to find Vidar."

"For the sake of Sigyn?"

Euthalia knew it now, knew Freyja's currency, knew she craved attention and power. "For the sake of bragging to Loki before all the feasting gods in Valhöll that he must thank you for his freedom." Loki would not thank her for this arranged humiliation, but humiliation was better than centuries of agony. "And you will help me to find Vidar."

"And I will find Vidar." Freyja smiled, a smug, knowing smile. "Is it a bargain, merchant girl? Or shall we haggle further?"

Euthalia had not realized her background was so plainly known, either. She pushed her shame—but no, there was no shame in being a merchant's daughter, not when she could not have been born a goddess—she pushed aside her confused feelings and acted for Sigyn and Vidar. "Yes, I will serve you."

"Good," Freyja said. "Our bargain is struck." She clapped her hands, and a thrall came from the far end of the hall. "Take this girl and dress her properly," ordered Freyja.

Euthalia looked down at herself. "But what is wrong with these clothes?"

One corner of Freyja's mouth curved upward, as sly as Loki. "Servants do not wear gold brooches, to start. And if you are to be a thrall in my hall, you should be collared."

"Collared?" repeated Euthalia in dismay.

"Shall she work in Folkvang, mistress?" asked the servant.

"Not in Folkvang," Freyja mused, smiling. "I think I will keep her here in Sessrúmnir. Now go, both of you; I do not appreciate repeating myself to my servants."

Euthalia lifted a hand to her throat, as if the rounded iron collar already hung there, and tried to think of something to say. "No—I didn't mean—"

"You struck a bargain, merchant girl," said Freyja, returning to her drink. "The deal is done."

The servant took Euthalia by the wrist and gently pulled her away.

That intolerable brother-lover.

Euthalia's hands shook with rage, humiliation, hurt. The jar of mead she held trembled with her suppressed emotion, and she thought she might spill when she poured.

Before her, a long table of the dead waited for her to fill their drinking horns. Valhöll was not the only hall of the dead; those who were not chosen for Odin's battle elite came to Freyja's hall Sessrúmnir, where her many thralls served them feasts in the evening.

Whore.

It was plain that Freyja used her body as a tool, not for love but for possession and gain. Euthalia did not think it wrong to enjoy a man's embrace, and now Vidar had taught her many pleasures—but that was for love, not for power. And she did not know if Freyja were even capable of love.

Liar.

And Freyja knew something. She had known Euthalia could have lost Vidar, which meant she knew about Vidar, and she enjoyed knowing what Euthalia did not. Euthalia would learn it.

Euthalia moved among the dead and filled their horns, answering their thirsty calls and ignoring the hands which brushed and groped her as she pushed among the crowded tables. She kept her eyes forward, her jaw clenched. She would not react, she would not allow Freyja to observe her discomfort, and above all she would not cry.

"What is this, little Greek?" Freyja's voice cut into her resolution. "No smile for your mistress?"

"My service is sufficient, I think," Euthalia said.

"Not if I say it is not," Freyja returned. "I am owed a smile, I think."

"You have my service," Euthalia said. "You do not have my heart."

Freyja's hand caught her upper arm and jerked her about with superhuman strength. "That is not an answer to give to your mistress."

"I am the wife of a god, as you said to me only this morning."

"You are a thrall."

"And even a thrall has still a heart and a mind."

Freyja slapped her across the face. "That is not an answer to give to your mistress!"

Euthalia stared, her hand to her stinging cheek, stunned. She had not expected to be mistreated, and while performing her assigned task.

Freyja leaned close to her. "You are a thrall now, and my thrall. That was your bargain, your trade to find the husband you lost and to help an eel-tongued wretch who wouldn't lift a finger to your aid. This is your choice. And you must understand that you are no god's wife, not now, not here." She shoved Euthalia into the arms of two of her table's guests, a short man and a stout woman. "Beat her," Freyja ordered. "Not too badly that she cannot work, but enough that she knows her place."

"No!" cried Euthalia, but the stocky woman was already drawing back her arm. She struck Euthalia just above the ear, and as Euthalia twisted away the man seized her arm with crushing force and struck her across the back hard enough to knock her down. They stooped to follow her, and she curled into herself defensively.

The beating was brief, and not as fierce as it might have been. Freyja had already turned back to her feast, and without her eye the two guests lost interest and wanted to return to their own food and drink. Euthalia uncoiled, trembling, and folded her bruised arms about her bruised torso. Her clothing was dusty and torn where they had pulled at her and kicked her, but she had no broken bones and only a few scrapes.

She got to her feet and looked toward Freyja, but the goddess was laughing with someone Euthalia did not know, and she did not look back at Euthalia.

Euthalia limped back down the hall, tears burning her eyes and stinging the abrasion on her cheek.

I will find Vidar, she swore. *I will find Vidar without you, despite you. And I will free Loki for Sigyn. And I will do it all without your help.*

CHAPTER 20

Freyja went to Valhöll the next night, instead of dining in her own hall, and Euthalia saw her chance. She followed at a distance and waited a few minutes after Freyja had entered the longhouse. Then she clenched her fists, took a deep breath, and pushed open the door.

Freyja was further up the tables, laughing with a table of men and women. She did not look back as Euthalia entered. Euthalia took a tray of food from another thrall. "I'll do it."

"Thanks."

Euthalia started up the aisle. Freyja did not look back. Euthalia tightened her fingers on the tray and passed the table, head rigidly forward. Freyja turned, said something to the table behind Euthalia to draw grins and cheers, and then turned back to the first table. She had spoken directly across Euthalia's path but had not noted her.

Euthalia's supposition had been correct: Freyja did not care to notice thralls, and one was as another unless she needed something in particular from one of them. If Euthalia did not draw too much attention, she could move about Valhöll without her mistress's knowledge.

Someone shouted and reached for the bread on her tray—one of the einherjar, sharing it out among his friends—and she looked over the tables nearest her. There were many tall men, many muscular men, many bearded men, but none she recognized as her husband. Of course, she would not know him. She had barely seen him, and his face had looked human for only an instant before twisting into its monstrous form.

Which form was true?

Her tray was empty. She moved away, her back to Freyja, and took up a jar of mead. She glanced at the table where her mistress sat and then started for the enormous and ornate chair at the head of the hall.

Odin's single eye shifted toward her while she was yet three long tables away. She swallowed and kept going forward under the heavy weight of his gaze. Finally, as she neared the reach of his arm, she glanced down and bowed her head. "My lord."

He made a curious gesture with his fingers and then held out a drinking horn to her. "You have not come as a guest to this hall."

She was ashamed of her torn clothing and bruised face, but there was nothing to be done for them. "No. I am a thrall to Freyja." She poured mead into the horn.

He frowned. "Why? You have no home of your own, true, but why Freyja?"

"She told me she could help me," Euthalia answered. Best not to say that Freyja had bragged she could sway Odin to her will.

Odin grunted. "Freyja helps only herself."

"I believe I have learned that," said Euthalia.

Odin laughed, dark and cold.

Euthalia steeled herself. "I came here tonight first to look for Vidar, and if I could not find him, then to ask again for your aid."

"And are you truly looking for him?"

Her whole body tightened. "Is he here? Now?"

Odin crushed her with a word. "No. No, he is not here tonight."

Euthalia nodded, swallowing her disappointment. "Can you tell me where he is?"

Odin shook his head. "He has not spoken to me."

Even if Vidar were not in the long hall, Odin's magic could still reach him. "Can't you see him?"

"It is likely, but not without some seeking." He gestured, and one of the ravens hopped forward from the throne to his hand, dwarfing even the Æsir's massive fist. "I can look for him, but he may not wish to be found."

Euthalia thought of the wail diminishing into the night and tried not to agree with Odin. "I want to speak with him. To—to apologize to him, and to ask his forgiveness, and to see if he will have me again."

"If he will have you?" Odin seemed surprised. "You still want him?"

Euthalia swallowed. "We were happy before I saw his face. I think we could be happy again."

Odin nodded slowly, considering. "It pleases me to hear you say this."

He spoke to the bird in words Euthalia did not know, and then both ravens lifted themselves into the air and blurred into the smoke trailing upward from one of the hearth fires.

"He looked like a man—an Æsir—at first," she said. "Then his face changed. I—which is his true face?"

Odin scowled. "He is cursed." He took a drink, but it seemed to be more an excuse to gather his words than to slake his thirst. "My son is cursed."

Euthalia kept her eyes on him. "What kind of curse?"

"It can be seen only through the eyes of love." Odin gestured down the empty hall. "When you were in Valhöll, among so many, you did not know him from the others. You looked upon none of the einherjar or the Æsir with love, and you did not know the face of him you loved, and so you could not perceive the curse's aspect in him you loved. When you knew him, however, and loved him, the illusion would manifest."

She worked her way through this. "The curse only affects him if I recognize him?"

Odin was irritated with her thickness. "It affects him always. But only those who love him see it."

So Vidar had remained in the dark, that she could never look upon him with love. It was heartbreaking to think on it.

"The curse was laid upon him with a powerful magic. Thus Vidar thought never to have a wife, or to father children only by force. To be offered a bride who did not know him or the curse, who might learn to trust him through his peculiar request that she never look upon him, that was his only hope of love and family."

And so he had been so very careful of her, needing not only her love but her unfailing trust. And she had betrayed him.

The wave of guilt threatened to overwhelm her.

A cheer went up as some of the einherjar finished a story or a brag, and Odin glanced sharply in their direction. Then he turned his attention again to Euthalia. "Go, and come again to me another day. I will tell you what I have learned."

"I do not know when I will be able to escape Freyja's eye again."

One corner of his mouth curved upward, the nearest she had ever seen of a smile in him. "I think you will find you may escape your mistress's eye whenever you find the desire. Not because she is careless of her toys—indeed, she is a jealous possessor of her baubles—but because I think you are clever."

Euthalia wondered if she should thank him.

"Now go," he said, "for you have stayed long to serve, and someone will wonder at our words." He made a sign absently and one-handed, and she realized he had worked some magic as they spoke. A concealment, perhaps?

She took her remaining mead to a table of einherjar and hoped Odin's ravens would find a track of Vidar, a cave where he had sheltered, a place she could pursue him.

Freyja was doing nothing. She had promised to work to free Loki and to help to find Vidar, and she was doing nothing.

Euthalia said as much to her as she swept the packed earth of the goddess's sleeping room. "Am I not doing my work well? And so should you not be doing yours, according to our contract?"

"One might think you would not be so demanding to your mistress," Freyja warned over her shoulder.

Euthalia did not care. "It is not my mistress I address just now, but a party in a business negotiation."

"And what do you expect of me at this time?" asked Freyja, peering in a handheld mirror and tugging at a stray eyebrow hair. "Do you think I can simply march into Odin's hall and demand that he free Loki? No, of course I cannot; I would only anger him and set him more firmly against us. I must build my appeal carefully, must first sway others to my petition, and I must tread carefully as Loki has offended so many."

"Surely there must be some who are not hostile to Loki," Euthalia said. "He cannot have offended all of Asgard."

Freyja made a sound almost like an undignified snort. "How optimistic you are. In fact, he made a sport of that very thing—set himself a task to do it all in one night, in fact, leaving no one unaddressed."

"Offended to the point of torture?" Euthalia frowned. "Didn't he have a previous wife—?" But she stopped herself, realizing that an abandoned wife might be the very worst of allies.

"Oh, yes," answered Freyja. "I suppose she might speak for him. But she does not come often to Odin's hall."

"Then I will go to her," Euthalia said firmly.

Freyja opened her mouth to laugh, but hesitated. She sat up and looked at Euthalia, really looked at her for the first time in the conversation. "You would go to seek her? In Jötunnheim?"

Euthalia nodded. "And you should not begrudge me the time, as I only go to perform the work you yourself should be doing."

"Oh, I begrudge you not a moment of it," answered Freyja with a smile. "Indeed, you spare me much effort with your willingness. But do you know the way?"

"I do not," admitted Euthalia.

"Well, you must either take the Bifröst or climb the trunk of Yggdrasill," Freyja said cheerily, "and the tree will take far too long. I don't want to send you away for days, you see. So I suppose it will have to be the Bifröst."

"I have traveled the Bifröst on two occasions," Euthalia said, "but always with others. I do not know how to take the road myself."

"Oh, it is a simple enough thing," said Freyja, rising. "Only be careful of the fire. The red of the rainbow is all fire, you know, to keep the Jötnar from Asgard. But it's safe enough if you keep your wits about you."

Euthalia blinked and followed her from the hall.

They went to a place of gently rolling hills, in which was nestled another dwelling, a homey place which Euthalia thought looked comfortable and somehow friendly. "This is Himinbjörg," said Freyja, as if that explained all.

"Who lives here?" Euthalia asked, trailing obediently behind.

"Heimdallr." She raised her voice. "Heimdallr! Open to us!"

The door opened, and Heimdallr waved to them. "Freyja, welcome! Come and drink!"

"He is always drinking," Freyja confided in a low tone, but Euthalia did not think she sounded disapproving.

Heimdallr waved them inside, smiling broadly. "Come in, come in! What brings you to the heavenly hills?"

"This one must travel to Jötunnheim," said Freyja. "Will you give her passage on the Bifröst?"

"By herself?" Heimdallr frowned at Euthalia. "You will be safe?"

"I think I know not to step into fire," Euthalia said, but without as much confidence as she wanted. She had only a vague impression of traveling the Bifröst, and she did not remember clearly seeing fire.

"Oh, I am sure of that," he answered with a chuckle. "Only I meant the trip itself."

"She asked to go," Freyja said. "Well, I will leave her to her business. Come to me when you've finished, girl." She nodded to Heimdallr and departed.

The big Æsir turned back to Euthalia and rubbed his hands. "Jötunnheim, then?"

"Could I choose to go somewhere else as well? Midgard?"

He frowned. "Do you wish to leave your mistress? You must know I cannot aid you in that."

"No, I have remaining business with Freyja—a contract. I wish only to perform an additional errand in Midgard and then return."

Heimdallr seemed faintly surprised at her claim of business but did not argue.

She had to take the opportunity. "My lord," she said, "have you seen Vidar? Do you know where he is?"

He looked at her strangely, and she realized that he did not recognize her as Vidar's wife, but only as Freyja's thrall. "Why would you ask that?"

"It is important—to my mistress." At least, Freyja had agreed to search for him, and Euthalia could not bear to confess that she was the wife who had betrayed Vidar, not to this friendly face.

"She has not asked me," he said. "Freyja knows I can see far and know much. But I have not seen him."

Euthalia's heart sank. "Odin is searching for him, too," she said, and her tone betrayed her loss.

Heimdallr was clearly perplexed by her investment in the missing god. "Do you seek him in Midgard? Where do you think to find him?"

149

"I don't know if I will find him there," she said, "but perhaps a clue to his location."

"Where?"

She told him.

Heimdallr's dismay was unconcealed. "I can send you there," he said, "but it is no small thing you ask."

"I will be brief," she promised. "Only help me, please."

"When you have finished in Jötunnheim, return to the exact place you arrived, and I will send you on to Midgard," he said slowly. "And then come back to that place in Midgard to return here. Do you understand?"

"Perfectly."

"Good. Then go." Heimdallr waved his arm, and the air opened before Euthalia, brilliant with sparkling color. It was less a bridge and more a tunnel, and Euthalia felt dizzy merely looking into it. She tried to turn away, but it was already around her, she was already inside somehow, and she put an arm out to keep from falling and then jerked it back, remembering the fire. She fell.

The colors swirled around her and then parted, so suddenly that she might have imagined them but for her stumbling landing against the cold ground. The hills of Himinbjörg had vanished. She sprawled upon an expanse of ice, its sheen blunted by packed snow and a dark grey sky spitting stinging flakes down on her.

CHAPTER 21

Euthalia ran her palms down her skirt, the fabric catching in the sweat of her hands despite the raw chill in the air. Falling snow blew about her and confused her vision. Her thin cloak from Freyja's equipping was not sufficient for this mountain climate, and she longed for the bearskin Vidar had given her via the dragon-helmed warrior. But it was lost to her with her house and her marriage.

The other worlds, she was learning, encompassed all the geographies of Midgard, and while she had never visited the snowy peaks of the human world, she was climbing their equivalent now in Jötunnheim. She had been told the object of her search lived on this mountain, but looking at the rocks and snow all about her, she despaired of ever finding her.

Freyja had laughed. "Don't worry," she had reassured Euthalia in a voice which was not at all reassuring. "She will find you."

Euthalia stumbled as a frosty rock gave way beneath her foot and she caught her fall only by bashing her knee into a stone. She clutched the wounded joint through her skirt and considered sitting on the rock for a good cry. No one would notice, and she felt she could use one.

"I hate you," she snarled at the offending rock. "I hate you, and I hate Asgard, and I hate Freyja, and I hate Odin, and I wish I hated Vidar."

The rock responded with a quivering growl, and Euthalia jumped. The sound grew, and the roar shivered the earth beneath her feet, making the stones tremble about her. She waved her arms to keep her balance and caught one hand on a boulder.

And then the sound faded, and the rocks stilled, and she stared at the offending stone, wondering what power she had awoken and whether she should apologize.

"Well," she said, trying hard to make her voice artlessly light and distant, as Freyja did so well, "well, perhaps not you."

The stone did not respond.

Euthalia hesitated, considered, and decided to make certain. "I did not mean to offend you, stone. I only am so frustrated with—"

Laughter arose behind her, deep laughter which must come from a chest like an aurochs's or a dragon's. Euthalia whirled, and for a moment she saw nothing but the mountainscape.

But then the stones shifted, and Euthalia saw emerging from them a figure, grey and mottled like the lichened stone so that it had blended perfectly in the falling snow. It was a woman, Euthalia saw, half-naked in the cold and enormous like a great tree. She rose from the mountainside and stood over Euthalia, who staggered back in surprise. Euthalia's head came to her mid-thigh.

She did not come close. She did not need to. If she wanted to reach or catch Euthalia, there was little Euthalia might do to escape.

"Tiny girl," rumbled the half-bare woman. "The stone cannot hear you, and I doubt it cares much for your words."

Euthalia burned with embarrassment and shivered with cold fear of the creature before her. "I—I thought—the shaking... Was that you?"

But no, the earth had not trembled when she laughed or rose from the rocks.

The woman shook her head soberly. "It is not my doing."

Euthalia swallowed and focused on her task. "I have come seeking Angrboda."

The stone-colored woman snorted. "That rock does not bear my name."

"You are Angrboda, then."

"I am."

Euthalia nodded. "I have come to ask your help for Loki."

She had the woman's attention now. Angrboda lowered herself to sit on a great boulder and looked down at Euthalia. "Why is that?"

"You—you were his wife, once. For love of him, you could aid him. Do you know how he suffers now?"

"I do." She nodded seriously. "But why should I go to help him now?"

Euthalia hesitated, confused. "But... you had three children by him." She reviewed the names Vidar had once given her. "Jörmungandr, Fenrir, Hel."

"Four," Angrboda corrected, her lips turning upward slightly. "I ate one."

Euthalia had no answer to that.

"Yes," Angrboda said, "I had children with Loki. But I do not love him. We do not love, Loki and I. We are Jötnar."

Euthalia thought of Loki kneeling in the net, stretching out to his sons and pleading for mercy on them if not for him, and she wondered if Angrboda knew Jötnar as she thought she did.

"He has a new wife," Angrboda continued. "Sigyn. Let her help him."

"She is trying, as best she can," Euthalia said, "but it is not enough."

"Then Loki should have chosen his bed more prudently," Angrboda said.

Euthalia nodded once, agreeing mildly for lack of anything else to say. She liked Sigyn, but she could not fault Angrboda for resenting her husband's second wife.

"What did Loki think a human wife could do for him?" Angrboda sneered. She looked at Euthalia. "I would eat her. Devour her, crunch her bones and stew her marrow and suck her skin clean. If that would help Loki."

Euthalia gulped and clutched the rock behind her. "She is the only aid Loki has now," she said quickly. "I am sure it would not help him to remove her."

Angrboda shrugged.

"What of your children?" Euthalia asked, trying to keep the desperation from her voice. "Would they help their father?"

Angrboda stared down at her for a few heartbeats and then burst into deep, rolling laughter. "Do not approach them, tiny girl," she warned, still chuckling. "You cannot face such as them. The Æsir and the Vanir fear them; you could not hope to survive them."

Jörmungandr's serpentine length encircled an entire world. Fenrir's strength frightened even Thor and the mightiest Æsir. Hel kept the underworld. Euthalia did not want to face any of these monsters, and it was easy to believe Angrboda's warning.

The ground shook again, and Euthalia grabbed for the boulder beside her. This time the shaking was fiercer, and the rock shifted beneath her hands. It shivered free of its foothold and began to fall toward Euthalia.

An enormous hand cupped her and swatted her out of the boulder's path. Euthalia stumbled and fell across the rocky slope, panting for breath, and watched the boulder tumble down the mountainside, cracking into another rock with a sharp sound. She glanced up at the stone-colored woman who had saved her.

But Angrboda had no further interest in Euthalia or her gratitude. "That bitch," she snarled, looking across the mountain at something Euthalia could not see. "She is no help to him."

"What?" Euthalia asked. "Who?"

Angrboda shook her head and turned away. "We will inherit at Ragnarok," she said, walking into the falling snow. "He will be avenged then, many times over."

"We can help him now!" called Euthalia, but the half-bare stone-colored woman did not turn back.

Euthalia retraced her steps to where she had arrived sprawling in the snow, watching for a burst of rainbow. She had a visit to pay.

It was possible, she supposed, to visit anywhere in Midgard, the human realm. She could return to Aros, or Byzantium, or even to her own home village. She felt a small temptation at the thought of appearing unexpectedly at home, learning what tale her father had spun to explain the missing warriors and daughter and then explaining the truth of things to all—but that was no home to her now, even if she knew how to go there.

Heimdallr must have seen her somehow, for the portal opened and she braced herself for the disorienting whirl of color. This time she kept her feet. She did not remember much of her first trip via the Bifröst, when Vidar had carried her from Aros to the mimic-village in Asgard, but the second was etched clear in her mind.

She walked out into the cool air of a Midgard autumn, light slanting golden. She looked about the hilly landscape, pretty in the early evening light. Then she steeled herself and turned toward the cave which lay ahead of her.

Her stomach wrenched even as she faced the opening. Too clearly she recalled Narfi twisting into a wolf, Nari screaming as he tried to fend off his brother's savage attack, Sigyn's long, agonized screams as she watched her sons destroyed before her.

Euthalia shook her head. If they were terrible things to her, they were more terrible still to Sigyn and Loki. She took a slow, deep breath and started into the cave.

The light faded quickly, and Euthalia made slow progress as she felt her way forward. She remembered the cave floor being stone-littered but solid, without crevasses or pits to engulf her, and the ceiling was low but sufficient for her head. Through the darkness ahead of her she could see a pinpoint of light, and she crept toward it.

Sigyn heard her stumbling and kicking stones in the darkness. "Who's there?" she called sharply. "I know you're there!"

Euthalia wished she'd thought to announce herself earlier; of course they would fear someone creeping upon them. "It's Euthalia," she answered. "I have no light, I'm sorry."

"Euthalia?" Sigyn's voice was not welcoming. Euthalia told herself it was not outright hostile, but she wasn't sure if she were lying to herself.

Loki said something, but Euthalia could not distinguish his words. His voice was low and the words were slurred.

Euthalia could see them now, lit by a single lamp. Sigyn leaned forward over Loki's supine body, her arms stretched to extend the bowl over his head. By the angle, the bowl was better than half-full and heavy. She turned her face from the bowl to watch Euthalia come into the light.

"What brings you here?" she asked, her voice a barely contained snarl. "Come to gloat? To see how far we have fallen?"

Euthalia felt as if a knife had pierced her gut. "No, Sigyn, no," she answered. "Of course not." She swallowed. "I came to ask how I can help."

"Help?" Sigyn bit off the word as if it were foul.

"I have been trying," Euthalia said quickly. "I have gone to Freyja and secured her pledge to help me persuade Odin, and I went to find Angrboda, and—"

Loki's cracked laughter interrupted her. It was horrid, crackling and wet, and she really looked at his face for the first time, shielded by the intervening bowl. It was pitted and scarred, red and black with scabs and oozing sores which ran down his chin and pooled in the hollow of his throat. Euthalia caught her breath, unable to look away.

But Loki was still croaking his laugh. "You went to Angrboda," he cracked. "You sweet-faced little liar. You never did, not you."

"I did," Euthalia said. "I found her on the mountain, in the snow. She—she was not eager to help you, not now that...."

"Not now that I have a human wife?" Loki snorted. "Perhaps you did speak with her, little lamb."

"Stop calling me a sheep!" snapped Euthalia, surprising herself. "I am only trying to help you!"

"It is your fault he is here," Sigyn growled.

"That is not true," Euthalia returned. "Blame Baldr for his taunts, blame Thor for his cruelties, blame Loki himself for his own actions, but do not blame me. If Odin had not heard my story, he would have chosen another punishment, but he never would have overlooked the death of his son. This is not my doing."

Sigyn looked at Euthalia for a long moment. Her arms were beginning to tremble.

Euthalia reached for the bowl. "Let me help you—"

"No!" Sigyn's voice was more worried than harsh. "No, we can't risk jostling it." She leaned further forward and bent her elbows, adjusting the strain from her arms to her back. "A little longer."

"Why?" asked Loki, looking to Euthalia. "If you do not believe this is your doing—and I do not agree or disagree, I only ask—if you do not believe this is your fault, then why work to release me?"

Euthalia made a gesture to encompass Loki, the serpent, the cave. "Is it not obvious? Even one guilty of heinous crimes should not be tortured."

"Never?" Loki asked. "Even if his crimes were heinous? Not, of course, that mine were."

Euthalia shook her head. "If he is awful, if he has done hideous, unspeakable things—executed, maybe, if he cannot live among men and the laws of men. But not tortured, or else we are no better than he."

Sigyn bit her lip as she shifted a leg. "It is nearly full," she said to Loki.

"No," Loki urged. "Not yet. A little longer."

The dark, viscous fluid glistened in the single candle's light, shivering near the rim as the bowl trembled. It looked malevolent even merely pooling in the bowl.

Sigyn shook her head. "I must, or it will overflow. A spill would be worse."

"No," began Loki. "Sigyn—"

"I will be quick," she said, her voice tight and pleading. "So fast, my love. So quick."

Loki began to curse, loosing such a stream of foul profanity as Euthalia had never heard even among her father's warriors, among the sailors of Byzantium, from men dying against their will. He squeezed his eyes shut and he shouted obscenities and Sigyn pulled the bowl of venom away.

The snake's mouth poured forth its acid poison, and drops fell into Loki's scarred face. He screamed in fresh agony.

Sigyn ran with the bowl, holding it extended and moving as smoothly and quickly as she could over the rough ground, and when she had reached the edge of the candle's circle of light she pitched the acid forward into the darkness. It hissed as it hit the stone, audible even over Loki's shrieks.

Loki wrenched as the venom trickled over his face and burnt into him, convulsing against the ropy intestines which held immobile. The stones did not break beneath him, but the ground began to shake with his paroxysm, groaning with the strain of his struggles.

Euthalia stumbled with the trembling earth. She snatched at her pinafore and extended it over his face, trying to shield him. The snake hissed at her, and fresh poison burned through the cloth like quick fire and struck him. Euthalia leapt back as her clothing hissed and smoked with the venom.

Sigyn ran back, faster now that she did not have to take care with the bowl, and shoved it again between the snake and her husband. Loki's convulsions slowed, and he moaned wordlessly.

Sigyn knelt beside the first protruding rock, the one which held his shoulders, and whispered apologies to him, pressing her cheek to his dark hair. Euthalia felt helpless and removed. She was useless here.

"Can't you remove the serpent?" she asked. She felt stupid even speaking. Of course they would have thought of that.

"More venom," Sigyn said softly. "I cannot reach it without setting down my bowl—and even if someone were to help me, angering it only produces more venom."

"And the binding?"

"Firm magic," rasped Loki. "They are a binding of my own flesh and my own blood. They will not break."

"Must you carry the bowl so far to empty it?"

"Look around you," snapped Sigyn.

The ground about Loki's three stones was slightly concave, Euthalia noted. If Sigyn poured the venom here, it would roll back and scorch Loki's feet. Perhaps that was how the ground had been etched, before she had learned to carry it further.

Euthalia's throat felt raw and swollen as if she'd been screaming along with Loki. "I only want to free you and find Vidar," she said miserably. "Only these two things, and I am helpless to do either."

"Not everything is yours to do," Sigyn said softly, and Euthalia looked at her. Sigyn glanced up briefly and then quickly returned her eyes to the bowl, already puddled with venom. "You cannot return my sons," she said. "No one can. They died in Midgard, and they were too young to be counted as warriors. They will not come to feast in Valhöll."

Loki licked his cracked lips. "Their sister will not torment the innocent."

"Their sister!" repeated Sigyn. "They are not siblings, Loki, for all they share a father. Hel is a monster, even by Jötunn standards. Do not think to comfort me with empty lies."

"I'm sorry," Euthalia said, her voice thick with grief for children she had not known and regret for a punishment she had not encouraged. "I'm so sorry. I will do all I can to see you released."

Sigyn looked at her, meeting her eyes for the first time. "Please."

Euthalia nodded. Then she looked at Loki. "You knew," she said. "You knew I loved him, and that if I looked at him, I would lose him. You did destroy what we had."

"No," said Loki. "You destroyed what you had. Was it I who screamed upon seeing what was in your bed? Did I recoil when you learned what it was you'd opened your legs to, what face you'd kissed, what horror you'd pulled close in the dark? No. I gave you vision instead of darkness. What you did with that vision is yours alone."

"Like you gave Hodr a mistletoe wand to throw!" snapped Euthalia. "If you are so full of knowledge, tell me how to break his curse!"

"Oh, I could," said Loki. He grinned, scabbed lips splitting, and rolled his eyes to meet hers. "But would you believe me?"

Ice lanced through Euthalia's chest. No, no she dared not. Loki spoke half-truths, crafted to work the greatest harm. He might tell her a charm which would instead worsen the curse. He might tell her how to break the curse but use the result to create a greater problem. It was a dilemma, needing to ask him and needing to distrust him.

Loki laughed, watching her. Sigyn looked away, avoiding Euthalia's eyes.

Euthalia turned and started toward the faint daylight and Heimdallr's escape.

CHAPTER 22

Euthalia went haunted about her chores in Sessrúmnir, with Loki's screams and taunts echoing in her head. Her discomfort reached beyond knowing his brutal agony. She did not want to see him tortured by the burning venom, but she could not stand how he mocked her and tore at her love with Vidar. Why? What made him so hateful?

Chaos, she recalled. Chaos, to counter harmony. Sigyn had warned her that Jötnar were meant to destroy. Perhaps Loki simply could not help himself.

But no, there were things Loki loved and wanted to preserve. Nari and Narfi—and Sigyn's peace of mind, reassuring her that they would not be tormented by his daughter Hel. There were bits of humanity in Loki, if humanity were the right word for an inhuman Jötunn.

"Little Greek!"

Euthalia had yet to hear Freyja use her given name. But she could not refuse her mistress's call, not without risking a blow to the head or a jerk to her hair. "Yes?"

"Come with me."

Freyja had looked startled, for just a heartbeat, when Euthalia had returned from her trip, and Euthalia had wondered, for just a heartbeat, if Freyja had hoped she would not return—that Angrboda would devour her like she had talked of devouring Sigyn. But the thought was too terrifying to hold for more than a moment, and Euthalia let it slip away, keeping only a lingering relief that she slept with the other thralls well away from the goddess.

She followed Freyja to one of the external storehouses made of earth and wattle. "I am having the Vanir and Æsir to feast tonight," said Freyja, "and I asked Idun to send over her magical *epli* for us. But they have been spilled in my storehouse and mixed with the other nuts and berries."

Freyja gestured, and Euthalia looked into the storage hut. The floor was nearly hidden beneath a thick scattering of nuts and berries, a tapestry of colors and textures in the sunlight spilling in from the door.

"It would be a grave insult to serve ordinary fruits and berries instead of Idun's magic," explained Freyja archly. "So you must sort them for the feast. You have—" Freyja glanced at the sky—"perhaps as much as two hours."

Euthalia stared at the harvest-rich floor. Berries of all colors were mingled with nuts of many shapes and sizes, and Idun's magic *epli* could be any of them. "But, how am I to tell which are which? There are so many—"

"How you accomplish your task is not my concern," snapped Freyja. Euthalia could see the small creases of pleasure about her eyes. "But if you are not finished before the guests arrive, I will beat you myself."

Equal parts rage and despair rose within Euthalia. "How have I offended you? This has nothing to do with Vidar or Sigyn! Nothing!"

"No," agreed Freyja. "But you are my thrall and you must do the tasks I set you. Do you think I will be able to bend Odin's ear if I am shamed before him for spoiled nuts and berries which carry no magic? Of course not. So you must do this, even if you think it has nothing to do with your lost husband."

She smiled, teeth flashing like a predator's, and turned away to return to her hall. She did not look back, confident in her swaggering triumph.

Euthalia stepped into the storehouse, taking care to work her feet gently down so not to crush any of the richly-colored berries. The entire floor was covered with the mixture. Had every container in the storehouse been inverted along with Idun's *epli*?

Euthalia pushed aside enough of the fruits and nuts to make space to kneel, and she folded her knees to the dirt floor. She scooped up a double-handful and stared at them in her cupped hands.

Impossible. Even sorting the produce just into the various types of berries and nuts would be a challenge within the limited time. Separating them also by magic was unthinkable. Euthalia had no idea which pieces were Idun's magic produce and which were merely nuts and berries. Who had brought them? Had Freyja created this chaos only to torment Euthalia?

She sifted the collections of berries and nuts in her hands, letting them spill messily through her fingers and roll across the floor. There was no difference among them. She knew each type of berry, each shape of nut, but there was no magic to them. Perhaps there was no magic at all—only Freyja's lie that somehow they were different.

The sobs had crept upon her before she realized, and her first tears took her by surprise. But she did not fight them, and she let her sobs build. There was no way to distinguish the magic, and no time to separate the produce, and no way to find Vidar.

Someone brushed past her, and she choked off a cry as she looked up, ashamed to have been caught weeping. But the woman who saw her did not slow. It was a thrall woman, dressed in dull and faded clothing, and she moved to the far side of the little hut and squatted to the floor.

Another person entered, and another. Two more thralls, a man and a woman. Each squatted or knelt and began to sort nuts and fruits into piles, using just the tips of their fingers.

Euthalia looked around at them. She knew them, recognized them from Freyja's hall and others, but she did not know them well—not so well that they should share in her task of their own will. "Why?" she asked. "Why are you helping me?"

A woman answered without looking up from her work. "We can help you in this thing which you cannot do."

Euthalia rubbed tears from her cheek. "Which I cannot?"

"You cannot tell the magic," the woman answered. She nudged two nearly identical beech nuts beside one another. "These are the same to you."

Euthalia shuffled nearer on her knees and reached out to pick them up. "They are both beech nuts. I cannot say anything more about them."

The woman smiled a pale, weary smile. "You can pick them up." She reached out and took one, rolling it in her hand. "We can handle only the natural *epli*." She reached for the other, lifting it slightly with her fingertips and dropping it to the floor, where it bounced and rolled. "The magical *epli* of Idun burn us."

"Burn you!" Euthalia reached for the woman's hand.

But the thrall pulled her fingers away. "It is not so severe as that." She began sorting again. "You are the wife of a god, so you are meant to take them. You have dined on them yourself. But we cannot hold them long, and we dare not eat them. Which is, I am sure, the purpose of it. Idun's *epli* are for the gods and goddesses alone. Not the thralls who serve them."

Euthalia thought of Birna bringing her fruits which she encouraged but never took herself. She had never guessed they were Idun's magical food which sustained the gods. But of course, Sigyn had been in Asgard long enough for generations of her Midgard family to have passed, and human brides would need the magical food to continue with their husbands.

But the magic repelled the human thralls. "Then you harm yourself to help me. Why? Again, why are you helping me?"

The woman deftly rolled berries and nuts to one side or another, testing each with a brush of the fingers. "You are kind to us," she said simply. "You said thralls were still hearts and minds. We are insects to her. She is a goddess, and we are not, indeed, but she relies upon us for her comfort. And we are insects to her. Not to you."

Euthalia stared at the woman who went on sorting, never looking up, and she felt a dull hollow open in her stomach. She had never thought of the thralls particularly, had never gone out of her way to be kind even after she had become one of them. Yes, she appreciated Birna and enjoyed her company, and yes, she had been polite to the servants when she had gone to Valhöll, but *kind*—had she ever been kind to them? Sought them out to give a gift, tell a joke, do a favor?

But the men and women around her paid little attention to her guilty wonder, as they slid berries and nuts from one pile to another, organizing neat divisions about the floor.

They would need baskets. Euthalia shook herself and rose to bring empty containers from the rear of the storehouse. "Which are the magical ones?" she asked.

They each pointed to a pile, a smaller selection of beech nuts or elderberries. As the magical *epli* did not trouble her, Euthalia knelt to gently gather each of the designated piles into a separate basket, taking care not to bruise the berries. She lined these along one wall and started gathering the ordinary fruits and nuts into baskets which she kept separated on the other side. Gaps began to widen in the multi-colored carpet of harvest.

If she could handle the magical *epli* as the thralls could not—then she was not entirely like them. The wife of a god could handle the *epli*. She was still the wife of a god. Vidar was still her husband. She had not been abandoned entirely.

The thought warmed her with a hot strength which made the baskets light. She was still his wife.

As the thralls worked, she collected their sortings. At one point she went out and brought back water and flatbread for them to share before returning to their task.

The sun had slanted through the door and was turning the earthen floor golden with its evening autumn light when the thralls began to rise from the floor. "They are sorted," the woman said. "You can collect the rest."

"Thank you," Euthalia said urgently. "Thank you, thank you."

The woman reached out and took Euthalia's hand. "Torfrid," she said. "My name is Torfrid."

Euthalia bit her cheek in quick shame. She should have thought to ask. "Thank you, Torfrid."

Torfrid pressed Euthalia's hand briefly, and then turned and left with the others.

Euthalia knelt and gathered the remaining piles, cupping handfuls into their respective baskets. She was crawling across the floor after an escaped gooseberry when a silhouette darkened the door.

"How is your work coming?" inquired a sweetly malicious voice.

Euthalia leapt to her feet and turned back to Freyja. "The task you've set me is finished," she said. She reached to roll the berry from her palm into the woven basket beside her. "All is sorted for your guests tonight."

But Freyja ignored her, staring around at the empty floor. "You—how did you work so quickly?" she asked. But as she turned back to Euthalia, it was plain she did not want to be answered. "That was good work, girl," she bit off in a tone which made the words a threat.

Euthalia bowed her head and suppressed a smile which could ruin her.

"As a reward for your diligence," Freyja said, "you may serve in my hall tonight."

Euthalia's heart quickened. Would Odin come? Of course he would—if the Æsir and Vanir were gathering, he would not be absent. Would she be able to speak with him about Vidar?

"Thank you," she said, trying to keep the anticipation and hope from her voice. Freyja glared at her, and she added, "Mistress. Thank you, mistress."

But she did not mind. Let Freyja think herself clever and cruel and controlling. She was sending Euthalia exactly where she wanted to go—to Odin, to ask after her husband.

That night, Euthalia carried the precious *epli* about the hall, distributing them to gods and goddesses who never thought of the pains they had caused that afternoon. When she had finished, and with a glance to be certain Freyja was looking elsewhere, Euthalia carried sweet mead to Odin's chair. "My lord," she said, "what have your ravens learned?"

He did not look at her. "Come to my hall tomorrow," he said, "and we will speak of Vidar."

Her heart spasmed in her torso. Was this an omen of good news? Of bad? "My lord—"

"No," he said firmly. "Not here."

And so she went away, her stomach twisted and her face held in a merciless mask of neutrality, lest Freyja guess she had been petitioning Odin for more than the honor of refilling his wine. And she served the rest of the night without looking again at the massive figure.

Tomorrow. She would know tomorrow.

"My ravens cannot find him," Odin said heavily. "This means he wishes to hide, and he is concealed with strong magic."

"Stronger than yours?" challenged Euthalia, facing his carved chair.

Odin frowned. "Strong enough," he muttered. "He wishes not to be found, at least not yet."

Euthalia set that aside for the moment and pushed to the next and most important question. "How can the curse be broken?"

Odin looked at her, faintly surprised. "Broken? It is a curse. It cannot be broken."

The words were nearly incomprehensible to Euthalia. "Cannot? Of course it can." Odin's placid answer infuriated her. "You are the father of poetry and wisdom! You hear all manner of things from your ravens! Your wife spoke to every material thing on behalf of your boasting and beautiful son— can you not do as much for your obedient son?"

Odin turned on her, his eye narrowed. The two ravens started up from the chair, alarmed, and the two wolves began to growl low in their throats. "I am Odin!" he thundered. "I am wisest of gods and men. If I know of no answer to this curse then there is—"

"You did not know the mistletoe could kill Baldr."

It was a dangerous barb, and cruel, but it stopped Odin, who could not deny its truth.

"Won't you ask?" she pressed. "Won't you look? Can you not do this much for him?"

Odin opened his mouth, said nothing, looked from one wolf to the other. "There is one to ask," he said. "But it will cost dear."

Euthalia gazed at him levelly. "My husband fled me in the middle of the night and I am homeless and enslaved," she said. "Not asking also costs dear."

Odin nodded once, a bare acknowledgment of her truth. "There are some few who are skilled in seidr, the discerning of destiny," he said. "And there are fewer still who can not only perceive the warp and weft of the Nornir's weaving, but can weave it anew."

Euthalia thought of the Moirai, the three spinners of her mother's tales who measured out and cut mortal lives. "But what is fated cannot be undone."

Odin raised an eyebrow. "Then why exert yourself, little bird? Why search for Vidar or a cure?"

"But I do not know if this is truly fated, or only what has happened." Her words sounded feeble even as she said them.

Odin leaned forward. "And I tell you, even if the Nornir have woven it, it can be unwoven." He reached out to pull her ragged and burned pinafore horizontal between them, and he took a thread from one of the rips and drew it across the surface of the fabric, pulling the hole wider and the thread free. "It needs only a weaver who can grasp the thread."

"And who can do that? Who has the power?"

Odin sat back on his chair and rested his hand on the back of a nearby wolf. "Though seidr is a woman's art, and I have been called unmanly for it, I am no mean practitioner. But I know I cannot undo this curse. It is beyond me."

"Then there is no one but the Nornir themselves?"

"No, there is one other." Odin's voice was level, heavy. "Freyja."

Euthalia's heart sank. "Freyja!"

"She came and taught the Æsir the magic of the Vanir, among whom she is the greatest practitioner. She possesses the greatest skill in seidr. If the curse can be broken, then she is the one to break it."

"Then tell her to help us!"

"No."

Euthalia stared at him. "No?"

"Understand this, little butterfly: when Freyja first came to us, we were in awe of her skill. Magic is not ours by nature, and we marveled at all Freyja showed us. But we desired too much, and we began to abandon our practical skills for magic, and we demanded more and more of her. In the end, the Æsir and the Vanir went to war."

The second wolf gave up watching Euthalia and went to curl behind Odin's chair.

"The war was hard, and we ended it only with hostages and the brewing of Kvasir. I will not make demands of Freyja again. If you can convince her to act, I will be most glad of her help, but I will not call upon her myself."

Euthalia bit back the bitter taunt which rose to her lips. Even a god could choose to avoid conflict, and a war among the gods would do Vidar no good. Nor would it be likely to help

Loki, as neither side would trust him to aid if released. She should be grateful for the information Odin gave.

"I will ask her," she said. "I will convince her."

Odin chuckled, and it was so unlike him that it frightened her. "Little spitfire," he said. "I doubt she will hear you, unless you can bargain with her. Freyja's taste is for fine things and power. I hope you can satisfy her."

"I will make her listen," Euthalia said.

And now that she stood before Odin, now that he had his ear and he was helping her to help his son, now she should ask....

"And Loki," she said, more abruptly than she'd meant. "Will you release him?"

Odin turned dark eyes on her. "What? Why?"

"For—for Sigyn's sake. His wife. And for the sake of your own bond with him. He has suffered—"

"He murdered my sons. Baldr and Hodr are both dead, by his scheming."

Hodr! But he had meant no ill! But Euthalia could not pause for this news. "Baldr tormented him, you must have known—"

"Enough! I will not hear more of this. Loki is bound where he can do no more harm, as should have been done long ages ago. He will stay where he can do no harm. And it will take more than your pleading to sway my mind on this."

Euthalia hesitated and then nodded. "I will go and speak to Freyja about the curse. Thank you for your help." She retreated from the hall, and Odin did not look as she went.

He had not said that he could not be persuaded to release Loki—only that she could not persuade him. She could still enlist another who might have more influence. There was yet hope.

And she could ask Freyja to help her find the answer to Vidar's curse. Her chest tightened. Poor Vidar, waiting long years to find a bride who had never seen him, who would keep his wish to never be seen, lest he lose her love.... It was terrible to think of. But she would petition her mistress, press Freyja to keep her part of their bargain, and together they would find the answer.

CHAPTER 23

Valhöll ran with mead and rang with shouts and songs, another night of feasting among the einherjar. Odin sat in his great carved chair, ravens at his shoulders and wolves at his feet. The Vanir and the Æsir cheered past exploits and bragged of future victories, while Euthalia and the other thralls bore endless food and drink about the long, long tables.

The change was small at first, subtle, and Euthalia did not comprehend its significance. Valhöll had many doors, and when the laughter and cheering at a table nearest one of them slowed, it was hardly worth noting, if the change could even be noted in the noise of the great hall. The einherjar at that table glanced at one another, smiles propped up on their faces as their eyes questioned. Had anyone else heard it? Should they carry on?

But then all laughter ceased, and heads at other tables swiveled to look at the door as well. Several men jumped to their feet, and several hands went to axe hafts and sword hilts.

The sound came again—hardly a sound, more a sensation, a deep, deep groan at the very edge of hearing as the massive timbers over the door flexed. A tiny rain of dust came down about the door and table.

The Æsir and Vanir were on their feet now too, glancing back to Odin on his chair.

"Go," he ordered.

But the einherjar were already crowding about the door, pushing to brace it and drawing weapons in a ring about the straining wood. It was bending visibly now, creaking with pressure. The heavy beam across the door cracked, and Euthalia wondered when they had begun barring the doors during the feasts. She remembered clearly the doors had been unbarred when she and Sigyn would leave the hall as the feast continued ever on.

The einherjar were shouting now, and the braggadocio of a few minutes before was gone. Their faces were serious, ready for fighting but worried, too, in a way Euthalia would have not expected in strong men who had died gloriously in battle.

Euthalia crept backward until she came up against the edge of a table.

The beam splintered only a heartbeat before one of the hinges, and the door half-swung, half-fell inward over the einherjar. The press of fighting men gave way as if everyone wanted room to swing his raised weapon, but no weapon moved forward.

A wolf came into the hall. But it was only a wolf for lack of any other ready word, for it was like no ordinary wolf. It ducked its head and shouldered through the gaping door, its withers scraping the upper lintel. It was enormous, dark and thickly furred, and its gold eyes glared about the hall with a keen understanding no wolf ever showed of the halls of men or gods.

It stepped forward, and once free of the door it straightened to its full height. One of the einherjar, bold or stupid with mead and boasting, rushed forward with a spear. The wolf twisted its head, opened enormous jaws and snapped the spear and the arm which held it. It slapped a paw on the unfortunate warrior and pinned him to the ground, tearing the arm partly free with the force. The man shrieked and then was muffled beneath the massive paw.

The wolf dropped the spear and arm and raked a mildly curious glance at the armed men around it. None stepped forward.

The wolf took its eyes from them and turned its golden gaze on the gods standing at their tables. Its mouth opened, showing white fangs like knives. In a deep voice which rolled through the hall like a grinding stone, it asked, "Where is my father?"

There was an awful moment in which no one answered.

Its father? How could such a beast seek its father in Valhöll? And then Euthalia remembered Vidar answering her questions about Loki. *He fathered Hel and Jörmungandr and Fenrir, Fenrir is a wolf, though that is the same as to say that Yggdrasill is a tree. He is a mighty beast, and fearsome.*

Vidar had not spoken plainly enough. Fenrir was massive and heavy with malice and they had—oh, they had bound his father for eternal torture.

The table pressed hard against Euthalia's back and she clenched her fingers uselessly on its rough edge.

Fenrir's ears rotated, flattening with annoyance. "Where is my father?" he repeated, and there was a snarl in the words now.

He is a mighty beast, and fearsome, and one day he will kill Odin, in the time of Ragnarok. And then I will fight him.

Odin had not risen from his chair, but Euthalia saw his knuckles tight on the armrest. "Your father is not here," he answered evenly. "You seek him here in vain."

Fenrir lifted his head. "I can see he is not here. I am asking you where he is to be found."

"By what right do you break into my hall and make demands of me?" snapped Odin. "Your father is not here. Seek him in any of the nine worlds, but do not trouble my hall with your insolence."

Fenrir sat and seemed to smile. "There was a time when I was welcome in your hall," he said. "Such games we played."

He ran his eyes over the watching Æsir and Vanir. "Such games."

"Your father is not here, Fenrir," called Tyr. He stood erect and, if not unafraid, at least uncowed. "And you have not been invited to this hall."

Fenrir turned a cold yellow eye on Tyr. "I shall go to find him," he said. "And I shall see you again in this hall."

"And we shall play again as we once did," said Tyr, and there was no hint of merriment or game in his voice.

Fenrir rose and turned, stepping over the body of the dying einherjar as if it were a bit of debris, and pressed through the big door which was too narrow for him. His black-furred tail waved through the door and disappeared into the dark outside as if the night were a sea which had swallowed him, immediately invisible.

For a moment no one spoke or moved. At last one of the einherjar stepped into the line of the door, well away from the threshold itself, and leaned to peer out into the darkness. After a moment he shook his head. "I cannot see anything. I believe he is gone."

It was unlikely he could see Fenrir in the dark whether the wolf had gone or not, but his words released a thick tension and the hall began to breathe again. Some men began to prop the door back into place, while others muttered to each other. All turned to the Vanir and Æsir and Odin in particular.

Odin's face was grim. "The feast is ended for tonight," he said. "We must talk."

CHAPTER 24

None of the einherjar were eager to go outside Valhöll and into the darkness where Fenrir had disappeared, so the Æsir and Vanir left for another of Odin's halls to discuss the wolf's visit. Euthalia, following discreetly, noted it was the same in which they had condemned Loki.

All through the moonless dark she imagined hot breath on her back and worried the fear-sweat dripping down her neck was drool. But if they were going to discuss Fenrir and Loki, she needed to hear what would be said. Loki's screams as Sigyn carried away the venom-brimming bowl were too fresh in her memory, too ready to return to her ears.

Sigyn could not free Loki. She depended on Euthalia to do that.

The gods and goddesses went into the smaller longhouse—still a great hall, even if not so grand as the enormous Valhöll—and closed the wooden door behind them. Euthalia's chest tightened. *Don't leave me out here, not in the dark, not with Fenrir....*

But she could not open the door and walk in, a thrall among the gods. They would throw her outside again, and

Freyja would beat her after. She pressed herself against the door, sitting with her shoulder and ear to the wooden planks, leaning close to listen and to shrink away from whatever might be nearby in the night.

The men's voices carried more clearly. "It's going to be trouble," said someone, possibly Tyr or Njord.

A woman's voice answered, and Euthalia strained to hear. "...Lie to him. He will learn."

"He already knows," said someone else.

"No, or he would have opened battle tonight in Valhöll."

"He will learn. And then he will return."

"We must keep him from learning. Or prevent him from waging his father's blood-feud."

"And how would you do that?"

"We bind him."

"We have tried that, again and again!" This was Freyja's voice, too recognizable to Euthalia's ear. "Always he breaks whatever chain you think to put on him."

"Then forge a better chain."

"You can say such a thing, Bragi, as if it is so simple. Why don't you spin us a worthy chain out of your sleek words, poet?"

"Stop! There is only one forge, and one smithy of craftsmen, which could make such a chain."

The speaker—Heimdallr? Tyr?—had the others' attention now. There was a moment of quiet.

"Whom shall we send to Svartalfheim?" Thor's brash accents and cocky tone were easy to identify. "Only two people have ever been able to wheedle gifts from the dwarfs, and we've bound Loki in a Midgard cave."

There was a pregnant pause, and then Freyja snapped, "You loathsome self-righteous ballsack. I won the Brisingr brooch for myself, and a dear price I paid for it."

"Four nights," said another masculine voice. "Four dwarfs."

"Oh, shut up. I'm not sleeping with any more ugly dwarfs for this. You bound Loki, you deal with his son."

"So you'll open your legs for gold, but not for the safety of us all?"

"Enough!" This was Odin's voice. "Freyr, send to negotiate with the dwarven smiths. Give them to understand that Fenrir's wrath will not leave them unaffected even in Svartalfheim."

"And when Fenrir is bound, then what?"

Euthalia froze. That voice! Was it the dragon's voice—Vidar's voice?

"Fenrir is not the only son of Loki who may come to demand repayment for his father's humiliation and blood. Jörmungandr will be a formidable foe."

"Then we must be certain they cannot join together," said someone else. "Bind Fenrir, and then find and kill Jörmungandr."

"Kill Jörmungandr?!"

Thor's hearty chuckle came clearly through the door, overloud and cocksure. "I will kill the serpent," he said. "Leave him to me."

Euthalia shifted against the door. If she could but see—if she could peer through the door....

They were arguing with Thor. They would not notice her. With her heart in her throat, she reached up for the latch. She could ease it open, so slowly....

But unlike the enormous Valhöll, with its many doors set along the impossibly long walls, this hall's door was set at the narrow end, with a short wall to baffle the wind gusting in when the door opened. Euthalia saw nothing but the dark wall and a soft glow from beyond the wind block.

The voice came again, more clearly. "This is stacking more logs upon the fire in the hope of smothering instead of fueling it. You mean to suppress them—but if you cannot? If this plan does not work? You will only have enraged the both of them. And what if they should enlist the aid of their sister?"

Euthalia's heart ached with the sound of it, for it was not Vidar's voice. He was not here.

"Leave her out of this," said Freyr curtly. "She does not trouble herself with Asgard, and we will not trouble ourselves with her. It is the sons we must take care to stop."

Or perhaps he was here, but not speaking, not just yet. They would not see if she entered. She could creep inside, listen, look around—

No, she could walk directly inside and call his name. He would turn, and she would know him, and—

And the curse would be activated. He would become a monster before her eyes. She would disregard his only request, again, and in a room full of watchers. How could that reassure him?

What if he did not wish to see her, if he rejected her again in front of all the gods and goddesses assembled?

What if she could not control her reaction when he changed, and she flinched upon seeing him? Before all the gaping eyes of the Æsir and Vanir?

Her determination crumbled before the thought. She could not humiliate him before all, not in the name of proving her love. And she could not shame herself by entering the gods' council and calling for her husband who—if she were honest with herself—was not there.

And then she realized that they had stopped speaking, that they were breaking apart and some were coming toward the door. She rushed away, too hurried to be silent.

"Who's there?" called a voice.

But it was not Vidar's voice, and so she did not answer.

She flung herself about the corner and hunched close to the wall, holding her breath in the dark. They came out in pairs and small groups, bearing lamps to light their ways to their own halls. Euthalia would need to grope her way home to Sessrúmnir without light, and she hoped she could find the way. She hoped she would find nothing else and no one else along the way.

She listened intently, but she did not hear his dragon voice as they left the hall.

Oh, Vidar....

She had to find a way to convince Freyja to unwork the curse. But Freyja would never do it for love of them; she would need payment. And Euthalia had nothing to offer, and certainly nothing of the richness that would motivate Freyja, would incite her desire as had the Brisingr brooch—

The brooch.

Euthalia's face stretched into a cold smile. If Freyja would play false with Euthalia, not properly seeking Vidar and setting her to impossible tasks, she would treat her mistress likewise. If Freyja did not keep her word, she would take the precious jewelry and offer its return only for the undoing of Vidar's curse. It was the only way to ensure Freyja's cooperation.

CHAPTER 25

"Little Greek."

Euthalia clenched her jaw. Some day, when Freyja called her by that disparagement, she would turn on her mistress and shout at her to use her proper name, else Euthalia would not answer.

Today would not be that day.

"Yes, mistress?"

But Freyja was not so mocking as usual. "They are collecting materials for the dwarfs' smithing. A chain as could bind a creature like Fenrir must be made of very particular components."

The goddess so skilled in magic might know what must be woven into such craftsmanship. "I am sure it is so."

"I want you to go with Thor."

"With Thor?"

"Do not argue with me," snapped Freyja, though Euthalia had not meant to argue. "Just as Fenrir is too dangerous to be left unbound, Jörmungandr is far too dangerous to let swim beneath the waves."

Loki fathered Hel and Jörmungandr and Fenrir, all with another Jötunn. Vidar had mentioned Jörmungandr, but he had not explained him as he had Fenrir and Sleipnir. "I know Jörmungandr is another of Loki's sons."

Freyja snorted. "He is, and he is a monster."

The word rang cold in Euthalia's ears.

"Jörmungandr is a serpent, the enormous serpent of Midgard. The entire ocean is his."

Euthalia nodded. "And Thor will go to find him today?"

"Thor will go to kill him today." Freyja looked at Euthalia seriously, for the first time lacking spite and malice in her voice. "Because if he does not, then at Ragnarok, Jörmungandr will kill Thor, and many others."

Euthalia felt a chill pass over her skin. She had seen Fenrir, terrifying and fierce, and she could not imagine what a serpent which filled the sea must be beside him. "And—and I am to help?" Her voice broke.

Freyja laughed, cold and mirthless. "As if you could," she said. "I am not certain Thor can do it. I am not certain his attempt will not open Ragnarok itself." She shook her head. "But there is no dissuading the bull-headed fools once they have set their minds to a thing. Thor has a mighty hammer and Odin considers his brood indestructible even as two lie rotting in the ground. No, I do not send you to fight alongside Thor. I send you to collect a rare material which can be found nowhere else. Bring me some of Jörmungandr's flesh. Scales will suffice."

Euthalia hesitated. "You want me to follow Thor to a battle which may open the end of the world and to take scales from the Midgard serpent as it tries to kill him?"

Freyja's mouth quirked, and the old malice was there again. "Yes." She pointed. "He will travel by the great tree. Go."

Euthalia wondered briefly if she should take additional items for the task, but she couldn't think of a thing which might be useful. Even if she armed herself with a small knife, what good could it do against a serpent the size of the sea? If she brought a net, even the largest, what could she accomplish with it which the mighty Thor could not?

Freyja's pointing finger had indicated the great shape of Yggdrasill in the misty distance. The tree grew through the center of the cosmos and each of the many worlds was nestled in its branches, and this branch—a mountain of wood—thrust here through the fabric of Asgard.

Thor was there already, clapping other warriors on the upper arms and running his thumb along the edge of his rune-worked belt. A woman with hair of gold—real gold, Euthalia realized with awe, draping from her scalp in a beautiful and hideous mockery of hair—stretched upward to kiss Thor, and he pulled her roughly close, drinking deep of her lips.

Another warrior stood beside Thor—a Jötunn, she recognized, pleased that she was beginning to know them apart. She did not know the name of this one.

Thor supplied it. "Come, Hymir!" he announced, finally releasing the golden woman when they had both run out of air. "Let us go to slay Jörmungandr!"

Hymir appeared to share neither Thor's confidence nor enthusiasm. He hefted a large axe and an enormous bag which dripped blood, and they started toward the tree.

Euthalia thought, watching, that neither of them would be likely to welcome a female thrall on their quest. She edged around the watchers and walked toward the enormous tree branch, her eyes on a place just beyond where Thor and Hymir would arrive.

Yggdrasill was an ash tree, its ancient bark rugged and thickly split with vertical crags. Now that she was near it, she saw the massive branch extended far to either side, faintly curving, with no end in sight through the light mist. It was like trying to look around a hill.

She watched Thor and Hymir approach the tree without looking at her. They tied their weapons and burdens securely about their torsos and then stepped into one of the bark's vertical splits, bracing hands and feet on either side, and began to creep downward.

Her stomach twisted. Could she? Dare she?

She looked at the thick bark. What if she took another fissure—would she go to the same place? Yggdrasill ran between entire worlds; it was possible she would follow the branch to another location entirely in Midgard. She walked to the place Thor and Hymir had started and looked down, seeing the two muscular men climbing down the fissure into the ground.

Euthalia licked her lips and stepped into the rugged fissure, facing the tree itself. She braced her toes against one side and quickly shoved her other foot against the opposite side, mimicking their descent and steadying herself with her hands as she pressed outward to keep from falling. She took a breath, trying unsuccessfully to slow her pounding heart, and began to inch downward like a spider.

It was slow going. It was only a moment before her limbs began to tremble and she thought she would fall. She did not dare to look down.

She did not know exactly when she descended below the thick grass of Asgard's ground and into the passage of Yggdrasill itself. She could not look around, did not dare to twist within the crevice of the tree. She could hear the men talking below her, but she did not know how near she was to them.

Something chattered, very near her head, and she froze. Beside her hung a red squirrel, head down and tail extending up the tree, clinging to the rough bark with inverted grasping toes. It tilted its head, twitching its long ear tufts, and gazed at her with dark eyes.

Euthalia stared at the squirrel, her arms and legs shaking with the effort of holding herself against the tree, and the squirrel stared back at her. She took a deep breath against the fatigue in her limbs and started downward again.

The squirrel scurried downward and ran over her hand and forearm, sharp nails pricking at her skin.

Euthalia cried out and jerked back, more in surprise than pain or fear, and she fell. She hardly had time to cry out before she landed on Hymir, knocking him with a grunt loose from his spider climb so that they both fell onto Thor below. Euthalia grabbed at any flesh or clothing she could reach, her scream caught silent in her throat.

"What is this?" grumbled Thor, braced in the fissure with Hymir half-resting on his shoulder and Euthalia clinging to his hair and Hymir's tunic. "What are you doing?"

Euthalia forced her fingers to release the handful of hair. "I—I—I was sent after you. By Freyja."

"Get off me." Thor shrugged Hymir toward the wall of the shaft, and the Jötunn looked down and laughed. Thor looked at Euthalia. "By Freyja?"

Euthalia started to nod, but she realized she was lying across the bloody bag across Hymir's back. She wriggled backward and slipped as she grasped at the bark.

Thor reached for her and heaved her over his shoulder, rump upward, as if she were another bag of meat. He started down the fissure again. "I thought you were Vidar's."

Euthalia was surprised. Despite her storytelling, she did not think many of the Æsir knew her, especially since her thralldom, and certainly she would not have supposed Thor would. "I was," she said. "That is, I was—"

"Did he sell you to Freyja?"

Euthalia stiffened. "He did not. I—"

Thor spoke over her easily. "I did not think so. You are his wife."

Euthalia's heart caught in her chest and she twisted on Thor's shoulder, trying unsuccessfully to see his face. "You said *are*. I still am his wife."

Thor shrugged her back into place. "Vidar did not want to be rid of you."

The words, simple and gruff, seemed to open the sky above Euthalia even in the twilight of the great tree. Thor, simple, self-centered Thor, knew her because of Vidar's love for her. Vidar must have spoken of her fondly, must have done so often and eloquently enough that Thor was surprised to find her serving Freyja.

It could not be that Thor was so dull as to miss entirely that Vidar had thrown over his bride. She would not allow herself to believe it. The truth had to be that even Thor knew of Vidar's love. Had to be.

The squirrel ran past them, flicking its fluffy tail in derision at their relatively slow pace. Thor snorted. "Silly thing."

"Do the animals travel between the worlds as well?"

"Only that one, Ratatoskr."

"Why?" Euthalia asked, partly from curiosity and partly to keep her mind from considering that she dangled between worlds from the shoulder of a spider-climbing man.

"He carries insults," Thor answered briefly. "Always looking for new tales to carry." He did not continue.

Euthalia could see little, draped over Thor's shoulder with her head dangling between back and bark, so she gave up trying to look about her and let herself swing with his movements. Thor wore a wide leather belt worked with both runes and curling figures chasing about the length of the belt. She had never seen such detail on a belt or on any leather item. Hadn't Loki said something about a magical belt which granted Thor greater strength? This must be it. For a moment Euthalia was tempted crazily to tear it away, but even if she somehow dared to thieve off the mighty Thor, it would be beyond foolish to do so as his augmented strength held the two of them in a crack of bark at some unimaginable height.

"I was sent for some of Jörmungandr's flesh," she said, feeling awkward.

Thor laughed. "You shall have as much as you want, once I have killed him. But I will take the head as a trophy."

The squirrel ran past them again, heading upward this time. He paused, looked at Euthalia, flicked his tail. Then he turned and followed their descent a few paces, moving quickly and then stopping, quickly and then stopping, as if bored with their glacial progress. If he sought stories and controversy to tell, Euthalia considered, he might be delighted by the appearance of Vidar's offending and abandoned bride who was now enthralled to the goddess seeking to steal her husband.

Euthalia looked back at the belt. Would it work only for Thor, or for anyone? Would it work only for one who wore it, or was mere physical contact the key? She knew so little of magic....

She stretched a hand to the belt and spread her palm and fingers against the tooled leather. Was that a tingle against her skin? Was she stronger?

She laughed at herself, swaying upside down over Thor's shoulder. It was all in her head. She had felt nothing. She looked up, half-expecting to see the squirrel Ratatoskr chitter-laughing at her, but he had gone.

She realized there was more light coming around Thor's broad torso and illuminating the bark around her, and she twisted again to try to see.

"Steady, girl," Thor said. "Don't make me miss my footing."

He braced himself against the tree, put a foot against the bark where Euthalia could see, and kicked backward. He landed a few seconds later and Euthalia grunted with the impact of his shoulder into her abdomen. He reached up and rolled her off him and to her feet.

Beside them Hymir landed, nearly as broad as Thor and still carrying the bloody bag. "This way, then?" he said, not really asking, and started forward.

Euthalia looked about them. The great ash tree was already well behind them. There were few other trees in sight, even of more normal size. The land was all windblown grass and jumbled grey stone. She could see some sheep scattered across a distant hill, but no people or other animals. "Where are we?"

"Midgard," answered Thor without looking around.

The human world. And the world where Loki was imprisoned and where Sigyn sat endlessly with him to catch dripping venom. "Where in Midgard?"

Thor kept walking. "The Wyrmhole."

CHAPTER 26

They came to a rocky shore—more of a cliff than a shore, to Euthalia's mind, for the grassland ended abruptly and a careless step could carry one straight to the pitted stone slabs extending below. Euthalia looked over the edge, resisting the urge to reach for Thor's arm. More than a dozen men could stand atop one another and not reach from sea to cliff's edge.

At the base of the cliff, worn stone extended out into the sea, and the waves crashed upon this plateau in a ceaseless cycle of foam and spray. As the white water receded, Euthalia saw the frothy waves pour not wholly back into the ocean, but also into a great rectangular hole in the stone.

"The Wyrmhole," Thor noted with satisfaction.

Hymir did not look so pleased. "He may not be here," he said, and there was a thread of hope in his voice.

Thor shook his head. "That is why we have brought the bull." He pulled the sack from Hymir's shoulder and tore it open, exposing great chunks of quartered bull. Thor next took out an enormous iron hook and began knotting a rope to a ring set at one end.

Euthalia tried not to think of what would need a quarter of a bull as bait. "I am—that is, my mistress sent me to bring flesh from Jörmungandr," she said.

Thor laughed. "You may have as much as you please once I have slain the beast," he said. "Only until then, you must stay well out of the way."

Euthalia looked down at the hole. Nine men might lie along its side, head to heels, without crowding. It was a strange door to the sea, set in the sea.

She wanted no part of what might come out of it.

Thor hooked the meat and lifted the haunch as lightly as if it were a small child. Then he flung it out over the cliff, the extending rope winging behind it, and into the dark water of the hole. He wrapped the remaining rope about his wrist, setting it on a thick leather bracer to spare his skin.

He turned and pointed across the rocky grassland. "Go over there," he said to Euthalia. "You should be safe enough—"

The rope snapped taut and Thor stumbled toward the edge. Hymir reached for him with a cry and Euthalia leapt too, catching him about the rocky bicep and pulling hard away from the cliff. She knew she should run, wanted to run, but she was afraid to release her grip lest Thor fly over the edge.

But Thor was already regaining his balance and crouching hard against the pull of the rope. "So fast!" he shouted with undisguised glee. "He was here already!"

The water below them frothed and heaved, and Euthalia stared down as a dark head broke the surface, nearly the width of the pool. It rose and swung at the far arc of the rope, a long, sleek body shedding water like a cataract as it swayed, and its mouth opened.

It was a snake, a serpent, a monstrous sea serpent like nothing Euthalia had imagined even when she looked at the hole and the haunches of beef. It was hooked through the mouth like a fish, and it was furious.

Jörmungandr reared back, threatening to pull Thor forward off the cliff, and the three of them braced hard to pull against him—though Euthalia knew she was lending no strength, that it was only Thor and his magical belt and Hymir the Jötunn who held the great serpent. Still she dared not let go, could not pry her fingers loose from Thor's arm, for fear he would fall or the serpent would come free.

And then, at the far end of his tether, Jörmungandr reversed and struck. His head dove at them with blinding speed, and they could not collect the rope fast enough, could not move quickly enough. All that saved Euthalia as she spun away was the serpent's indifference. It struck at Thor.

Euthalia hit the ground and rolled onto a rock which painfully stopped her. She looked back and saw the enormous head strike where they had stood, mouth open to take a bite of the cliffside. The eye which rolled to look at her was the height of a man.

She flinched back, scrabbling for purchase, and the snake tore the ground away, dropping soil and stone into the foaming sea below. Euthalia crawled backward from the eroding cliff edge, her eyes on the enormous head as it shook debris from its mouth and hissed in rage as the hook flexed in its jaw.

The rope on the hook snapped tight, and Euthalia tore her eyes from the monster to see that Thor still stood, rope about his arm, grinning with unnatural joy as he wrestled against the strength of the enormous beast. He had escaped to the other side, letting Jörmungandr bite where he had stood.

Where Euthalia had stood, she realized.

Jörmungandr, caught by the rope, twisted his head one way and then the other. His eyes blazed, but not with the fearful intelligence Euthalia had seen in Fenrir. This son of Loki would not treat or negotiate with his tormentors. He sought only to kill and to free himself.

She glanced down to where endless coils of serpent were writhing up from the sea, grating through the hole and heaving the ocean aside as it came.

"Thor! Cut it loose!"

Hymir was shouting from his place on the ground beyond Thor, but the Æsir ignored him. The singing rope burned against the leather bracer, steaming faintly with the seawater.

Euthalia got to her feet. She could run back to the tree, to Yggdrasill, she could—

The serpent struck again at Thor, mouth wide to expose fangs longer than a man's height. Thor dodged aside, frantically gathering slack rope, and pulled one arm back to deliver a hooking punch just behind the snake's nostril. Jörmungandr, unfazed, twisted and lashed his body against the cliff.

Euthalia's foothold crumbled.

She screamed and flailed for grass, stone, anything which might save her. Her hand struck sleek scales. She wrapped her arms about the broad, broad curve of the serpentine body and fell, sliding along the scaly curves and being carried with the coiling body.

She tumbled off the writhing snake and into the ocean, and the cold took her breath. But the waves bore her up again with Jörmungandr's fury, and she gasped air and looked about for safety. She could see the snake rising from the Wyrmhole to her left, and somehow she knew that hole was death. If she were drawn into it, she would certainly be crushed against the stone sides by the massive serpent—and if she somehow escaped that, who could say what horrifying oceanic pit it opened onto below?

She kicked hard, but the swelling water lifted her and carried her back, away from the rising cliffs. She could see the wide stone ledge, marked with seaweed and bristly plants and pocked with wear, and then frothy water crashed over it once more and she was swept toward the Wyrmhole, and she could not even scream for her mouth was full of seawater.

And then something moved beneath her, caught her, and she clutched again at the thrashing body of Jörmungandr. The great serpent lunged upward from the sea, bearing her high, and she fell as he twisted over the battered cliff.

She hit the ground hard, and for a moment she could only choke and spit and try to clear her vision. When she looked up she saw Thor braced against the serpent's head, feet planted on the lower jaw as he hauled back on the rope fixed in it, holding himself in place as Jörmungandr shook his head in pain and rage. Hymir ran for them, a sheep-sized boulder in his arms, and leaped to bring it down on the serpent's skull. Jörmungandr shook off the blow and struck Hymir aside with a swipe of his head.

"Cut him free!" shouted Hymir again.

Thor shook his head and shifted his grip on the rope. Jörmungandr reared high, higher than Euthalia thought possible, carrying Thor with him. Thor took one hand from the precious handhold to pull the hammer from its place on his belt. Euthalia saw him raise the weapon, silhouetted against the sky, and bring it down against the serpent's head.

There was a crack like thunder and Jörmungandr actually staggered beneath the blow. Then the serpent's head snapped and Thor was flung high and hard, the rope burning free of his arm. Jörmungandr bellowed with fresh rage and shook his head, and then he tipped his enormous eye down to search for the fallen Thor.

Hymir was already running. Euthalia looked past him and saw he was not running for Thor but for the rope lying slack between Thor and Jörmungandr.

"No!" shouted Thor, rolling to his feet. He ran to seize the end of the rope near him.

Jörmungandr opened his mouth and hissed, a sound like a steaming ocean. Blood ran from his maw where the hook had torn him.

Thor snatched up the rope and twisted it about his leather-bound wrist once more. Jörmungandr jerked backward against the renewed pressure, shaking his head in fury and pain. Thor roared incoherently and lifted Mjollnir in challenge.

Jörmungandr's head remained in place, held by the agonizing hook and Thor's strength, but his body began to rise and coil about him, gathering on the cliff edge. Euthalia's breath choked in her throat as she saw loop after loop edge over the cliff and spill across the grassy plain, obscuring the wide sea behind.

Jörmungandr was leaving the sea. He would cross the world and destroy everything. He could not but destroy everything.

Thor laughed with manic joy and tightened the rope another twist about his wrist.

Hymir reached the taut rope straining between them. He made a mighty leap into the air, and at the pinnacle of his jump he brought his axe down against the rope. Strung so tightly, it parted like a released bowstring.

Thor tumbled backward with the release, shouting in fury. Jörmungandr recoiled and slid off the cliff, sending towers of spray into the air.

"You fool!" roared Thor. "You coward!"

Euthalia peered over the edge, afraid to look and equally afraid not to, and saw Jörmungandr sinking again into the Wyrmhole, mouth open and hissing in bloody agitation.

She waited, staring, more than half expecting the serpent to rise again from the hole, but the waves settled into their usual pattern of advance and crash and retreat, without the turmoil of an angry beast below.

Hymir was on his knees, panting, his axe beside him. Euthalia decided to emulate him and dropped heavily backward to sit on the grass. Her limbs felt weak and cold, though she told herself it was just the frigid water.

"You released him!" shouted Thor, closing on Hymir.

The Jötunn looked up at him. "Yes, I did. Because your fight was not going to prevent Ragnarok, Thor—it was going to open it. Jörmungandr would have destroyed Midgard if we had not cut him loose to return to the sea."

Thor squeezed the haft of his hammer and gave an inarticulate cry of rage. "But now he is gone!"

"And we should be grateful for it," answered Hymir.

Gone. And Thor had not killed him, and Euthalia had not collected his scales. Thor had not prevented Jörmungandr's attack, and Euthalia had not found the material to prevent Fenrir's.

Freyja would beat her, but that was only pain and humiliation. If the Æsir feared Fenrir enough to bind him, his impending attack would be worse than Freyja's punishment. Fenrir's attack would kill her friends. Would kill Vidar.

My husband, my love, I only ever fail you.

She turned away from the sea and started toward Yggdrasill, leaving Thor and Hymir arguing on the rocky grassland. Jörmungandr had gone, and they had failed.

She reached the enormous tree and looked at the craggy bark. It would be a long, long climb, and she dreaded asking Thor for help.

Her wet clothes clung to her, making her shiver. The shade of Yggdrasill blocked all sun.

She set one hand to the bark, testing a grip, and then twitched backward as a squirrel ran down to her. It paused, peering at her at eye level.

"Ratatoskr?" she asked, feeling foolish. Was it even the same squirrel? Did it understand her?

The squirrel chattered and darted downward, pausing where the tree slipped into the earth of Midgard. It looked up at her and twitched its fluffy tail.

"Are you—are you waiting for me?"

The squirrel scampered downward and then upward again, peering up at her.

"But that's the wrong way," she said. "I have to return to Asgard."

The squirrel made an exasperated noise and ran downward again.

"All right!" Euthalia pulled a handful of wet skirt through her legs and tucked it into her belt, and then she stepped onto the rough bark. She started climbing downward after Ratatoskr—if it even was Ratatoskr and not another red squirrel.

I am following a squirrel, she thought, and felt foolish. *And yet, I just fought a sea serpent. So perhaps a squirrel is not to be wondered at.*

They descended into the earth of Midgard and the shade rapidly became the subterranean dark. They had not gone far when the ground opened about them and Euthalia perceived they were in a cavern.

Was this the same cave where Loki was bound? She held her breath and listened, but there were no voices, no cries of pain. No, this did not look like the same cave; it was smooth with endless wear, without stalactites or stalagmites. The air hung humid and salty. This was a sea cave, enormous and round—

Euthalia's heart stopped. This was a passage used by Jörmungandr. It was the serpent's passage which had worn the stone round and smooth, as much as the ocean. This was one of his endless ways about Midgard.

She froze, afraid even to breathe lest the sound summon him.

Ratatoskr suffered no such hesitation. He leapt from the bark and landed running some paces away, twitching his tail and chattering at her. It was so clearly an instruction to follow that Euthalia moved despite her fear, dropping to the sloping stone floor and splashing through a pool of residual water.

The faint light which had filtered through the crevices of bark faded entirely, and Euthalia slowed as the cave dimmed to blackness. "I can't see," she said aloud, hoping the squirrel would understand her. "I can't see."

An impatient chatter came back to her.

Euthalia took a breath. She had seen no obstructions previously; the cave had been worn smooth, and Jörmungandr's bulk would have paved the way long ago. She put her hands out before her and crept forward, testing each step but following the sound of the squirrel.

"Ratatoskr?" she called. "Not so fast, I can't keep up with you. Ratatosk—"

Her hand touched scales.

Euthalia leapt backward and swallowed the shriek which rose in her throat, fighting to keep from rousing the monster with her fear. But surely Jörmungandr had heard her already, heard her stumbling in the dark and calling to the squirrel, to the stupid *squirrel*, which she had followed into the dark like an imaginative fool.

She stood frozen in the dark, her heart pounding in her throat, and waited.

There was no movement in front of her. The scales did not slide rasping over stone. And then there was a sound, a tiny sound much too small to be Jörmungandr, a sound like small claws on rock. Ratatoskr squeaked at her and ran forward again, to where the scales waited.

Euthalia took a breath and edged forward, hands extended. When her fingers brushed scales, she jumped, but she did not flee. The scales gave slightly beneath her pressure, as if there was nothing substantial behind him.

Insight came to her with dizzying relief: it was a shed skin. Jörmungandr the serpent had shed like any other, and this was his discarded skin, with the retained impression of his scales.

She laughed with released tension, and Ratatoskr chattered as if agreeing about her foolishness. Euthalia stepped close to the skin—even empty, it piled high above her head.

Freyja had asked for Jörmungandr's flesh. Euthalia smiled with giddy relief and joy and took the tiny utility knife dangling from her belt to begin cutting free a hide's-breadth of old skin.

CHAPTER 27

It was an exhausting climb up Yggdrasill, and Euthalia had already worn herself out when she heard voices closing beneath her and looked down to see Thor and Hymir ascending. Thor was still angry, but Hymir had placated him somehow, and Thor only grunted as he caught up to Euthalia and held out an arm to her. She accepted, leaning into his grip, and he shifted her to his back where she clung like a child as he continued to climb, fast and sure.

She wondered at his inarticulate offer, to a thrall and in his frustration at losing Jörmungandr. Might it be that Thor was not quite the brute she had imagined him to be? Certainly he had participated in the brutal beating of Loki, but that might have been more at Baldr's inciting than his own. And Vidar had said that Loki had more than earned retribution from Thor. Certainly Thor was not only a bully—facing the enormous Jörmungandr had required courage, not petty cruelty.

She was tired, now that the battle with the Midgard serpent had ended and after the heart-stopping moment in the dark cave, and she found herself nodding as Thor climbed. She woke herself with a start—what if she should lose her grip and fall?—but the rhythmic motion of his climbing lulled her back to drowsiness. She blinked fiercely and bit the inside of her cheek in an attempt to fend off her exhaustion.

But she did not notice when they emerged into the sunny realm of Asgard once more, not until Thor stepped off the tree and reached back to dislodge her. He lowered her with neither roughness nor particular care to the ground and then looked to Hymir. "We go and tell them, now."

Hymir nodded. "We go and tell them."

They started away without looking back at Euthalia.

She did not mind. She was a thrall, she was a woman, she was a hindrance to their task and had been only a literal burden to them. They owed her no special courtesy now that they had returned to Asgard.

She, however, must report to Freyja. She got to her feet, shook out her damp skirt, and started toward Sessrúmnir.

Freyja appeared to be deep in thought when Euthalia arrived. "Mistress," Euthalia said, prompting her to turn away from the hearth, "I have brought it."

Freyja stared at her a moment, as if sorting through her memories for what it was Euthalia was to have brought. "Yes?"

"The flesh of Jörmungandr." Euthalia unbound the rolled skin from the shoulder strap she had cut for it and held it out. "As you wanted."

Freyja took it gently, staring. "You—how did you?"

Euthalia wasn't ready to explain that she had followed a squirrel into a cave. "You said it was important." She nodded toward the skin, like a roll of vellum or parchment. "How will it help?"

"Jörmungandr and Fenrir are blood," Freyja answered, examining the skin. "Blood binds."

Euthalia thought of Loki bound in place by the entrails of his son, unable to break free. It seemed logical that the strength of Jörmungandr might likewise hold his brother Fenrir.

"Leave me," said Freyja shortly, still looking at the skin.

Euthalia was only too happy to obey. She went to her own corner and curled into it, head leaning against the wall, and slept.

Euthalia woke with a sense of satisfaction and contentment she had not felt in a long while.

She remained still for a moment, testing the feeling. She had found the flesh of Jörmungandr, simultaneously fulfilling her mistress's impossible demand and securing Vidar's safety by helping to bind Fenrir, prophesied to fight him. Yes, she had done well, and now that she had slept, she realized the grand extent of her accomplishment.

She should ask Freyja now. Now, while her mistress was both pleased with Euthalia's obedience and success against all odds and too distracted with her own concerns to engage in petty cruelty. She should ask Freyja how to break the curse on Vidar.

It would require careful presentation and more than a little flattery. But so much depended on it. All depended on it.

Euthalia rose and washed, brushing the dried sea salt from her clothing as best she could. It needed a proper laundering, but she was a thrall now with a thrall's possessions, and laundry would have to wait until she could take the time to wash and dry what she wore.

But it did not matter. The cloth would loosen with wear, and she would ask today how to free Vidar from his curse. Then she would do whatever was required, and he would return to her and forgive her, and they would love again.

Freyja was sitting on a stool in the sun, combing out her hair. Euthalia approached her. "Good morning, mistress. May I help you?"

"Yes." Freyja held out the comb.

Euthalia took it, a well-made thing of finely-carved antler, and took a place to one side where she could watch

Freyja's face. "Will they bind Fenrir soon, now that the necessary pieces have been gathered?"

"What? Oh, yes, I suppose so. The dwarfs have been hard at work forging a chain unlike any other."

Euthalia felt mingled unhappiness and joy. Fenrir had spoken well and fairly, demanding to know where to find his father, and they had lied to him. It felt wrong to chain him against nothing he had done, but what he might do. And yet, he was prophesied to fight Vidar—and she would do all she could to prevent that.

"Of course, having a chain is one thing," Freyja mused. "Putting it about a wolf is another."

Euthalia's hands slowed with the comb. She had not considered this difficulty.

"But that is always the trouble," Freyja continued. "Plans are simple. Actions are less so."

Euthalia swallowed. "I wish to know something of plans and actions," she said. "You promised that if I would serve you, you would help me to free Loki and to find my husband."

Freyja's mouth curved. "Yes?"

"I wish to know how the break the curse on Vidar."

Freyja raised an eyebrow. "A curse?"

"I know the nature of it, that it shows itself only in love. That is a horrid curse, brutal and cruel. I do not know what monster made it, but I know I will unmake it. I only need to know the way."

"Only," repeated Freyja with some amusement. "Who told you of this curse?"

"Odin," said Euthalia, wavering between admission and pride. She had gone behind her mistress's back, but she had been resourceful. "Odin told me of the curse, and he told me it could be undone."

"And did he say how?"

"No."

"And why is that, do you think?"

"I think perhaps Odin knows how to do it," Euthalia said. "But I think it requires something of him he is not willing to sacrifice. Not even for his own son."

"Odin has sacrificed much for his knowledge."

Euthalia's temper flared. "His knowledge, maybe, but not his own blood!"

"He has lost two sons."

"And that is no reason to make another son suffer." Euthalia warmed to her subject. "It's not right. Baldr was Vidar's brother. Hodr was Vidar's brother. He grieves them just as Odin grieves them. It is not right to let him suffer further only because Odin does not want to extend himself for his son who survives."

"Little Greek," snapped Freyja, "have a care for my hair."

Euthalia dropped the handful of hair she'd been unconsciously pulling tighter as she spoke.

"Listen to me," said Freyja, "and I will tell you what you should have seen yourself."

Euthalia dropped the comb to her side.

"You have asked me to help free Loki," Freyja said. "And I will do no such thing. It would not please Odin, and it would not please me. What would please me most would be for Loki to *know* that I had the power to free him and to beg me to use it. That would please me. For me to petition Odin for his release when Loki has done me no deeds? That would be foolish indeed."

Euthalia tried to argue. "But—but he would be under obligation to you. Think of the joy in that. Didn't you say it would be a precious thing to have Loki indebted to you?"

Freyja shook her head. "It would indeed. But Loki has no honor. He would acknowledge himself indebted and then laugh and wave it all away. He is *utgard*, don't you see? He is outside of order. He is destruction."

Chaos, Euthalia thought. Chaos would never serve a debt to harmony. Chaos could not be bound to a debt.

"But you are not outside of order," she said desperately, "and you promised to help me in exchange for my service. I have done careful service for you, and for all the Æsir and Vanir, by bringing the flesh of Jörmungandr. Now by your honor, you must help me!"

Freyja looked faintly confused for only an instant, and then she nodded and smiled. "Ah, the flesh of Jörmungandr. Indeed, such brave service should be rewarded."

"Then tell me!" repeated Euthalia. "Who cursed Vidar? How can it be broken?"

"And again," Freyja said, "I will tell you what you should have seen yourself. Who cursed Vidar?"

Euthalia stared at her.

"All others see Vidar as he is," Freyja said. "He changes form only under the eyes of love. It is an illusion spell, or a shapeshifting spell."

Euthalia could not look away.

"What fool could stand before me and say she does not know who in Asgard is responsible for a shapeshifting curse?"

Euthalia's stomach sank. "No...."

Freyja grinned with sadistic pleasure. "You have worked so hard to free him, thinking him wronged, and you never considered the wrong he has done you."

"Loki," breathed Euthalia. "Loki."

Did Sigyn know? But she must know. She had spoken first of the curse. She must have known.

Ice chilled Euthalia's limbs and she felt faintly nauseated. She had done so much to set Loki free from his torment, and he was responsible for all of hers.

All of hers.

Freyja nodded with pleasure at Euthalia's realization. "Why do you think Odin refused to break the curse? Because it would mean releasing Loki, and he is not willing to let two sons go unavenged for the sake of the third."

Euthalia let the blonde hair slip through her limp fingers.

"Knowing now what Loki has done, not just to Baldr and to Hodr and to Odin and all, but also to you, do you still wish to free him?"

Euthalia felt numb.

"You must choose, little Greek—would you win your husband's love, or free his tormentor?"

Euthalia opened her mouth, but no words came.

Freyja stood, sweeping her hair into a braid and settling a catskin cap over her head. "And now we should go. They've called Fenrir."

CHAPTER 28

The hall was large enough to hold all the Æsir and Vanir together, and yet it felt cramped once Fenrir had entered and cast his golden eyes about at them.

"Where is my father?"

The enormous wolf's voice grated like stone. Euthalia swallowed and was grateful that she was no one, that she would not be expected to answer the beast. What could one say to Fenrir's question?

"I have not seen him," said Ullr, which was probably true enough. None of them ever went to the cave, so far as Euthalia knew.

Fenrir's ears flattened in irritation. "I have sought him all over Asgard and found no scent or track of him."

"There is no reason he should be here in Asgard," said Njord. "You know he likes to make mischief in Midgard. Or," he continued, perhaps thinking it was unwise to prompt the wolf to explore the world where Loki lay bound, "he may be in Jötunnheim, where he is wont to go."

"Perhaps he's with the dwarfs again in Svartheim," suggested Freyja.

"He will turn up," grumbled Bragi the bard. "One cannot be rid of him for long."

This insult seemed to placate Fenrir more than any supposition, perhaps for its familiarity. "That is true," he acknowledged.

"In the meantime, then, play with us," said Freyr. "As you used to."

Fenrir curled a lip. "When I was a foolish pup? But you have been content to leave me in the wastes all this time. Why should I come to entertain you now?"

"Oh, come," said Bragi. "It is not entertainment solely for us. You enjoy showing your prowess and strength, which has no equal." He turned, his eye falling on Thor.

Thor stiffened. "My strength is equal to Fenrir's," he said gruffly. "My strength exceeds Fenrir's."

The great wolf sneezed.

"In truth," said Bragi, "since we have lost Baldr, we have suffered for entertainment, as there is no one to meet our challenges. And while I have my stories and songs to share, it seems—"

"No one wants your songs," growled Fenrir with a curl of his lip. He looked at Thor. "You are quite proud of your muscles."

"They are the match of yours and more," declared Thor firmly. Euthalia could not guess whether he was baiting Fenrir into a trap or had been baited by Bragi.

"Shall we test this?" asked Freyr, stepping forward. "What about a contest of strength between Fenrir and Thor?"

Fenrir's ears went back as he looked from Freyr back to Thor. "And we shall see whose blood runs red first?"

"No," said Bragi quickly, holding up his hands. "No, this is a match of strength, not combat. We will test who can break chains."

Fenrir laughed. "But I have already broken many chains," he said, tongue flashing red behind his white teeth. "That is no challenge."

"Then you have no reason to refuse," said Bragi, "and you may laugh loudest if Thor is trapped."

"I will not be trapped!" Thor protested predictably.

Fenrir grinned. "Bring the chains."

"Oh, not here," Bragi said quickly. "It's too narrow in here for a test of strength. You and Thor would break the walls with your striving."

Fenrir and Thor both grinned agreement.

"Let's go out to a field," Bragi suggested. "Where we gamed with Baldr."

Where Loki had engineered Baldr's death and Hodr's. Euthalia shivered.

"Let us say the marsh," Njord countered. "It seems wrong to sport where Baldr died."

"The little island," suggested Freyja.

"There is a small island there in the marsh," said Freyr. "That is a good place."

Euthalia watched them, all dissembling in unison, luring Fenrir to his doom. Part of her wanted to warn the wolf, and part of her wanted to rush to help bind him herself.

Fenrir agreed to the marsh, which seemed, if an unlikely spot for games, at least an equally unlikely spot for battle. They walked out together from one of Valhöll's many doors and came to an island in the midst of a clammy fen. They gathered beside an enormous boulder pierced with a wide hole.

Bragi gestured, and thralls came after them, each laden with a staggering amount of draping chain. Euthalia gaped at the sheer quantity of metal and metalwork—this was a kingly game, indeed, to judge by the expense of the playing pieces.

Ullr and Freyr directed the dividing of the chains into two lines, sorted by craft and size of the links and the matte sheens of the metals.

"I'll go first," said Thor, and he reached down to the first chain in the row beside him. "Here!" He thrust his arms out before him, wrists together. "Bind me!"

Freyr and Ullr wrapped a length of chain about his wrists three times and secured it with a pin. The spectators fanned into a broader semi-circle to watch, and Thor gave Fenrir a quick grin. "Thus," he said, and he flexed his massive arms and tore his arms apart, snapping a link easily.

"Such fragile goods are made in Asgard," Fenrir said. "Now it is my turn."

Freyr visibly hesitated before approaching the wolf to wrap the chain about his fetlocks, and Fenrir noticed and grinned faintly. But Freyr did his work, and as he stepped back the wolf lifted one massive paw free, breaking the chain with a sound like cracking rock even before Freyr had gotten clear.

Euthalia clenched her fists. If Fenrir could break these heavy chains so easily, then he could break Loki's bindings. A tiny flame of an idea took light in her mind. Fenrir was looking for Loki; he would free his father, if Euthalia led him to the place. And then Loki, in gratitude for his freedom and relief from eternal torture, would tell Euthalia how to find Vidar and break the curse.

Hope swelled in her for the first time in a long while. She would stay until the games had finished, as it looked as if Fenrir's great strength would leave him at liberty, and then she would gather the courage to somehow approach the great wolf and tell him she could lead him to his father.

Thor was scowling at the wolf's accomplishment. "Let us forego the daisy chains and test ourselves against the dwarfs' work."

Fenrir grinned, white fangs flashing. "Let's do."

Ullr pointed to a set of chains further up the two rows. "This one, perhaps?"

The next chain was cast of rough iron, with links the size of Euthalia's open hand. It was too wide to wrap about even Thor's broad arms, so they passed it about his torso, binding his arms to his sides.

"Stretch hard, little pup," rumbled Fenrir.

Thor took a slow breath and then thrust his arms outward, roaring as he stretched a link and then snapped it. He gasped for air after his effort and beamed his pride at the cheering spectators.

Fenrir's lip curled. "There must have been a flaw in that link," he said dryly. "I thought the dwarfs were better smiths."

"Our smithing is the finest of the craft!" shouted a short, bearded figure. Euthalia had nearly missed him among the spectators for his height and his soot-black skin which blended with the dark thorn bushes behind them. Two other dwarfs stood beside him, silent but similarly scowling defiance of Fenrir's insult.

"Brokk." Njord stepped close and bent to whisper assurances or conciliations, pointing at the lines of chains.

Which was the chain forged especially to hold Fenrir? When would they test it—and would it work?

Fenrir was submitting to the over-sized iron chain now, amused at the way the two men wrapping his legs and shoulders tried to avoid touching him as they worked. When they stepped back, he took a deep breath and bent his head, straining.

Euthalia dug her nails into her palms. *Come on, Fenrir.*

And then the massive chain gave, a link fracturing cleanly and dropping the entire heavy mass to the ground. Fenrir straightened and grinned, tongue flashing between his white fangs.

And then it was Thor's turn again, and this time the dark dwarf was coming forward in short, angry strides. "I will settle this," he said. "Let us see if any of you can stand against Gleipnir."

"Gleipnir?" repeated Fenrir dubiously.

"When a work is wondrous enough to win a proper name," snapped Brokk, "you should speak its name with respect."

Fenrir's lip curled at the rebuke.

The dwarf and his two companions went to the far end of the array of chains and selected a line from the ground. It was dark with the dullest of gleams, and it was forged of links so fine it appeared almost to be rope rather than chain.

Thor and Fenrir laughed together. "It is made of hair!" accused Thor. "It is no chain at all!"

"Then put out your hands, if you would mock the craft of the dwarfs," said Brokk.

Thor obeyed, and the fine links were wound about his forearms. Brokk stepped back and nodded his satisfaction.

Thor smiled and pulled his arms apart—or tried. He frowned and pulled again. Then he placed his bound hands against the wide belt he wore, as if to pull strength directly from it, and tried again, elbows quivering with the strain. He grunted, he sweated, he moaned.

Fenrir laughed toothily.

At last Thor stopped, panting, and covered his angry humiliation with a nod of acknowledgment to the dwarfs. "That is fine work," he said. "Gleipnir is the greatest of its kind."

They received his praise as their due and unwound the links from his bare arms, revealing the spiderweb-fine impressions of his struggle.

"How is it made?" asked Freyr, inspecting the chain in the dwarfs' hands. "For this is a wondrous piece of work."

"It is forged from materials which are very difficult to work," answered a dwarf with the falsest of modesty. "A cat's footfall and the beard of a woman, the voice of a fish."

"The spittle of a bird," contributed another.

"And the root of a mountain," said another.

"It is woven like the words of a poem," said Brokk. "It is fine work, and no one can undo it."

The dwarfs turned to Fenrir, and for the first time he hesitated.

"This means of course," suggested Bragi, "that if Fenrir can break the chain Gleipnir, then he is stronger than Thor and the strongest of all."

Thor's face darkened. "Not so," he said. "I only couldn't get my footing on this marshy ground."

"That is a lie," refuted Fenrir. "You had every chance to show your strength. You simply could not break the silken ribbon of the dwarfs."

"Then test it yourself," growled Thor, "and you'll see it cannot be broken! You'll be as trapped as I was!"

A ripple of protest moved silently through the spectators as Thor came too near the truth in his angry taunts. It was terrible to entrust such a critical plan to a dull braggart like Thor, Euthalia thought. How the Æsir and Vanir must hate the necessity of depending on him.

But she did not mind. She needed Fenrir now, and if he refused the test of Gleipnir, she would have him so much the sooner.

Fenrir's eyes shifted over the onlookers, who stirred and shuffled beneath his gaze. "This is a curious game," he said, "and I wonder what would happen if I were indeed as trapped as Thor."

"Why, we would free you," said Freyja with a placating smile. "Just as we freed Thor."

"Is that so," Fenrir said, and it was not a question. "What surety do I have of this?"

"Thor was freed, wasn't he?" Freyr said. "You saw it happen. And this question is meet only if you are bound by the chain, which could happen only if you were no stronger than Thor."

Fenrir's lip wrinkled. "I should like some greater surety," he said. "Or it seems this game is no game."

Freyja spread her hands. "What surety can we offer you beyond our word?" she asked.

Fenrir looked at her. "Flesh," he said.

Freyja recoiled despite herself, fear and disgust showing in her face.

Fenrir looked about at the gods and spectators. "One of you should place a hand in my mouth," he said, "and then I will be bound. I will release the hand when I am free, by my effort or yours. This is fair."

They stared at him. Bragi shook his head. "You might bite down in your effort to break the chain," he said. "That would maim someone undeservingly. We can find another—"

"A hand," Fenrir repeated, his voice grinding like rocks. "I can be careful of it. But a hand will prove your trustworthiness."

Someone seized Euthalia's forearm, and she turned her head to see Freyja's hard face. "Here," her mistress called, and she dragged Euthalia stumbling forward. "Take this one. Keep her hand in your mouth."

"No!" gasped Euthalia, pulling back against Freyja's iron grip, and it had nothing to do with the fear of treachery and everything to do with the nearness to the great dark beast.

But Fenrir was laughing humorlessly. "A thrall? Do not mock me or take me for a fool. The life of a slave is no surety from you. Give me the hand of one of your own."

Euthalia twisted her arm free from Freyja's grasp and retreated, her heart pounding. How had she ever thought she would simply approach the wolf? He was terrifying.

Silence drew out, and she looked around her at the silent gods. Their scheme was undone, and Fenrir would go free. Equal parts fear and relief warred in her, wanting the wolf to help to free Loki and yet so afraid that he would be left unchecked.

"I will do it," came a voice, and Tyr stepped forward. He kept his eyes fixed on Fenrir as the spectators shifted around him. "You know me of old, Fenrir. I raised you, I fed you, I cared for you."

"After a fashion," murmured Fenrir.

"Take my hand in your mouth," Tyr continued, his chin high, "and when you have broken the chain, you will release me unharmed. And if the chain proves stronger and you do not break it, then we will unbind you, and then you will release me."

Fenrir nodded once. "This is acceptable surety to me."

Tyr nodded in return. Euthalia thought he was the most gloriously brave and stupid man she had ever seen.

Tyr stepped close to the enormous wolf and extended his left arm.

Fenrir lifted a lip. "The other."

Tyr took a breath and then raised his right arm to the wolf, who lowered his head to take his hand and forearm in his jaws. They disappeared behind the glistening teeth.

"Bind him," Tyr said, and his voice was nearly steady.

The dwarfs began to wrap the fluid chain about the wolf. Fenrir's eyes followed them over Tyr's head and shoulders, watching them wrap Gleipnir about his forelegs, his shoulders, and then back to his flanks and rear legs. Fenrir growled at this, but the dwarfs continued, their hands trembling only slightly.

Fenrir turned his head, his teeth dragging Tyr with him. His question was muffled by his fixed jaws and the forearm in his mouth, but the meaning was clear enough.

"We are securing it now," said Brokk, stepping back. "You will have more leverage against it."

Fenrir growled again and flexed his forelegs. Then he shifted his weight and tested his rear legs against the chain. Then he took a long breath through his bared teeth and flexed, pushing outward against all of Gleipnir all at once.

Gleipnir held.

Fenrir's growl became a snarl, fierce and furious, and the dwarfs scattered with no pretense of fearlessness. Tyr set his free hand against Fenrir's jaw, whether to brace himself or to attempt to pull his arm free, Euthalia was not sure. He stumbled back and forth with Fenrir's massive head as the wolf flexed and twisted.

The slim chain held.

Fenrir's eyes widened, white-rimmed, and then he paused and looked at the watching gods and dwarfs. The unspoken question hung heavy and suffocating in the air.

Freyja laughed.

Fenrir's snarl became a roar of rage as his eyes narrowed and turned down to Tyr. Tyr looked back, desperate courage in his face. Fenrir's jaws closed.

Tyr cried out despite his courage as the bones all through his forearm and hand were crushed. Fenrir lashed his head from side to side, shaking Tyr as a dog shakes a rabbit, and Tyr was flung back and forth. He screamed as his broken body tore and gave way.

Euthalia screamed with him and then shrank back with the others as Fenrir began to thrash in earnest. He reared up on his hind legs, straining against the chain winding about his torso, and then fell on his side, kicking against the loops. Nothing shifted, and tiny lines began to appear where the thin cable cut his shaggy hair. Fenrir snarled and snapped at the air.

Euthalia felt tears on her cheeks. *No.* She needed him, needed his help, needed him in order to find and help Vidar, and he was going to be bound just as Loki was.

Vidar.

Desperation overwhelmed her and she started forward, her hands already reaching for the dark chain.

"No!" Gefjun pulled her back as two enormous linked paws scythed the air. Fenrir bit at his own legs, blood flecking his teeth. Euthalia could not guess if it were Tyr's blood or his own.

"You can see from here," Gefjun said, and Euthalia realized she had not guessed her intention. That was just as well; they would never let her finish, not when they finally had Fenrir as they wanted.

The dwarfs were moving again, and she watched them gather about the thrashing wolf. When Fenrir twisted his head to snap at one of them, another leapt forward and slipped another chain through the binding on his forelegs. When Fenrir lunged at this one, another threw a chain over him to a dwarf on the far side.

Fenrir realized what was happening and tried to roll to his feet, but the dwarfs were quick and coordinated. He got his bound legs beneath him and tried to stand, pulling stout dwarfs up with him, but the Æsir rushed to their aid, bracing themselves and using their strength against the trapped wolf.

"Hurry!" shouted Ullr.

Thor stepped forward and took one end of the dwarfs' chain. He passed it through the hole in the great boulder and a dwarf fastened it again to itself.

Euthalia shook her head, crying in earnest now.

Thor reached beneath his shirt and took out a small hammer, which seemed to enlarge as he swung it high overhead and then drove it full-sized against the great boulder. The ground shuddered and earth heaved on all sides as the boulder sank into the ground.

Thor struck it again and again, so that the boulder sank from view and the wolf was dragged across the ground to the pit. Euthalia seized Gefjun's hand and squeezed it as the wolf was pushed into the pit after the boulder, snarling horribly. He twisted in the hole, his forelegs scraping together at the edge, and snapped viciously at his tormentors out of reach.

Someone threw a sword. It tumbled end over end and flew into Fenrir's open mouth, lodging at the rear with hilt against his tongue and point wedged against the roof of his mouth. Fenrir's eyes widened and his snarl rose in pitch, but his snapping jaws stilled.

"Well done!" cheered a host of voices. "That's the best of gags and muzzles!"

Freyr stepped forward, feigning bravery but flinching with each of the wolf's movements, and finally he drew near enough to reach out and touch the dark muzzle. Fenrir roared but could not bite down, and Freyr turned to posture for the spectators.

Euthalia's knees went weak. Saliva ran from the wolf's frozen jaws, like endless streams of serpent's venom. She wrapped her arms about herself and cried, but her sobs were drowned in the general cheers and merriment of victory.

There was another sound which did not fit, and it drew her like one lodestone to another. She followed it to the side, away from the jeering crowd, to where Tyr lay folded on the ground around what remained of his arm.

Euthalia rushed to him and knelt, trying to make sense of the pulpy red and the too-pale bone and the blood pooling atop the marshy ground too saturated to receive it. She pushed away his remaining hand and pressed her pinafore hard over the mushy stump, making him cry out again.

"It worked," he breathed between moans, his breath fast and ragged. "It worked."

Euthalia looked over her shoulder at the crowd shouting and taunting the great wolf, brave in their cruelty now that he was helpless. "At what cost?" she asked. None of them seemed to remember Tyr or his gruesome sacrifice even as he lay bleeding behind them.

Tyr's eyes were closed. "Victory is everything."

Euthalia stared at him, pale from bleeding, and she remembered Vidar talking about fighting courageously for lost causes, proving valor not in victory but honorable combat. She turned and looked at the crowd surrounding the trapped wolf, throwing and slapping and jeering.

No, the heroes of your tales are not heroes, they are bullies who use their strength against opponents who cannot hope to resist, cowards who attack only those they are certain to defeat without risk to themselves.

Insight came blazing to her with nearly painful intensity. The great gods and goddesses, the mighty ones of Asgard, were corrupted. What they had been was not what they were, and they were too near to see it in themselves. It was not only Vidar who was cursed; they were all monsters and did not know it.

CHAPTER 29

She'd said nothing.

She had said *nothing*.

She had watched as the people she relied upon to survive together lied to a searching son and sacrificed the hand of one of their own, to avoid facing the consequences of what they had done in murdering his half-brothers and binding his father.

And yes, both father and son were monsters in their own way—but how could they be more monstrous than those who killed innocent children? Who promised safety in knowing lies? Who let a brave man have his arm torn away so that they did not have to explain themselves to the son seeking his missing father?

And she had let it happen, just as she had done nothing to stop the murders of Nari and Narfi and the torture of Loki. And she had done nothing for the same reason then and now: she needed their good wishes to survive.

Or she'd thought she did.

She had asked for help in finding Vidar, and little had been given. She had traded her freedom for the promise of aid and had received none. She had been bound with false promises just as Fenrir had, and she had let it be done to him.

She would break her own binding first.

Freyja and the others did not return from the marshy prison until the sun had fallen too low to light their mockery. They would celebrate the next day, once they had rested for their feast. Euthalia felt as if her determination were humming within her, surely audible to the other thralls around her and to her mistress. But Freyja showed no sign of interest in Euthalia's tense movements or frequent glances, an inattention which both enraged and relieved Euthalia.

When the last lights were extinguished, Euthalia curled her knees to her chest and began counting. But her thoughts ran uncomfortably over one another, tangles of Vidar's rich laugh and Freyja's fallen promise and Odin half-blind to his own son and terror for what she was about to do, so instead she told herself the story of how Ariadne had aided Theseus when he was doomed to the Minotaur's maze. She would tell this story one day to Vidar, she promised herself—her heart caught—later, she promised, when his curse was broken and when the tale of a man-monster could not offend him. One day, she would tell him.

When she had finished the story, even to Theseus abandoning Ariadne in the night on the island of Naxos—*I will tell this story to him one day when it can no longer hurt us*—she got to her feet and stretched her hands into the dark.

No light came into the hall, and the darkness was perfect. But Euthalia had served in this hall, had cleaned it and cared for it, and she knew it as well as anyone. Her eyes picked out the faint orange lines of the ash-banked embers deep in the hearth oven. They gave no illumination, but she knew by them the oven's location and was able to orient herself.

Freyja slept at the far end, in a sleeping nook well-padded with skins and furs. Sometimes she stayed here in Sessrúmnir, sometimes in her hall Folkvang, and Euthalia was glad she had chosen to bed here tonight. Euthalia crept toward the nook, breathing as softly as possible, fingertips questing urgently for any furniture or item which might jostle and betray her.

It must have taken her an hour to reach Freyja's sleeping place. She felt exhausted, as if she had walked much further than the length of a longhouse. But the greatest task lay before her still. She tucked her fingers into her armpits to warm them to flexibility, and then she slid back the panel to Freyja's bed.

She needed a light to find the brooch quickly, but something in her recoiled at the thought. Though her lighting of Vidar's face had nothing to do with her theft of Freyja's brooch, the feeling was too near. And if a light should wake Freyja...! No, she had to do this in the dark. She leaned closer and stretched out her fingers, moving them too gently to prod a sleeper to wake, waiting to feel the soft brush of wool or fur.

A hand closed about her wrist.

Euthalia jerked back, banging her head into the panel's frame, but the grip was firm. Another hand seized her hair. "Who is it?"

"Stop!" gasped Euthalia.

Freyja hesitated, then laughed, squeezing her fingers against Euthalia's scalp. "You! And what did you think you could do? Only one person has ever stolen the Brisingr from me, and he's no danger to anyone now."

"You killed for it?"

"What? No, girl, I coupled for it. But if you mean what happened to the thief, he's shaking the earth with his agonies in Midgard."

Loki. Of course it had been Loki.

But none of this helped Euthalia. "I wasn't taking it to keep." She winced against the grip on her head. "I don't want it."

"Then why come for it?"

"Because you want it." Euthalia swallowed. "I would have held it as collateral for your half of our agreement."

She had surprised Freyja, she could feel it. "Tenacious little thing," the goddess said at last. "And what makes you say I must be motivated by collateral?"

"You have done nothing to find Vidar, and you—"

"And already you are wrong," interrupted Freyja. "I know exactly where he is."

"But—but then—why have you not said anything?"

The cat-smile was audible in Freyja's voice. "What was the wording of our agreement, merchant girl?"

"That I would be your servant until you found Vidar and—"

"No, no, oh, no. The agreement, little fishmonger, was that I would find Vidar, and you would be my servant until you and he were reconciled. I never agreed to tell you where to find him."

Euthalia stared into the dark, her thoughts spinning with this caustic betrayal. Odin had not been able to find Vidar, had said he was concealed by strong magic. Odin had also admitted that Freyja had magic to rival or even surpass his own. All this time, she had been keeping Vidar from Euthalia.

She shrieked in fury and lunged at the prone goddess.

Freyja caught her easily and slammed her with the hair-grip into the sliding panel. "No, little fishmonger, that is no way to conduct business. If you did not like the terms of the contract, you should not have agreed to them."

"You lied—you kept him—"

"Hush, girl, and listen. Yes, I have hidden him, as he wished to be hidden. You wounded him greatly, you heartless bride, and I have been comforting him."

Fire burned through Euthalia's blood, and she trembled with rage.

"But I am not so heartless as you," Freyja continued, her voice weightless in the dark. "I will be flexible with the terms of our agreement. Continue to serve me well, and I will tell you where to find him."

"You lie."

"Little fishmonger, I have no need to lie. Let me be perfectly clear: I will keep you as my thrall while I keep Vidar protected as he wishes. I will comfort him and win him, and when he loves me, I will let you see one another. And he will be shamed by his former love for a wretched thrall and will love me all the more, and you will still see him as a monster, and you will never, never be reconciled." Her breath warmed Euthalia's cheek. "See? I do not lie. I do not need to lie."

Euthalia felt alternately cold with horror and hot with rage. "And you think I will serve you in this?"

"Of course you will." Freyja's cat-smile returned. "What choice do you have? I am the only one who knows where Vidar is, and I have promised to take you to him."

She was right. Even Odin could not find Vidar, not through Freyja's charms, and so Euthalia had no chance of finding him herself. She would be Freyja's slave until she reconciled with Vidar, and so she must serve Freyja in the hope of speaking with him once again and trying to rekindle his love, even when he had been poisoned against her.

Freyja was right. Euthalia had no choice.

Freyja laughed and released Euthalia. "You understand." She slapped her hard across the face. "That's for the idea of stealing my brooch. It's not enough, but I'm tired and in bed, and I think I've pained you far worse than any more material blow I might give you." She lay back upon the skins and furs. "Good night, girl."

Euthalia stumbled away from the sleeping nook and dropped to the floor, shaking. She grasped her knees to her chest and rocked, burying her face into her skirt to keep the sound from the monstrous woman lying just paces away.

"Little Greek!"

Euthalia clenched her fists.

"Little Greek!" Freyja swept into the house, her hands wrapped in her gleaming hair. It was not the shining pure gold of Sif's unnatural hair, but it was beautiful enough, especially beside Euthalia's tangled mop, uncombed since the drama of the Midgard serpent.

"Freyr is coming to walk with me. There is a great feast to celebrate the binding of the wolf," Freyja said, "and I must look my best." She picked up the comb of carved antler and smoothed her hair. "Would Vidar prefer my hair braided into a tail or hanging loose, I wonder?" She looked at Euthalia, lip curved in the faintest of cruel smiles. "What do you think?"

Euthalia tightened her jaw. "I will not help you to win my husband."

"No? Even if I am your mistress and I command you?"

"He is my husband. I love him, and you do not."

"Which means," Freyja answered smoothly, "that I can enjoy him as you cannot."

Heat burned Euthalia's skin, but she could not argue. Vidar's curse made Freyja's words true; the woman who loved him would never appreciate his physical aesthetic.

"You are a serpent," she breathed, clenching her hands into fists. "You slip around the fences and the walls and you take what is good and corrupt it."

"A serpent?" repeated Freyja. "Those are the words of jealousy, little Greek. They are not becoming for a philosopher or songweaver like you. Slip around walls? I enter openly, little Greek, and with eager invitation. I sleep where I want, with whom I want, and who are you, puny human, to judge me?" She pinned her hair in place and then turned arch eyes on Euthalia, scornful and proud. "Men desire me, men strive for me, and that is more than you can say."

"Men desire you," snapped Euthalia, "and that is *all* you can say. Does that golden necklace you prize have power itself among the Æsir because you wanted it? Or isn't it true instead that you consider yourself more powerful when you wear it? You do not love the necklace for itself, but for what it makes you in your possession of it." She pointed at Freyja, not caring what beating the words would earn her if she could but once strike down the goddess with truth. "Songs are sung of the great deeds of great men who made great names for themselves, but of all the most desired women in history and legend, it is said only that men fought over them, and it is the men who are praised and admired for their winning. We have thousands upon thousands of stanzas on the men who fought for Helen of Troy, but what was ever written of her after their fighting? Not a word. Not one word."

Freyja eyes blazed. "Stop—"

"Who admires the prize rather than the victor? What skald sings of a treasure without mentioning more of the hero who won it?"

"Enough," Freyja warned. "You twist words to make yourself seem clever."

"You make yourself an object to think yourself powerful. But when you make yourself an object, you become a mere possession. You are a mere necklace to them, a bauble to be displayed and admired." She raised her head. "You may be a goddess and I a mere human, but even I have known more true love than you have."

Freyja lunged at her, and Euthalia twisted away. The goddess screeched in rage and snatched at Euthalia's hair, striking her face again and again. "It is a lie! Say it is a lie!"

"The sky is dark green," choked Euthalia.

Freyja's hand hesitated, but she kept her grip knotted in Euthalia's hair. "What?"

"My ears are like those of a goat."

"What are you saying?"

"If you stand upon that stool and step off, you will float away to Midgard."

"You speak nonsense, girl."

"Exactly." Euthalia met her eyes. "When I lie, you are annoyed, but you are not angry. You are angry when you hear unwelcome truth."

Freyja hurled her against the wall, the wood cracking with the impact. Euthalia sank to the ground in a cloud of dust. She was too breathless and stunned to move, and she felt like she should be in great pain, *would* be in great pain as soon as she had a chance to realize it.

"Bitch!" screamed Freyja. "Bitch!"

Euthalia lay still, lest she provoke the goddess further. But a tiny part of her was satisfied to see that her observation had struck home.

Freyja clenched and unclenched her fists, breathing hard. "I should kill you."

"For speaking the truth?" Euthalia said. "Just as Loki said as much in Odin's hall? Will you destroy me as you did him, and hide the truth until the next person speaks it aloud?"

Freyja picked up the antler comb and shattered it in her fist, leaving a stiletto point.

"Or would it not be better to change the truth?" Euthalia said. "Make the truth a thing of pride instead of shame?"

Freyja froze, a tiny frisson of shock passing visibly through her. "They respected me once," she said, and her voice was nothing like Euthalia had ever heard it, small and hollow. "They were in awe of my magic."

She came and taught the Æsir the magic of the Vanir, among whom she is the greatest practitioner, Odin had said. *She possesses the greatest skill in seidr. If the curse can be broken, then she is the one to break it.*

Euthalia swallowed. "Then earn their respect again. Odin knows you are powerful in seidr, he told me so himself. Show your skill. Earn their admiration."

"And start another war?" Freyja shook her head. "We are hostages here, my brother and I, surety for peace between the Æsir and Vanir. That war began over the possession of magic."

Euthalia's breath caught, but this was her only chance, and she pressed recklessly on. "Then show them what good you can do with your skill. Earn their respect by saving one of their own. Unwork the curse on Vidar and—"

"Ha!" Freyja's laugh was nearly a roar, full of derision and fury. "And help myself by helping you? You are exactly like everyone else, working toward your own desires and nothing else. Who are you to scold me, little Greek?" She reached down and seized a handful of Euthalia's dress and apron. Pain lanced through Euthalia as she moved. "And here is my final order to my thrall—go to Hel. Ask Loki's vile daughter for the help you want. I am done with you, you pathetic whining bitch. Get out of Sessrúmnir, get out of my sight."

She hauled Euthalia off the ground with effortless strength and plunged the broken antler into her throat.

CHAPTER 30

It was dark. And cold, in a way that chilled to the bone.

Euthalia was lying on her back, and she was cold. The dark pressed heavily on her, like a fur without warmth. She tried to open her eyes, but her lids felt as if they were pasted closed, and she couldn't summon the effort. Someone was near her, though—not Freyja, somehow she knew that. Perhaps by the hand on her shoulder—yes, there was a hand, quiet and firm, not holding her down but keeping a steady contact in case she needed to feel a hand.

There was a light on the other side of her, low and orange, perhaps a rawhide-shaded lamp. But it was cold, so cold, and so quiet, and the floor seemed to be moving like breathing beneath her. And—she remembered now—and she had been killed.

She worked her eyelids, trying to free them, and cracked open her lips. "Am I dead?" she asked.

The hand jumped, and someone bent to look at her. "Less so than I'd thought," he admitted. "But considering where we are, perhaps more so than you'd like."

She had heard the voice before, but did not know it well. Freyr?

He called to someone. It *was* Freyr, Euthalia thought, squinting upward. Cleaning his sister's mess of a dead thrall.

"Is she awake?" Someone else came to kneel beside her. She brushed Euthalia's face, pushing back hair and checking for fever. "I told you, you should have remained a virgin." Gefjon gave her a reproachful smile. "So much trouble might have been saved."

"But so much love might have been lost," answered Bragi behind her. "And so many stories would not have been told."

"Not every story is worth telling," returned Gefjon. "Ask her if she likes her own story just now."

"Where are we?" asked Euthalia. "Why are you here?"

"Freyr called us," said Bragi. "He saved you."

Freyr looked embarrassed at this accusation of kindness. "My sister has her reasons for what she does," he said gruffly, avoiding eye contact. "But they do not extend to murder, and not the murder of the wife of a man she wants."

Euthalia did not feel particularly charitable toward Freyja's reasons, whatever they might have been. "She meant to kill me."

She reached a hand to her throat, and her fingers found a thick wrapping before Gefjon caught them away. "Leave it be," she said. "It needs peace to heal, like the rest of you."

Euthalia closed her eyes. "I don't understand. How did I live?"

"I helped you," said a fourth voice. This one was female, too, and it sounded wrong to Euthalia, as if it were not meant to say kind words. She had heard it before, but always angry, or grieving, or—

"Frigg," she recognized. She tried to turn her head, but she felt so weak.

Freyr rose and took hold of a taut rope stretching above Euthalia. Frigg stood stiffly beside him. "Freyr brought me a thrall his sister had meant to kill. I recognized her as the wife of my husband's son. Like Freyr, I felt Freyja's reasons did not extend so far. I am a healer, and I did my best to mend the wound."

"Thank you," breathed Euthalia.

"It was a poor strike, or you should have been dead," Frigg said. "You came very near to death."

Euthalia blinked as a lance of energy ran through her. "Not near enough."

"What?"

Go to Hel. Ask Loki's vile daughter for the help you want.

Euthalia smiled. "I want to go to the land of the dead."

"We know," said Freyr. "You would not stop speaking of it, even while Frigg was wrapping bandages about your bleeding throat. That is why we have come."

Now it was Euthalia's turn. "What?"

Gefjon helped her to sit up, and she looked about her, careful of turning her wounded neck too far. They were on a ship, rolling slightly with a strong wind in its bellied sail. Freyr squinted at a blocky crystal he held aloft, and then he unlashed the steerboard and made an adjustment to their course.

"You said you wanted to come for Vidar," Frigg said, and Euthalia saw for the first time how much restraint she was exercising. "You—you don't think he's dead?"

"No, I'm sure he's not," Euthalia answered hurriedly, anxious to assure her. "But I think Hel can help me to find an end to his curse." If she could not ask Fenrir for aid, she could ask his sister. "And, Freyja told me to go to Hel, and I am bound to obey my mistress."

Frigg sighed. "Your wound will trouble you less here," she said. "Mortal pains have less power in the world of the dead."

Euthalia nodded as if this made sense, though her stomach twisted at the unnatural implications.

"You will need directions," Freyr said. "I cannot take you all the way, even in this the finest of ships." He patted the wood fondly.

"Tell me," Euthalia said.

"Go north," Bragi said. "You must go north, across the river Gjöll—it is a torrent of battle—and then on to Nágrindr, the Corpse-Fence. North to death, always."

"And then?"

"Continue north, and you will come to Eljudnir, Hel's own hall. She will be there."

"We are nearly there," Freyr announced quietly.

The ship slowed as Freyr worked rope and steerboard, and Bragi and Gefjon put out oars to brace against the pebbled shore which crunched under the keel. Euthalia looked out upon the land they'd reached, grey and misty and bleak. There was no sun—it did not ascend above the horizon in this place. "Which way is north?" she asked with mounting panic.

Freyr lifted his piece of crystal, the length of his palm, and peered through it. He rotated the stone, swiveling in place and then pointed. "There. That is north."

"Are you certain?"

"This is a sunstone," he answered. "Let me show you, and you can use it as you walk to stay on course." He put the crystal into her hand. "Put the mark at the skyward side. The stone breaks the light into two, see? Now lift it, and rotate the stone until the two views are the same."

Euthalia did so.

"When they are identical, then this edge points to the sun," he said, tapping the crystal. "It is morning, so now that will be east."

Euthalia nodded. "But won't you need this to navigate home again?"

Freyr gave his ship another caress. "Skidbladnir will find a good wind," he said. "She always does. Take the stone."

"Thank you."

Euthalia climbed over the edge of the ship and up the pebbled shore. She turned back and met Frigg's eyes, worried beyond what the goddess would ever admit. Euthalia forced a smile. "I will find him," she said. "I will find him and end his curse."

Frigg nodded, once.

Euthalia turned and began walking in the direction Freyr had indicated. Behind her, she heard the keel scrape again as Skidbladnir slipped back into the water, leaving her alone in the land of death.

CHAPTER 31

The wind was cold and cut through her clothing, and disorienting mist swirled about her and sucked the heat from her limbs, but every few hundred steps she would stop and check her course with Freyr's sunstone. Despite its promise of a sun just out of sight, she felt as if she were in an enormous cavern, that the muted sky above was more stone than air.

At last she came to a chasm filled with what Euthalia first thought was rushing water, crashing against rocks and frothing with rapids, but as she started across a narrow bridge Euthalia could see that it was instead a riot of vicious fighting, warriors striving against one anther in an endless flood of war and death. Their weapons rose and fell like waves, their blood-flecked breath rose like foam, and they took no notice of the woman passing overhead.

Bragi had called the river Gjöll a torrent of battle. She was on the right course.

"North to death," Euthalia whispered to herself.

North had always been death, she realized. Her fate had been sealed when she started north again with her father from Byzantium, not having found a husband there. The river-pirates had carried her further north to Aros, where she had been sacrificed. Now she was going yet further north to Helheim, the realm of death itself.

A wall rose before her, a work of earth and stone, tall and forbidding. She stopped and stared at it. This was certainly the ring of Hel's domain, but how was she to enter?

A rapid alerting bark startled her, and she looked around. There was no dog to be seen, however, only the dead plain and the distant river of battle. She looked back at the wall as the sound came again, and she realized the dog was behind the wall, though it sounded much nearer. Such an earthwork should have muffled the bark, but it sounded sharp and near, clear enough that she could tell it came from a large throat.

The wall of earth shifted before her, shaking down rivulets of dirt as the dead grass parted. Euthalia leapt back.

A wolf pushed through the splitting earth, shaking dirt free of eyes and ears even as he roared and pushed forward. *Fenrir!* Euthalia recoiled and whirled, looking for escape, but there was only the dead plain, offering no shelter. She looked for a weapon, anything to stave off the ferocious jaws, perhaps something dropped from the river of battle, but there was nothing.

The beast's shoulders had just emerged when a hand appeared and caught it by the neck, staying its progress. It continued to snarl at Euthalia, but it did not come for her as the earthwork opened to reveal a tall woman holding the animal by a collar.

A collar. Euthalia's breath came more easily. Fenrir wore no collar, and this creature was much smaller, an ordinary beast.

The woman dragged the wolf or dog away and fastened him to a chain, which he bit at futilely before turning back to growl in their direction. The woman looked at Euthalia with a faintly disapproving expression. "We have few guests who arrive by the Nágrindr."

The Corpse-Fence. She had found the way. "I come to seek an audience with Hel," Euthalia said bravely, straightening.

The woman looked from her to the chained animal, now growling with mouth closed, and back. "You have not much liking for Garm."

"He has not much liking for me," Euthalia answered. She hesitated and then admitted, "There was a moment I thought he was Fenrir."

The woman shook her head without smiling. "Fenrir is greater," she said simply, as if Euthalia should have realized this while fleeing in terror. "Garm is the hound of Hel. Fenrir is her brother."

Euthalia nodded. "The earth made him look darker than he is," she agreed. "But he was digging out, and I thought—" She stopped herself, suddenly wondering if this woman in Helheim knew yet of Fenrir's binding.

The woman's stoic face gave no indication either of knowledge nor of curiosity for Euthalia's choked-off words. "What do you wish with the lady Hel?"

Euthalia took a breath. "I was sent by my mistress, the goddess Freyja," she said. If Freyja could offer her no real help, she could at least lend her name to carry Euthalia past the gatekeeper.

The woman did not react.

Euthalia licked her lips. "And I bring word of Hel's father and brother," she added. Perhaps family could succeed where Vanir prestige could not.

The woman did not react.

If she could not be brave at the very gates of Hel, when she had nothing left behind her but failure, when could she be brave? Euthalia pushed her shoulders back. "And I wish to see Hel and speak with her."

For a moment the woman still did not react, and then she nodded slowly, once. "Enter," she said, "and she will receive you."

Euthalia did not want to step past the growling beast, but she fixed her eyes on the far side of the passage through the earthwork and forced her feet to move.

North to death. North to death.

It was easier to keep going once she had started, and she kept walking. Behind her she heard the deep rumble and she looked over her shoulder to see the earth closing again, once more the wall of Nágrindr. The woman and Garm stayed where they were, looking after her. Euthalia wondered if they were there to prevent the dead from escaping over the Corpse-Fence, and for a moment she had a terrible vision of trying to scale the earth and stone wall with Garm snarling and dragging her down by the calf.

She shook her head free of the vision and kept walking.

A longhouse appeared in the foggy distance—Eljudnir, if she recalled her directions correctly—and she directed her steps toward it. It was cold here, and damp, and she felt as if the very air drew the warmth from her skin. The not-sky above her remained distant and muted and eerie.

There was no door visible in the longhouse. She circled it and found the door facing north.

She opened the door of Eljudnir and went inside.

CHAPTER 32

There were long tables for the dead, just as in Valhöll, but these guests did not boast and jocularly fight one another as they ate. They sat on long benches before lean tables which bore watery gruel, and the faces they turned to Euthalia as she entered were gaunt and hollow.

She looked beyond them for the chair she knew must be present in this mirror of Valhöll, and indeed she saw it, a great carved chair very like Odin's. Unlike Odin's it sat at the end of a table, joining the guests in dining. She started toward it, ignoring the rows of wondering dead on either side of her.

She looked up, vaguely conscious of movement, and jumped mid-step as she saw the roof move. They were snakes. The roof was thatched with living snakes.

Someone grasped at her sleeve and she jumped, looking down despite herself. It was not a face she knew, and she pulled away. Someone else took a handful of her skirt, and she redoubled her pace, forcing herself down the aisle toward the chair and through the hungry dead. She had to reach Hel.

Deep in her mind, where she had not properly thought of it but only unconsciously assumed, she had imagined Hel to be a queen of the underworld in the same way she had heard stories of Persephone, the beautiful wife of Hades. But the figure on the throne was nothing like what she had unconsciously expected.

Hel was a woman, as was more than revealed by her rotting clothing which hung in rags and half-covered, half-exposed her frame. She was piebald, with mottled white and black skin, and much of her flesh seemed soft and rotting. One of her arms held a drinking horn half-raised, and the other was a skeletal corpse-hand, white bone visible through the ragged skin and muscle. Silver glittered from her arms and neck and fingers, bright jewelry, but as Euthalia neared she saw it was not silver, but frost, faceted like intricate knotwork.

Hel turned her eyes on Euthalia, one blue and beautiful, one dull and dried and unseeing.

Euthalia swallowed hard against the mingled nausea and horror which threatened to choke her.

"I greet you, godswife," said Hel, and her voice was dusky and piebald too, rich and rasping. "What brings you to my hall, when you are not yet ready to join it?"

Euthalia's tongue refused to move. "I—I...."

Hel pursed her lips, as if accustomed to this hesitation, and took a drink from her horn.

There were two figures on either side of Hel's great chair, and Euthalia knew each of them. Baldr stared down at his bowl of gruel, uninterested in the newcomer approaching them. The other figure was Nari, Sigyn's younger son, sitting and staring out at the hall as if he were not seeing Euthalia or anyone else in it.

Hel followed Euthalia's staring eyes. "Do you know my brother?"

Euthalia nodded slowly. "Not well. I know his mother. I saw him only—only once." *Only in the moment that he died.*

Hel reached out to brush the boy's shoulder. "I knew my own flesh when he came to me," she said. "His mother is not my mother, but we share a father, and so I have kept him here in a place of honor with me."

"You did not know your father had taken a—human wife?" Her voice made only the smallest stumble over the word.

Hel shrugged one shoulder, tearing a bit of flesh further to expose a stark white tendon. "What has the living world to do with me? All will come to me in the end."

Then she did not know. She did not know about her father Loki, her brother Fenrir, Thor's attempt to kill her brother Jörmungandr.... She did not know.

Euthalia's heart quickened. "Let me tell you why I have come, Lady Hel."

Hel gestured with her skeletal fingers. "Do."

Euthalia took a breath. "I am the wife of Vidar, son of Odin. I have been separated from my husband by a curse which distorts his image to all who love him. I did not respect his wish that I not look upon him, and so he has fled me. I travel now to find him and break the curse."

Hel nodded in acknowledgment. "I know this much, for did I not greet you as a godswife when you entered my hall? But your husband is not here, so you seek here in vain."

"I did not think to find him here," Euthalia said. "I came here to ask for your help for your father."

Hel's head shifted to one side, as if fixing her good eye on Euthalia. "Yes? How so?"

Euthalia looked at Nari, wondering if the boy would speak, but he only stared ahead at the hall. Euthalia swallowed. "Odin changed Nari's brother Narfi to a wolf, and he killed Nari. Odin then used Nari's intestines to bind Loki to three rocks, where he is tormented constantly by a serpent with burning venom. All this was done in return for Baldr's death." She pointed at Baldr, who was listening now with visible interest.

"Then I am avenged," Baldr said, and he grinned.

Nari's eyes shifted to stare at Euthalia. She looked back at him, and slow emotion came into his flat face, a recalled horror.

Hel looked between her two guests. "Is this true?"

Baldr shrugged. "It is no secret that there is bad blood between Loki and me, or many other of the Æsir and Vanir."

Hel's expression did not change. She turned and looked at Nari. "Is this true?"

Nari's eyes filled with tears, and his face crumpled. "Narfi—it wasn't Narfi—he wouldn't—"

Hel nodded, as if hearing a suspicion confirmed. She reached to embrace the boy, a comfort of rot and bone, and he leaned into her black and white body, shivering as he at last faced his death.

"And is my father indeed bound?" Hel asked Euthalia over Nari's bent head.

"Yes," Euthalia said. "In a cave, in Midgard."

"Then we will go to him," said Hel. She looked down at Nari, clinging to her. "I must go to our father, and then I will return. When I come back, there will be much to do, and you will have many guests to greet. Do you understand?"

Nari did not understand, but he nodded, and after a moment he released Hel. "I will wait for you," he said.

Hel kissed the top of his head with desiccated lips. Then she rose from her chair, revealing a leg as rotted and bony as her arm, and drained the drinking horn. She strode from behind the table. "Bring my horse."

A gnarled and bent servant limped into the hall, leading a three-legged pale horse which limped alongside, so they appeared like mismatched wheels. They made their painful way up the aisle, slow and halting.

Hel went to them and mounted the horse. Then she looked at Euthalia. "Show me the place."

Euthalia shook her head. "I do not know the way from here."

Hel put out her hand. "Death always knows the way," she said. "You need only say where. Take my hand."

Euthalia stared at the hand, intact but with mottled skin and the soft look of rot, and she made herself think of Sigyn, cupping venom away from her husband's face and eyes. She took the hand, flinching only a little when the flesh gave beneath her grip. Hel pulled Euthalia behind her on the horse, which shifted uncomfortably with the weight and imbalance. Euthalia wondered if it would collapse beneath them.

"Now think of the place," ordered Hel.

Euthalia closed her eyes and saw it, saw Loki bent backward over the rocks, saw Sigyn's arms trembling with the weight of the bowl but unwilling to remove it until the last possible moment.

"Good. We will go."

The crippled horse surely could not carry them, Euthalia thought. But then Hel turned the animal's head toward the door, and the pale horse leapt forward with blazing speed, skimming through the lean tables and plunging through the narrow door of the hall to the dark world beyond. Hel guided it around the longhouse and headed south. Euthalia clung to Hel's waist, all slick flesh and bone too near the surface, and tried to think of none of it.

Narfi, she realized. She had not seen Narfi in the hall. Hel had said she recognized her blood, and she had not kept Narfi with his brother. That meant Narfi was still alive.

The thought thrilled her for a moment, until she had to close her eyes and clench her teeth against nausea as the horse whirled up Yggdrasill at dizzying speed and Hel's torso squelched and shifted within Euthalia's encircling arms.

They burst free of the dark confines of Helheim and into the open air, and Euthalia gasped for it, quenching a thirst she hadn't known she had. Now she could taste the foulness of Hel's body more than ever, and she closed her eyes and moaned.

And then the horse slowed, and Euthalia opened her eyes and saw trees passing on either side of them, still too quickly to be normal. They turned, clattering over broken limestone karst which should have shattered the legs of any horse, and finally halted at the entrance to a cave.

Euthalia slid to the ground, legs shaking, and braced one hand against the hip of the pale horse. It gave before her weight and staggered, precarious on its three legs. She caught herself and the horse recovered, standing before the cave with head lowered as if it could not walk another step.

Hel dismounted and turned to the cave. "Let us find him."

Euthalia followed Hel inside. They had no light, but the cave seemed to lighten around Hel as she walked, the underworld recognizing its queen.

Sigyn noted them coming. "Who's there?" Her voice was wary, haunted, exhausted.

"Hel has come," Hel answered. "Father?"

"Hel!"

It was the voice of a hopeless man suddenly experiencing joy, and Euthalia's throat closed with the sound of it. Hel moved forward and then stopped suddenly, looking over the scene: the three broken stalagmites, Loki's arched body, the acid-scarred floor, worn deeper now than Euthalia remembered, Sigyn's extended arms and the half-filled bowl.

Sigyn stared back at them, her eyes jumping between Hel and Euthalia, a step behind. "Hel," she repeated, half-whispering.

Then Hel strode forward and reached down to the ropy intestines which bound Loki, extending her skeletal hand to touch the middle strand. As Euthalia watched, the stretched tissue began to rot, blackening and softening. Loki began to laugh, a fierce, high laugh which chilled Euthalia's blood, and then he flexed against the rotting flesh and it pulled apart. He jerked upright and leapt away from the rocks, stretching his arms and laughing still.

Sigyn set the bowl on the abandoned stone, and then she rushed to Loki, arms open. "Loki! Oh, Loki! You're—"

He shoved her away, hard enough that she fell back against one of the broken stalagmites. "No," he said firmly. "I will not let you sway me. I have work."

She stared at him, eyes wide, mouth agape.

Loki turned to Hel. "Have you my army ready?"

"I have everything you require, my lord," said Hel without looking at the stunned woman. "All awaits you."

Loki did not look back at Sigyn. "Let's go."

CHAPTER 33

Euthalia looked at Sigyn, but her once-friend did not seem to see her, staring into the darkness after Loki. Euthalia wanted to go to her, but Hel was leaving with Loki, and they were her final chance to find and help Vidar.

She ran after them, calling, but she heard no response. She followed the glow of Hel's travel and exited the cave shortly behind them. Hel was mounting her pale three-legged horse, and Euthalia ran to her. "Let me ride with you!" she cried, knowing she sounded rude and desperate but unable to stop herself.

Loki crouched low to the ground and then leapt high into the air, folding his knees and arms at the peak of his jump so that he became first a tucked ball and then unfolded as a falcon. He beat wings against the air and rose away from the cave, moving fast.

Euthalia stretched out a hand to Hel. "Please!"

Hel seemed to hesitate, but then she extended an arm, and Euthalia swung up behind her on the lean horse. They set off at the terrific pace, and Euthalia clutched Hel without regard for the rotting body, knowing that if she lost her grip now she would lose all hope of asking Loki for his help.

They dove back into the earth, returning to Hel's underground dominion, and Euthalia closed her eyes against the smell of Hel's rot and the sight of the Corpse-Fence rushing toward them. And then they were making a wide turn and Hel ducked as the horse pounded through the door of Eljudnir.

Loki swept in with them, banking once around the hall and then sweeping up and settling to the floor on man's legs. He looked around the long tables and grinned with satisfaction.

"Father!"

Loki whirled to face Hel's table and saw Nari. Instantly his demeanor changed, and he rushed to the table with outstretched arms. Nari met him halfway, flinging himself hard into his father's embrace.

Euthalia's throat closed, watching them. Again, she felt she had seen past the veneer Loki wore, the heartless disguise he kept for all others. He loved his children. He was not a monster.

He would help her.

Baldr rose from the table, facing Loki, and Loki saw him over Nari's shoulder. He did not move. "Save your breath, shining corpse," he said. "You have had your vengeance."

Baldr looked on Loki, on the rivulet scars rippling over his face, on the boy who clung to him. "I would not have involved a child," he answered, and it was almost an apology.

Loki looked down at Nari. "And your brother? Is he here?"

Nari shook his head.

"No matter," said Loki to Nari. "He shall be here soon."

"And Mother?"

"And your mother."

Euthalia's stomach tightened. "How will they come here, Loki?"

He ignored her and turned to Hel. "I see my first ranks," he said. "Do you have my building materials?"

Hel led him to a storage room at the hall's end and opened the door. An enormous pile spilled out, but it was no grain Euthalia knew. The pieces were coarse and misshapen, and as she scooped a handful she realized with sick horror: "Fingernails!"

The pile was fingernails and toenails, thousands of them, tens of thousands of them, and Euthalia recoiled as if they could harm her. She twisted and looked behind her, and Baldr held up one nail-less hand and wiggled his fingers. She looked down the rows of tables and saw none of the dead had their nails.

"These will do," Loki was saying, and he seized two great handfuls and began to crush them together in his fists. Euthalia stared as he smoothed them into a pebbled plank, each nail visible and distinct within the solid piece and yet inflexible, and set it aside. Then he started another. "To work!" he called, and the dead rose from their empty tables and came to him.

Euthalia stretched out a hand to Nari, watching beside her, and together they watched Loki mold the nails into planks and beams and then into a long curved piece which Euthalia finally recognized as a keel. *A ship. He is making a ship of nails.*

"Loki," she said, trying to pitch her voice correctly, "as I have done you a benefit by freeing you, I wonder if you could do me a benefit."

Loki glanced up from his work without speaking, his expression curious.

"My husband Vidar," she said. "He is under a curse. You warned me of it." *You told me he was a monster and prodded me into betraying him,* she thought, but she dared not accuse him while she needed his help. "I need you to undo it."

"Undo it?" He grinned. "What makes you think I can do that?"

"You are skilled with magic," she said, taken aback by his answer. It had never occurred to her that he would pretend he could not. "Only just now I saw you make yourself a falcon. Surely you can return a god to himself."

"I shift my own shape," he agreed. "But I do not shift others."

"But this is an illusion," she protested. "He is not really a monster, he only looks like one, and only to me. I believe you can do this."

Loki gave the final planks to the gathered dead and crouched to mold the last of the nails into a beast's head for the ship's prow. "That is a powerful spell," he said, his eyes on his work, "and it was done by a powerful worker of magic. It can be undone only by the one who did it."

"Then please—in return for your freedom, give Vidar his. Undo it."

He did not look up from his work, drawing out the jaws of some horrific creature and shaping jagged teeth from the nails. "Do you not listen when you are spoken to? Only the spellworker can unwork it."

Euthalia did not want to accuse him, did not want to blunt the gratitude he must feel for his release, but she had to answer. "And isn't that you? Weren't you the one to curse him?"

He stopped his shipmaking and turned surprised eyes on her. "Me?" He rotated to face her, drawing his knees to his chest and clasping them. "Me?" He began to laugh, a deep, mirthful laugh that should have been infectious but instead iced her blood. "I did not work that curse," he told her, rocking back and forth. "That is not my work."

"Who?" demanded Euthalia. "Who did it?"

Loki stopped rocking and looked at her, still grinning with wild delight. "Can you not guess?"

She came and taught the Æsir the magic of the Vanir, among whom she is the greatest practitioner. She possesses the greatest skill in seidr. If the curse can be broken, then she is the one to break it.

"Freyja," she breathed.

"Freyja," repeated Loki, grinning as if his scarred face would split. "Your mistress, whom you have served faithfully all this time, hoping for her aid to find your husband."

Euthalia sat down hard, dropping Nari's hand.

"Vidar spurned her," Loki said, "and everyone laughed because he would not accept her only trade good. In a rage she cursed him—but only a few have experienced the curse, because love is scarce in Asgard."

"Freyja," Euthalia repeated stupidly.

"And not only did you betray his trust, looking upon him when he forbade you," continued Loki, "but you went straight to the hall of the witch who cursed him and pledged to serve her. What must he think of you now?"

Horror exploded in Euthalia's chest, sending fractal branches all through her like expanding frost. She stared wide-eyed at Loki, unable to speak.

Loki laughed again, a cruel cackle which cut at Euthalia's soul. "You little fool," he said. "You stupid little fool."

"But I saved you," she said desperately, grasping for any straw to stay afloat. "Help me."

"I will help you in one way." Loki pressed his thumbs into the beast-head and shaped fearsome glaring eyes. "I will end your problem. It won't be long until you will not mourn your lost husband, because you and he and everything else will be ended."

Loki stood and lifted the great beast-head, carrying it to the ship which the many dead had assembled. He dropped the head into place at the prow and stepped back. "You are Naglfar," he declared. "Ship of the Dead, may you carry us to victory and utter destruction."

"How ended?" asked Euthalia, getting to her feet. Rising panic tinged her tone. "How ended?"

Loki turned back to her. "Odin said I would remain bound until Ragnarok," he said. "And I am unbound. So let Ragnarok begin." He placed a hand on each side of her face, trapping her, and kissed her forehead. "Thank you for your aid."

He turned and stepped into the ship, which rose gently into the air, filled with staring dead people. Nari ran after him and climbed over the edge. Loki gave him a long knife from the ship's store, and the boy clutched it, grinning. The dead, including Baldr, swarmed after the ship.

Loki pointed forward. "Let us go and show Heimdallr that we are coming."

The ship pushed through the walls of the longhouse, destroying timbers and planking. The cracking walls and roof sagged and fell, blockading the end of the hall as Loki sped away across the dead plain.

Euthalia was left alone in the underworld, alone in Helheim. She had no way to return.

She folded her arms across her chest and held herself, cold in the fireless hall. She had to return to Asgard, had to warn them of Loki's impending attack. She had to find Vidar and explain she didn't know Freyja had been the one to curse him. She had to find a way out of Helheim.

She looked around as if she expected a door to appear. It did not. She took a few steps one way, then another. She was numb.

A hissing sound seized her attention, and she looked up just as a snake fell to the ground beside her. She leapt to one side, too startled to scream, and it slid away from her into the rubble. The hissing continued, however, and she looked up.

The broken thatch was writhing with angry snakes. And now that the roof was collapsing, they were falling.

Euthalia ran for the rubble pile. She would climb to the top, somehow, and then she would just leap to the ground beyond. Surely that risk of injury would be better than staying in a collapsing hall thatched with serpents.

But the rubble shifted beneath her, and snakes slid from between the fallen beams, hissing and drawing back to threaten strikes. Euthalia scuttled back, hesitated, and then pressed forward again. She had no other exit.

Motion blurred simultaneously with a bloom of pain on her hand, and Euthalia yelped and, recoiling, lost her grip and tumbled back to the floor. Two punctures marked the back of her hand. She had not even seen the snake as she climbed.

The venom burned in her hand, and she saw her hand swell even as she watched. She turned back to the rubble and started climbing, but already her fingers were going stiff and numb, and it was difficult to flex them about the handholds she found. She lost her grip and slid nearly to the floor again.

Another beam fell, and two more snakes dropped in front of her. Euthalia spun, looking for another exit, but there wasn't one. She was trapped, and she would die here in Helheim, and Loki would destroy Asgard and all the nine worlds, and she would never apologize to Vidar and tell him she loved him.

She dropped to her knees. "Vidar," she whispered. "Vidar...."

The hall was going dark, no matter how she blinked her eyes, and she was swaying. She cradled her wounded hand and let the tears finally come. No one was there to see. She had betrayed Vidar and she had begun Ragnarok. There was no reason to hold back the tears.

She slumped to the ground, snakes dropping around her, and lost her vision.

CHAPTER 34

An enormous crash roused Euthalia enough to open her eyes, and she saw the opposite wall of the hall had cracked and sagged. There was a second blow, and timbers cracked and a hole gaped wide, trickling dust. A figure moved, silhouetted in the opening.

There was a snake in front of her. There were snakes all around her. She could not move; a drowsy inertia sat heavy upon her. Snakes hissed all around her, and she could not move.

Then a heavy boot appeared before her face and kicked the nearest snake away. The boot returned, pushing each hissing serpent back. The snakes hissed and a few struck, but none could penetrate the heavy leather boot.

Euthalia blinked, trying to make her eyes focus, and then a hand took her shoulder and rolled her face upward. "Euthalia!"

"Vidar!" She found strength she had not believed she had and extended her arms upward, trying to grasp him, to pull him close.

But he was already gathering her, one hand beneath her head, one beneath her chest, cradling her to him. "Euthalia," he breathed. "I thought—I thought you were lost to me."

"Vidar." She was crying now. "Vidar, I'm sorry, I'm sorry, I never meant—I didn't know—Vidar...."

"Hush," he urged. "Later. First, eat this." He pressed a berry into her mouth.

It was bitter and sweet all at once, and as the juice burst in her mouth she felt a curious tingling through her tongue and throat. She swallowed, and the tingling spread through her torso and ran down her arms, concentrating in her injured hand. "Idun's?" she asked weakly.

"Yes, Idun's *epli*," he answered. "They will heal you of the snake's venom. Take another."

By the fourth berry her vision had sharpened and she was able to speak clearly. By the seventh, she was able to rise and fling her arms about him properly. Cold metal brushed her cheek; he wore a shadowing helmet. He was in armor and bearing weapons. He had come to Helheim to fight.

"You came for me," she whispered. "Freyja—I'm so sorry, I didn't know it was Freyja...."

He pulled her closer to him. "Freyr told me you were here," he said in a rush. "He came to Folkvang and shouted until I came outside, saying that Freyja had tried to kill you, that you'd been serving her, that you somehow thought to petition Hel for me."

A spark of rage stirred within Euthalia's too-heavy body, not as strong as it should have been but promising to grow. Folkvang was another of Freyja's halls. Freyja had kept Vidar in her very own hall, even as Euthalia slaved for him. "Folkvang? You have been in Folkvang?" Then the spark caught. "You went to *Freyja*?"

He went still. "I—I asked Freyja to conceal me. She was the only one who could. I couldn't bear for all to know that my... that my face had—"

"No." She didn't want to hear him admit he was ashamed that his wife had recoiled from him, that he had needed to hide from those who knew he had gambled and failed.

"I didn't know she also had you." His dragon's voice was dangerous.

She pulled him more tightly to her. "Vidar," she murmured into his neck. "I never—"

"Euthalia, my love," he interrupted, "I should have given you a reason, I should have asked you, I should have stayed, we both—let us forgive one another? Start again?"

"But I didn't know it was Freyja—I thought I could ask Loki to undo the curse, and instead I have set him upon Asgard—"

Vidar stiffened and pulled back from her. "What about Loki?"

"He is free," Euthalia said, her voice nearly a sob. "He has gone to lead the Jötnar against Asgard."

At that moment a sound burst through the broken hall, setting the stones to vibrating and making the snakes hiss and strike at whatever was nearest them. Euthalia ducked her head against Vidar's chest and pressed her hands over her ears, but still it pierced her and set her heart pounding anew.

When it ended, Vidar said grimly, "That is Gjallarhorn, blown by Heimdallr," he said. "He has seen Loki's army."

"What do we do?" asked Euthalia.

"We fight," answered Vidar immediately. "We fight. It may not be true Ragnarok, and we will push back this assault. Or if it is indeed the end of all things, then we will meet our end with courage and valor."

He took her hand and they got to their feet, and they picked their way through the disturbed snakes to the hole he had kicked with his heavy boots. Outside there was a horse—Sleipnir, she realized with a start.

Vidar noted her surprise. "He was the only horse who could reach you in time," he said. "It takes nine days for an ordinary horse to ride to Helheim." He lifted her onto the saddle and then mounted behind her. "But Odin will need him now."

Euthalia wrapped her hands in the horse's mane and wondered if the horse, another son of Loki, would betray them. So far he had seemed to be only a horse, albeit one with eight legs, but he was a spawn of Loki just as Fenrir and Jörmungandr and Hel were Loki-spawn.

But the horse obeyed as Vidar turned him back toward Yggdrasill and set him at a gallop. The gait was unnaturally smooth, with twice as many legs, and Euthalia relaxed her grip on the mane. There was no sign of the gatekeeping woman and Garm the hound, but Vidar put a hand about Euthalia's waist and rose in the stirrups, and Sleipnir leapt the Corpse-Fence Nágrindr as if it were a fallen log on a forest path.

They ran on, pounding over the chasm bridge so fast that Euthalia could not see below to see if the battling warriors remained or had gone to fight with the others. On they flew, until they reached the massive tree and Sleipnir launched onto it, neck outstretched with speed.

They galloped all the way back to Asgard, and as they left Yggdrasill and plunged into the open field, Euthalia sat tall and looked around, straining to see Loki or any sign of battle.

She did not have long to look. All the einherjar were assembling, looking toward the distant sea and falling into rows along the many gods and goddesses. Euthalia's heart sank.

Vidar reined the sweaty horse to a halt. "Stay here," he said. "I must get Sleipnir to Odin, and I will fight with them. You stay by Yggdrasill. If there is any safety, it will be here at the World Tree."

"No!" protested Euthalia. "Don't leave me now, now when I have just found you again! You said we would fight!"

"I will fight," repeated Vidar. "You are a songweaver, Euthalia. Stay safe."

"Vidar!" She grabbed at his arm, but he was already setting her down, and as he kicked Sleipnir forward her grasp was torn free.

She ran after him, knowing she could never catch the wind-swift horse but needing to do *something*, something other than standing and watching in the safety of the tree.

But Vidar sped away from her, going to join the massing einherjar and gods near Valhöll. Euthalia stumbled to a halt and squeezed her fists, sobbing with lack of air and anger and despair. She turned from Valhöll and looked toward Sessrúmnir. "Freyja!"

The goddess was arrayed for war, bearing a shield and spear and riding in her two-wheeled cart drawn by two large cats. Euthalia started toward her, but the low wagon was already moving quickly and it was impossible for Euthalia to intercept it. She would have to chase it all the way to Valhöll, and what would she do when she caught it? Accuse Freyja of cursing Vidar? Who among the Æsir and Vanir would care, as Loki and the Jötnar advanced upon Asgard?

But she could not stand where she was.

She ran toward the lines forming for battle.

CHAPTER 35

What a fool you are, Euthalia, she told herself. *A useless fool. A destroyer, like Loki and his kin.*

She clenched her fists and wished she could stop everything. She would give up Vidar, anything, to keep Loki from destroying Asgard and Vidar, and Midgard and her lost family, and every other thing she had ever known or not known.

But there was no way to stop this now. Fate had rolled over her and all of Asgard, and—

And I tell you, even if the Nornir have woven it, it can be unwoven. It needs only a weaver who can grasp the thread.

Odin's words burned through her like fire through a threshing floor. She gasped, caught at her throat, and then whirled to search the sky.

Riders circled above the battle, wild women with spears and dangerous eyes. Their usual task was to choose those who would die in battle and then to collect the slain once fallen, to carry them to Valhöll against the time of Ragnarok. But there was no choosing of the slain this day, not with Ragnarok upon them. They circled, waiting to close upon Jötnar and the dead of Helheim.

Euthalia tore her apron free and waved it above her head, running after the nearest valkyrja, "Stop!" she called, knowing she could never be heard above the din. "Stop!"

But the valkyrja saw her signal and descended, reining in her snorting horse. She looked puzzled when she drew near enough to realize she did not recognize Euthalia. "Who are—"

Euthalia flung herself at the horse, grasping at the woman's waist and sliding back to the ground as the horse bounded sideways and snorted. "Take me to the Nornir!" she demanded.

"What?" demanded the woman. "We are closing for battle!"

"I can stop this," Euthalia promised, hoping it was not a lie. "But I have to reach the Nornir."

The woman stared at her, holding in check the prancing horse. "Who are you to speak to the Nornir?"

She was a ragged mess, Euthalia recalled, with a thrall's collar and matted hair and still bearing Tyr's blood over her dress and the apron she waved like a banner. "I am Euthalia the Songweaver," she declared. "And I know what to say to them. I need only to reach them."

The valkyrja hesitated, looking back at the ferocious battle. For a moment Euthalia thought she was considering escaping the danger, but then she realized the woman feared leaving the impending fight. "I need a warrior to carry me," Euthalia said quickly. "Loki will send someone to stop me if he realizes where I am going."

The woman turned back. "Loki knows you?"

"By name and face," Euthalia assured her. "He taunted me even as he was building Naglfar, but I was alone in Helheim and could not stop him myself."

The woman's expression relaxed into a grim smile and she extended an arm. "Come on, then."

Secure in her position of having an exalted enemy, Euthalia climbed behind the warrior and wrapped her arms tightly about the armored woman. The valkyrja let the agitated horse go and they launched forward fast enough to snap Euthalia's head backward.

They climbed steeply into the air and turned toward Yggdrasill. Euthalia looked down and then tightly closed her eyes instead. That was a mistake, for she had no warning when the horse plunged sickeningly.

Whatever she had thought of Hel's three-legged horse, that ride was nothing compared to this. This horse was faster, nearly as fast as Sleipnir, and its rider skilled at aerial and ground maneuvers which left Euthalia's stomach two turns behind. They dove, they soared, they wove through the tree's branches and flew down the narrow channels of its rough bark. Euthalia clung to the valkyrja and made no attempt to shield her face from the woman's snapping hair or to brush the wind-tears from her face.

Urdarbrunnr, the Well of Destiny, lay among the roots of Yggdrasill, so they had to travel even beyond Helheim. When at last the horse's motion slowed, Euthalia opened her eyes. They were galloping along an enormous root, with the horse's hooves firmly on the tree itself. Euthalia tried to breathe a sigh of relief and found she wanted to vomit.

Then the horse slowed to a trot, and a walk, and a halt. The woman half-turned in the saddle. "We are here."

Euthalia tried to slide from the horse and couldn't; her muscles were too stiff and locked in position. The valkyrja took her arm and lowered her, and Euthalia's legs gave beneath her as she reached the ground. She fell to her knees and bent forward, spitting saliva and dry heaving.

The valkyrja looked down on her with doubtful silence.

Euthalia spat a final time and wished for water. She did not look up. "What is your name?"

"Hildr," came the prompt answer.

Euthalia nodded. "When this is finished," she said, "I will tell Odin what a great aid you have been." If Odin cared about her words. And if this ended in any way which permitted speaking to Odin or anyone again.

Hildr seemed to understand the unspoken condition to the promise. "Thank you."

Euthalia pushed herself upright and got to her feet. She looked around and saw three women standing some distance away, watching their arrival.

They had watched her fall and heave. Euthalia's stomach twisted again, this time in shame.

But somewhere in the tree above them Loki was destroying all the worlds, and Vidar might already be dead. She wiped her hands on her stained skirt and started toward the women, her heart pounding in her throat.

CHAPTER 36

The Nornir were three women, all stately and wise and of indeterminate age. They stood beside a silver pool nestled among the man-height roots, and they watched Euthalia approach without moving or speaking.

She drew within arm's reach of them, and then she worried she had come too close. They were not gods like Odin or Vidar; they were more powerful than gods. They were unalterable fate.

No, not unalterable, she reminded herself. That was why she had come.

She hesitated, and then she bowed low. How best to address them? "I suppose you know who I am," she said.

One of the women nodded. "But even if that is so, it is rude not to introduce yourself properly."

Euthalia cringed. She had no room for error in this. "I am Euthalia, wife of Vidar and a songweaver. I have come to ask your assistance."

The woman who had spoken lifted a hand. There were runes in her fingernails, grown into the horn. "I am Verdandi," she said. "This is Urd, and this is Skuld." They all nodded a greeting to Euthalia.

"You wish to weave a song with us?" asked Skuld.

Euthalia folded her hands together to stop their shaking. "You must know what is happening right now. Loki is opening battle against Asgard and intends to destroy all the worlds."

"What is it you want?" prompted Verdandi.

Euthalia was surprised at the question. "I want to stop him!"

"And you think you can do that here?"

Euthlia took a breath. "There is nothing which cannot be unwoven," she said. "It only needs someone who can find and pull the thread."

"And you wish us to pull the thread of Ragnarok? Stop this battle? Save all the nine worlds?"

Euthalia squeezed her folded hands. "Please. Tell me what to do. Please."

"Oh, songweaver." Verdandi shook her head. "You do not understand your power."

"My power?" Euthalia stared at the Norn before catching herself. "What is my power in this?"

"Did you not say it yourself?" asked Urd. "That you had opened Ragnarok, by your own doing?"

Euthalia went rigid, her hands and feet going numb and horror squeezing her heart to a halt. Yes, it was true, and she was beyond foolish to think the Nornir would not know it or judge her for it. "Yes," she whispered, all that she was capable of. "I went to Hel, to free Loki, because I wanted to save Vidar."

"Vidar was not in danger," Urd said. "He only wore an illusion, and that only when your eyes were upon him."

The dagger of her words twisted hard in Euthalia's gut. "I know. It was my eyes alone which were affected, and if I had only listened to him—if I had not told the story of Apollo and Hyakinthos—if I had not told Odin the tale of Prometheus—all of this has been my doing." She tried to swallow past the stone which had appeared in her throat. "All of it is my doing."

"And again," said Verdandi, "again you do not understand your power."

Euthalia looked at her. "I don't understand."

"Do you think you can goad the All-Father with a stick of words and direct him like an ox?" demanded Skuld. "You did not make him kill the boy Nari. Do you believe you have the power to sway the Lie-Smith to your will? You did not convince Loki to kill Baldr. They are responsible for their actions, just as you are responsible for yours."

"What does it matter who is responsible?" asked Euthalia desperately. "Does it not matter more that we stop it?"

"If it is stopped," asked Skuld, "and no one knows their responsibility, then it will start again. It is not enough to stop disaster if all remain as children."

Skuld gestured to the pool beside them, and Euthalia saw that it reflected not only the great roots and the women around it, but faintly showed also a silent battle raging, translucent against the peaceful reflection of the tree. She leaned to look down at it, trying to peer around the surface glare, though the pool was in shadow. "Is this—is this Ragnarok?"

She could see a long line of einherjar forming along a rocky shore. On the horizon floated the nail-ship Naglfar, with Loki standing visible at her prow. Arrayed below and on either side ranged all the dead and all the fearsome Jötnar, a spread of dark armies.

Euthalia dropped to her knees and leaned over the pool, her stomach clenching. "No," she whispered, her face near enough for her breath to disturb the water. "No, please."

"Songweaver, come away," said Verdandi. "You—"

And then Euthalia fell. She plunged into the pool and instinctively twisted to find the surface—but she was suddenly so near the einherjar, and she was floating just above Odin, and she felt she could reach out and touch him.

She did.

The water shifted around her, becoming air, and she fell hard to the packed earth behind the one-eyed god. She scrambled to her feet, looking around at the ranks of Æsir and Vanir and einherjar.

The einherjar had formed a shield-wall, overlapping each shield with the next in line to form a sturdy barricade, and they beat their spears and swords upon the wood and iron as they shouted defiance and taunts to the approaching Jötnar. Some gods joined their line, linking shields, while others stood alone, ready to make independent stands or charges.

Someone shouted and pointed at a massive black shape rushing along the coast, sweeping toward the nail-ship Naglfar. A shout went up along both opposing lines, one cheering and one despairing, as Fenrir came near enough to be recognized.

He ran directly to Naglfar and reared up, putting his front paws on the side of the ship and stretching inside to greet his father. Nari shrank from his terrifying half-brother and the memory of a wolf tearing him apart, but Fenrir and Loki spoke for a moment, and then Fenrir turned his great head toward the Asgardian line and curled his lips into a snarl.

Euthalia, standing on her toes behind the shield-wall, felt her stomach shift within her as the wolf turned his malice on them. The warriors in the shield-wall, trained and seasoned though they were, shifted their weight and changed their grips on their sweat-slicked hafts and handles.

"I will take the wolf!" shouted a familiar voice, and Euthalia's heart sank. She turned and saw Vidar, his face safely hidden within his helmet, pointing with his sword. "I will take the wolf! He is mine!"

Vidar, no! But there was nothing she could do.

Odin rode Sleipnir down the shield-wall, shouting instructions and encouragement. The two ravens followed, grim reminders that death came close this day and it would be victory if ravens remained to feast on the dead. If Loki's warriors prevailed, not even scavengers would remain.

The clattering of weapons on shields began to synchronize, falling into a steady pounding rhythm. Thor raised Mjöllnir to the sky and bellowed defiance. Across from them, Euthalia recognized the enormous rock-colored figure of Angrboda, wielding a massive tree like a club.

The rhythmic pounding increased in speed, building to a crescendo which would ultimately launch the wall of warriors forward, intent on destroying their opponents for the survival of the very worlds.

And then the sea foamed like a maelstrom opening without warning, and a towering form rose out of the water. Jörmungandr opened his mouth to bare his fangs, swaying above the waves, and writhed forward onto the rocky shore.

The pounding of weapons on shields faltered and broke. Euthalia's heart sank.

"For Odin and Asgard!" roared Thor, his voice cutting through all other sounds. "I swear by my hammer Mjöllnir that you are my opponent this day, and you shall fall!" He leapt into his two-wheeled cart, drawn by two powerful goats, and drove directly for the serpent.

A cry went up as he charged, and the defenders of Asgard recovered and started forward. Battle closed.

Thor met Jörmungandr as he promised, swinging his hammer as the serpent struck at his cart and knocking the great mouth enough aside to spare his goats. Fenrir howled his fury and leapt forward, and Euthalia's heart throbbed in her throat as Vidar raced to meet him.

And then the lines were closing and she could see nothing but a clash of bodies and weapons like seas crashing together, a tumult of shouting and weapons clanging. She hung back—she had neither shield nor spear, she was useless, no, worse than useless, she was responsible for it all.

Lightning cracked as Thor and Jörmungandr struck one another, and the battlefield opened about the two of them as they entered combat.

Euthalia covered her ears and ducked, looking desperately around for Vidar. If she could reach him—if she could help him—Fenrir was so large, so powerful, so dangerous—

A coil of Jörmungandr's long body rose and fell across the stony field, crushing warriors of both armies.

Something seized Euthalia from behind, twisted in her dress and apron and hair, and hauled her upward. She pulled against it, stretching toward the battle and Vidar, but something close and muffling and invisible pressed around her face and eyes, smothering her, so that she gasped for air and choked on water.

She burst into air, streaming water, and was deposited beside the silver pool. The Nornir looked down on her with concern.

"The well of destiny is not for mortals," cautioned Verdandi. "Nor most immortals."

Euthalia coughed and spat water. "Was that—I was there—the fighting—"

Skuld shook her head. "You were not there," she said. "You only saw."

"But I—I felt—"

"You saw what will be."

In the pool, a dark wolf leapt into the air and seized the sun in its jaws, savaging it as it fell again to earth. The light dimmed as it tore pieces away from the whole.

Hot tears slipped onto Euthalia's cheeks to mingle with the pool's water. "Please," she said. "Undo me. Remove my thread, if that's what it takes—take me out of the weaving. Save Vidar, save everything."

"You cannot barter with Fate," scolded Skuld gently. "What we decide must be, must be. What you decide is what you do with what is yours."

"And Ragnarok? Is that what must be?"

"It must be," Skuld answered, holding Euthalia's eyes. "It is a debt. The future must be paid. But there are ways and ways to pay a debt."

Euthalia shook her head. "Tell me clearly—can this be stopped?"

"No," Skuld answered. "The future must be paid."

"But it need not be paid now," said Verdandi.

They watched her, waiting. The words caught at Euthalia. "Then it can be put off?" she asked breathlessly.

"It is not hard to change the pattern of a cloth not yet woven."

"How can I stop it?"

Urd smiled, calculating. "How was it started?"

Guilt lanced Euthalia once more. "I released Loki."

They waited.

"Then I must—I cannot bind him again! Even if I wanted to, I could not—I don't have that kind of power."

"Come with me," Urd said. "Let us speak of power."

Verdandi stooped and dipped a cup into the pool, and then she and Urd turned and started away along one towering root. Euthalia followed. Skuld remained where she was.

They walked along the gentle undulations of the root, turning so that the pool fell in and out of view behind them. Euthalia looked up and saw that rows of wooden slats hung from the root of the tree, each etched with runes. She could not read them, but she knew they must be powerful talismans—no, not talismans, for it was not the piece of wood itself which was the charm, but what it represented. The runic words it held.

Urd pointed at one as they passed. "This one has Freyja's name," she said. She traced the runes. "Do you read them?"

Euthalia shook her head.

Urd pointed elsewhere on the wood. "This is the name Odur," she said, as if that explained something. If it did, Euthalia did not understand it.

Verdandi crossed her arms. "How do they know you? The Æsir and the Vanir?"

Euthalia still did not understand. "I am Vidar's wife."

Urd shook her head. "No—what do they know you as? What did you present to them first?"

"What? I told a story." She had told the story of Prometheus, had tried to entertain Odin and the others with only moderate success. She had not guessed how that story would haunt her later.

"Exactly," said Verdandi, pointing a rune-carved fingernail at Euthalia. "They know you as a storyteller, a songweaver. They knew you first for your skill."

"And?"

"Is that how they think of Freyja?"

Euthalia started to protest that this meant nothing, but insight came to her. "No—no, they don't. But she is very skilled. She can work very powerful magic." Even to curse a god.

"How does Freyja present herself? What is her pride?"

Euthalia's breath caught. *I am beautiful. I am desired. Men desire me, men strive for me, and that is more than you can say.*

Urd nodded at Euthalia's expression, understanding before she spoke. "She was not always like this," she said. "But after the war, when she feared her own power—she found the simple magic of allure to be easier. Easier to wield, and easier to blame. She did not realize the trap it would become."

"She should have avoided beauty?" asked Euthalia faintly.

"What? No!" snapped Verdandi. "Have we said beauty or desire are wrong? Does not your husband think you beautiful? Do you not lie with him and take hot pleasure in each other's touch?"

"But...."

"But he knew you first for yourself and he loves you for that. Not for the gap between your legs, nor the hope of it."

Euthalia was silent.

Urd smiled to soften the bite of Verdandi's words. "Freyja was once loved and respected for her skill. It was fear which changed her." She paused. "And grief."

"Grief?" echoed Euthalia.

Verdandi passed her the simple cup, half-filled with water. Euthalia looked into it, seeing nothing but water, and then closed her eyes and took a drink.

Instantly she saw Freyja, stumbling by night, her hair unkempt and her clothing muddy. She was sobbing, repeating one name over and over. "Odur," she wept. "Odur. Odur." Golden tears fell from her contorted face to the ground.

Euthalia opened her eyes and stared at Verdandi. "She loved him?"

The Norn gave her a sad smile and took the cup, and then she walked on ahead.

Euthalia looked at Urd, who shrugged. They continued down the row of wooden slats.

"That one has Vidar's name," Urd said casually. Her eyes flicked to Euthalia, and her manner was so light, so indifferent, that it felt anything but.

Euthalia turned her head and looked at the indicated wooden slat. She could not make out the meaning of the rigidly carved runes, much more than Vidar's name alone as they wrapped about the long surface. She reached out and touched it, and she looked tentatively at Urd.

Urd was examining her fingernails, tracing the runes there with the pad of her thumb, her eyes carefully away from Euthalia. Verdandi had gone ahead, not waiting for them.

Euthalia grasped the slat and pulled it free. It was half the length of her forearm and about as wide, and carved runes lay thick over it. She tucked it into the torso of her dress.

Urd seemed to come to herself. "Oh, Urdarbrunnr is this way," she said. "Follow me."

They started again, and Urd wove back and around until they came again to the silver pool and the two waiting Nornir. Euthalia glanced around, trying to determine if this were a trick or illusion, but all seemed as it should.

"This is Urdarbrunnr," said Urd, indicating the pool. "The well of destiny."

The pool lay quiet, but Euthalia did not look into it, not wanting to see Ragnarok raging.

"The water is an endless cycle," said Urd, dipping her fingers into the pool. The runes in her fingernails seemed to brighten. "It has already fallen and pooled here. It is the past. But it is drawn into the tree Yggdrasill, where it becomes the present."

"The past always shapes the present," said Verdandi. "But it does not enslave it."

"We can still make the present," breathed Euthalia, a faint sense of relief coming to her though she felt no nearer to solving the puzzle. The knowledge that it *might* be solved was enough. "Then fate—fate is not absolutely destined?"

"The dew falls again," said Skuld. She touched a leaf, jarring silvery droplets into the pool. "The present will become the past, and it will shape what becomes the present."

Euthalia nodded. "But are we not bound to the past?"

Urd looked at her and turned away. She took several large stones from the ground and set them among the sloping smaller roots of the great tree. "If I pour water above these stones," she said, "the water must flow around them, yes?"

She demonstrated, dipping a pitcher into the pool and pouring steadily above the highest stone. Water ran smoothly about the stone, splitting into two streams which met briefly a handsbreadth below before separating again around the next two stones.

Euthalia nodded. "Yes, of course."

Urd handed her the pitcher. Euthalia hesitated and then mimicked her action, pouring a thin stream above the stones and watching the water take the same path through the already-dampened earth.

"And you might think that, since those stones have already been placed, there is no possibility of changing the water's flow." Verdandi reached out and lifted Euthalia's wrist, stopping the fall of water. Euthalia looked at her, and the silver-blue eyes gripped her more tightly than any chain. "But you choose where to pour the water."

Euthalia stared at her.

Verdandi shifted Euthalia's hand a few inches to the side. Euthalia tipped the pitcher again, and water ran out onto a stone, splashing outward in a spray over the roots and stones and showering the ground.

Euthalia took a shaking breath. "Then it can be changed," she said. "It can all be changed."

"This is magic," said Skuld. "There is great magic, in the weaving that we do. But there is small magic in the daily choices of every living thing. The past is the stones in the path of the water, but you choose where to pour the water."

Euthalia nodded. "The great magic," she said. "How do we perform the great magic?"

Verdandi smiled indulgently. "You do not," she said. "That is the task of the Nornir, and occasionally of those who practice seidr. It is not for the untrained."

"But I have to change it," Euthalia said. "I have to break Vidar's curse. I have to stop Ragnarok. It is my fault Loki was freed, my fault they are fighting. The gods are dying, and it is my doing."

Urd looked to her fellow Nornir, and for a long moment they seemed to be sharing a thought without any regard for Euthalia waiting anxiously beside them.

"Please," Euthalia begged. "Not for my sake. For theirs. All of them. Please."

"You set Loki free to lead an assault upon Asgard," said Urd.

"And I must stop Loki," Euthalia agreed. "But tell me how."

Verdandi turned a palm upward. "Move a stone."

"What?"

"Find a rock to set in Loki's way."

Skuld spoke next. "What does Loki desire above all else?"

"Revenge," Euthalia answered without hesitation. "Ragnarok."

"What does he want above revenge?"

She thought. Honor? No, she could not imagine it. Sigyn? No, he had shoved her aside even when she had borne the venom for him.

His sons. Loki had been genuinely grieved to see them destroyed and genuinely glad to find Nari again in Hel's domain. "His sons! Sigyn's sons!"

"Odin bound him with a son," Urd said. "So will you."

Euthalia tried to bend her mind around the Norn's words. A son.... "Nari is with him, and I don't know—Narfi." She looked around at them. "I believe Narfi is not dead," she said. "But where do I find him?"

One corner of Verdandi's lips curved in a cool half-smile. "Why do you ask questions to which you already know the answer?"

"Because I do not know the answer," Euthalia answered, frustrated. "Or I do not know that I know the answer. Can't you tell me?"

Urd answered. "Why do you believe Narfi is not dead?"

"I did not see him in Helheim," answered Euthalia. "Hel kept Nari, knowing him for her half-brother, but she did not have Narfi with them."

Urd nodded. "You did not see Narfi in Eljudnir."

Euthalia started to speak and then stopped. Urd had not repeated Euthalia's words. "Then... then he is not in Eljudnir, but he is in Helheim?"

The three regarded her patiently.

"Then he—oh!" She gasped, bringing her hands to her mouth in horror. "I have seen him!"

Skuld nodded. "You know him."

"I do now." Euthalia swallowed. "I nearly did then. I thought—I thought he was Fenrir, coming through the Corpse-Fence. But of course, they are brothers, and even more alike now."

"Then you know how you will try to stop Loki," said Verdandi.

Euthalia was keen on their slippery words now. "Try?" she repeated. She looked at Skuld. "Only try?"

Skuld gestured to the pool, the damp stones, the roots, the tree. "It is a cycle," she said, "But a complex one, with many fine details and intricate pieces. And the debt must be paid."

Euthalia closed her eyes. "I have nothing to lose," she said resolutely. "Ragnarok will come, now or later. If I do nothing, it will come now. If I fail, it will come now. If I succeed, I save us all."

"Until Ragnarok comes," agreed Skuld with depressing accuracy. "But safe for now."

Euthalia nodded firmly. "Then I must find Loki."

"First you must find Narfi," Verdandi reminded.

"But how can I return to Helheim?"

"Did you not come with a valkyrja?" asked Urd pointedly.

Euthalia looked back to where she had left Hildr. "Will she take me?"

"Considering what you mean to stop," said Skuld, "I think she will."

Verdandi gripped Euthalia's hands, pressing them in hers. "You choose where to pour the water."

CHAPTER 31

Euthalia went back to Hildr. "Can you carry me to Helheim?" she asked. "I must find Garm, the hound of Hel."

"The one that lives near Nágrindr?" asked Hildr.

Euthalia was surprised. "You know him?"

"And how would a valkyrja not know the world of the dead?" asked Hildr with a smile. "Yes, I can take you there. Let's go."

And Euthalia clung again to the armored woman as they were carried up, up Yggdrasill and into the nine worlds and to Helheim. They galloped over the bridge, and Euthalia was nearly relieved to see the river of battle beneath them. She had faintly worried that they would have gone to choose sides at Ragnarok, and seeing them still in Niflheim gave her slim hope the final battle had not yet begun.

And then they came to Nágrindr, and Hildr drew the horse to a halt. Euthalia could hear the snarls coming from within the mound of earth. She slid from the horse and faced the battlement. "Narfi?"

The ground began to crumble, and she could see the signs of the unnatural gate opening. The snarls grew louder, and

Euthalia's stomach tightened. What if she and the Nornir were wrong, and this was not Narfi at all? What if it had been Narfi, but he had lost all his humanity and could no longer recognize his name or an effort to help him?

"Narfi?"

The dark head burst from the earth, teeth flashing, and Euthalia noticed Hildr was beside her with sword drawn.

"Narfi!" Euthalia called, shrinking back. "Narfi, wait."

The shoulders worked free of the earth and Narfi lunged. Hildr jerked her sword to readiness. But Narfi was checked midair and fell backward, snarling.

The crack in the earthen mound split and the gate opened, and Narfi pulled against the chain which held him back from the women. His ears were flat against his skull, his teeth fully bared. Euthalia wanted to weep for him. "Oh, Narfi," she said. "Don't you know yourself?"

"Sing to him," said Hildr.

Euthalia looked at her. "What?"

"You are a weaver of songs, yes? And the skein of his life has been twisted. Sing to him and unknot him."

Euthalia doubted her ability could meet such a task, but there was nothing to lose and everything to gain. She swallowed. "I knew your mother," she began, her voice not a melody, but the commanding singsong of a skald opening a saga. "We dined together in the longhouse of Odin, in the Hall of the Fallen, Valhöll."

The snarls subsided to a long growl, as the wolf tried to decide what this intruder was doing.

"I knew your father," Euthalia continued. "He too dined in the Hall of the Fallen, and he spoke to all the gods, pulled all their beards, named all their faults."

The wolf's ears flicked forward and back.

"I knew you when you walked on two legs." Euthalia clenched her fists and forced her voice to steady. "I saw you bend beneath Odin's word, I heard your bones twist and shape by his curse, and I watched what was done. I saw Nari bite his captor's wolf-joint, and I saw him run, and I saw Sigyn weep as her children became wolves and the food of wolves, and—"

The wolf's growl stopped, and the golden almond-shaped eyes became round with recalled horror and comprehension. He stared at Euthalia with a disturbingly childlike expression of shock and regret and shame.

"And I have seen your brother," she went on, holding his nearly-human eyes. "I have seen him sit in a place of honor beside the sister he did not know, the lady of the deep, the Lie-Father's daughter. I have held him in my arms and I have seen him embraced by his father the Smith of Lies."

She was not being kind to Loki, but she felt it was important not to lie in a song meant to restore the truth of Narfi's mind. And surely Narfi must have known, must have heard the stories of what his father did throughout Asgard.

The wolf's ears sagged—not now the flat fierce warning of battle, but of hurt and despair.

Euthalia took a breath and knelt, opening her arms. "Narfi," she said. "Let me take you to your brother."

Narfi stepped into the limit of his chain, pressing against the collar, and she leaned forward to embrace him, keenly aware of how exposed her throat was and how little wolves might like being grasped about the neck.

But Narfi was not a wolf, not entirely and not now.

Euthalia lifted her head from the dark fur, wiping away tears, and looked around. She did not see the woman who had been at the gate before. Perhaps she had gone with Hel and Loki and the others. "How can we free him?" she asked, pulling at the chain.

Hildr gave her a flat look and took an axe from her belt. She lay the chain flat against a hard patch and swung the long-handled axe with enough power to drive the fractured link partly into the ground as it gave with a metallic *chink*.

"Where do we take him?" she asked, holstering the axe.

Euthalia looked at Narfi. Loki was not the only one grieving him. "The cave in Midgard," she said. "The one where they bound Loki. Do you know it?"

Hildr shook her head. "But I can find it."

"His mother Sigyn is there. And she is Loki's wife—she may have some idea of how to stop him." Though it seemed Loki would not stop for her, not by the way he had cast her aside upon being freed. Would Loki be angry to see her? It seemed wiser not to bring them together—not at first.

More, it seemed unwise to confront Loki before all the Jötnar he had gathered to make his attack. She could not ask him to abandon his assault before his army of destroyers; pride would prevent him from agreeing even if she could sway him. She must get him away from the Jötnar, bring him to Narfi.

"I will go ahead myself," Euthalia said. "Take Narfi to his mother, and I will bring Loki there. If I can."

CHAPTER 38

Naglfar was beached on the stony shore, nails against pebbles and dried bones, and Loki's army spread out from it like blood.

Loki sat among the Jötnar, running a long whetstone against the edge of a sword. The venom scars showed dark against his face. The giant Angrboda crouched beside him, cradling an uprooted oak tree with most of the branches torn away—the sight chilled Euthalia, for she had seen this tree-club in the well's vision—and other Jötnar of all shapes and sizes were clustered in groups around them, talking or jeering or laughing. They hardly glanced at Euthalia as she approached.

Loki noticed, and his mouth curved into a crooked smile. "Oh, little butterfly," he said, lifting the sword to examine the unnaturally perfect edge. "What question brings you to me this time?"

"Will you stop?" The words escaped before she could consider them.

Loki chuckled. "No."

He regarded the sword and, seeing Euthalia's eyes touch it, turned it to display it better. "She is a fine thing, isn't she?"

Runes lay in the steel like smoke within ice, fading into and out of sight as the firelight played over the surface. The sword was unblemished, the hilt intricate with knotwork and tiny images Euthalia was not near enough to make out.

"Her name is Laevatein," Loki said with obvious pride. "Wand of Wounds and Destruction." He rotated the sword, letting light run down the blade like water. "I forged her myself. You thought I was a smith only of lies, didn't you? I forged her in Niflheim and there is no weapon like her, nor shall there ever be."

"You created a sword for the ending of the world."

He chuckled. "If a thing is worth doing, it is worth doing well."

Euthalia straightened and met his eyes. "Loki, stop this attack. You will destroy everything, all the worlds. And you will not survive this, there is no profit in it for you, and—"

"Ah, you have been to the Nornir," he said. "And you think that makes you knowledgeable? Powerful? We have all seen the end, my fragile little butterfly. How did you think Odin knew his danger? He fears Fenrir because he knows Fenrir will kill him. Thor, that bold and stupid goatsack, knows Jörmungandr will be his death. And you think to stop me by telling me what I already know?"

Euthalia clenched her fists. "There are so many lives," she said. "Lives which had nothing to do with you, or your humiliation, or your pain, or...." She faltered, trying to think of his cherished wrongs.

Loki chuckled. "Do you think this is for revenge?"

She stopped and looked at him, surprised.

He shook his head. "You foolish little storyteller, thinking everything has a tidy reason you can explain away in a clever turn of phrase." He lowered the sword and came toward her, very close, and she fought the impulse to retreat. "Well, perhaps it is a simple reason, after all. Think, little butterfly. What am I?"

Euthalia licked her lips. "You are Jötunn."

"Yes," Loki sighed with nearly sensual pleasure. "I am Jötunn. I am a destroyer. It is my nature. And all that they have done to me is my justification—but it is not my reason." He grinned, his narrow tongue visible between his teeth. "You seek to trap me in your puny, narrow, *human* reasons. But I am Jötunn. I am a destroyer. And that is all the reason I need."

He turned back and took up his work again, cheerful. A little distance away, Angrboda raised the stripped tree overhead and smashed it into the ground, scattering rock and bone.

Hope slipped away from Euthalia. "Loki," she pleaded. "You can stop this."

"Yes," he agreed. His eyes met hers, and he grinned. "But why would I?"

This was her chance. Her only chance. Their only chance. "Would you kill your own son?"

"Ha!" barked Loki. "My son is already dead, or didn't you see him sitting with Hel in Eljudnir?"

"Narfi," she said. "Narfi is not dead."

Loki's hands slowed, and he did not look at her. "I saw Narfi turn."

"He turned, but he did not die."

Loki set aside the whetstone and sword and faced Euthalia, and then he seized her upper arms and pressed her hard into the planked side of the nail-ship. "Where is my son?" he demanded.

For a moment Euthalia couldn't speak, confronted so close with his dangerous eyes. This near, she could see all the mounds and cracks of the venom scars over his face, could see the pinprick scars where the dwarfs had once sewn his mouth shut. She gulped and answered, "With Sigyn."

For a moment Loki did not move, and she wondered whether the mention of his wife had caught at his heart or infuriated him. At last he set Euthalia down and released her. "Narfi is alive?" The muscles of his jaw worked visibly. "With her in the—the cave?"

She nodded. "I did not know where else to look for her. She could not travel back to Asgard without help." Help Loki had not offered.

He was silent.

"At least go and see him," she urged, hoping she did not press too hard and break the fragile spell. "At least speak to him before you kill him and destroy his world. He thinks you abandoned him."

"No!" said Loki, and the word seemed to surprise him as much as her. "I did not."

"You went to Helheim and greeted his brother," Euthalia said, pitching her voice with faint accusation, "and left him behind there. What else could he think?"

Loki's eyes shifted. "He was there?"

"He was. Hel did not know him. He was not in Eljudnir."

Loki's mouth flattened, and he looked at Naglfar and the assembled army. "I will go to my son," he said. "But I will not give up my day of destruction."

Euthalia did not answer. One battle at a time. Loki's flow had shifted about the first rock.

Loki made some sort of gesture which seemed to rip a hole in the air, revealing a passage through thin air where there should have been nothing. Its walls sparkled like a geode's cavern, but with all the colors of the rainbow, brilliant and penetrating. He stepped into the Bifröst passage, and Euthalia leapt after him, anxious that he not leave without her.

He seemed neither surprised nor displeased at her hasty following, but he did not reach a hand to her as the opening sealed behind them. The colors blurred into a dazzling and disorienting swirl, and they fell. Euthalia shielded her eyes, squeezing them closed, and then the sensation of falling slowed.

She felt ground beneath her feet, and she opened her eyes to see the mouth of the Midgard cave.

Loki snorted. "Is this what it looks like?" he said dismissively. "I had forgotten, if ever I knew. What a dull place." He went inside.

Euthalia followed.

She nearly knew the way by now, hands outstretched for the stalactites and stalagmites she knew were there. Loki did not seem to feel his way nor falter. Perhaps he could see in the dark.

When they came to the broken stalagmites, lit by an oil lamp, he hesitated only for a heartbeat. And then he looked around, ignoring the scarred floor and the serpent still writhing in its place and shouted, "Narfi!"

There was a sudden scrabble of sound from the dark, and a wolf streaked into the circle of light and plunged toward Loki. He bent and caught the animal effortlessly, his muscles bunching beneath the onslaught of weighty wolf. Narfi pressed into his father, hard and still. Loki put his face into the animal's fur.

Behind the wolf came Sigyn, more slowly but with the same anxious expression.

Narfi must have felt his father tense, for he wriggled free and dropped to the cavern floor. Sigyn and Loki faced each other.

"I stayed with you." Sigyn's voice trembled but did not give way. "I never left you—only to pour out the bowl and rush back to you. I never left you."

Loki shook his head. "You think you are at the center of this?" His voice was surprisingly gentle. "I was bound, and now I am free. It has nothing to do with you."

"It does!" Sigyn answered sharply. "Because I am here, and your son is here, and you are not here. You mean to go out and destroy our world, all the worlds, all when you could stay here with us." Her eyes blazed. "You are going to kill our child!"

That caught Loki. He stared at her, speechless for perhaps the first time.

"If you do this," Euthalia said quietly, "Narfi will die. And not Narfi alone. Fenrir, and Jörmungandr, and Hel. Sleipnir. All of them."

Loki's lips parted, but he did not speak.

Sigyn put a hand on his forearm—light, resting, not holding. "Stay with us," she said softly, her eyes on his scarred face. "Please."

Loki looked at her hand, and then at her eyes, and for a long moment neither of them moved.

Euthalia found she was holding her breath. *Please. Please. Please.*

A cat meowed.

Sigyn looked up as Loki whirled into a battle crouch, his hand already grasping for Laevatein. But Freyja spoke a word, and he froze.

Euthalia stared as Freyja descended from her low wagon, driven straight into the cave. Two large cats sat before it in harness, unconcerned with the scene around them. One of them raised a paw to lick and wipe at its cheek in slow disdain or a mockery of tears.

Freyja's smile was equally catlike. "Lie-Smith."

Loki tried to speak through his gritted teeth.

"Oh, no," Freyja said. She gestured behind her, and Euthalia saw figures in the dark. Freyja raised a light from her wagon, illuminating a half dozen valkyrjur gathered about a wooden framework. Ropes stretched and sagged across it, swinging with weights, and they were busily working the shuttle—a loom, Euthalia realized. It was a loom, and they were weaving.

Loki's face screwed in furious concentration.

The valkyrjur together worked their weaving, winding bloody fingers over the weaving bar, the beating bar. The weights swung with their rapid motions and Euthalia realized with horror that they were heads, human heads, keeping tension as the women worked and bumping gently together. And it was not linen or wool which they worked, it was ropy intestines, pale and bloody and slick with yellow fat.

Sigyn was locked in place as if a spell held her too, but it was not their magic. "No," she breathed. "Not again."

Freyja glanced behind her. "Is it ready?"

"It is ready," answered one.

"Now," said Freyja.

The valkyrjur moved, leaving the loom and splitting across the cavern. Two seized Sigyn and Euthalia and pulled them away from Loki, setting them against a wall and a long stalactite. One, Euthalia saw, was already pinning Narfi in place with a threatening spear to his back. Others with Freyja caught up the rigid Loki and flung him down onto the broken stalagmites.

"No!" shrieked Sigyn, lunging against her valkyrja.

The sound or the movement or the place seemed to break Loki free, and he wrenched and struggled against the armored women pinning him. But they were already binding him, winding pale tissue about him. The trapped snake hissed at their struggle, and Loki screamed as the venom struck him.

Sigyn fought, but she was no match for an armored shield-maiden, and she fell sobbing against her captor. Euthalia tried to push free. "No!"

"Euthalia! Why?"

Euthalia blinked, recognizing the woman who held her. "Hildr?"

Hildr's face bore no shame, only confusion. "You wished to stop Loki from opening Ragnarok," she said. "Now we do that. The world is saved."

Loki howled in agony.

The valkyrjur moved away from the Jötunn and the snake, regarding their work.

Freyja laughed and straddled Loki, looking down upon his torture. "Mock me now, Lie-Smith," she challenged as he writhed and contorted between her thighs. "Mock me now."

He shook his face clear of dripping venom and grinned at her. "Still like a she-goat in a herd of rams."

Freyja's face twisted and she slapped him hard. She cried out and jerked her hand back, shaking burning venom from it and cradling it to her chest. Loki laughed.

Freyja snapped an order, and the valkyrjur started toward their loom. Sigyn dashed forward, snatching up the abandoned bowl and extending it over Loki's head. He gasped and relaxed trembling onto the stone.

Freyja stopped and smiled upon Euthalia. "Don't look so distraught, little Greek," she said smugly. "Nor surprised. The valkyrjur are all my handmaidens, and it was you who brought me the flesh of Loki's flesh, the skin of Jörmungandr to bind him anew. And now Ragnarok is forestalled and all is well." She inclined her head toward Loki's prison-bed. "All is as it was."

Euthalia swallowed. "Vidar came to me."

Freyja's smile became a mask.

"We love one another, and we will love one another regardless of your curse," Euthalia said. "I know now it was you."

Freyja's mouth twisted. "Who told you that?" she asked sourly.

"Loki. And I believed him," Euthalia added quickly. "He does not always lie, not when the truth serves him better."

Freyja glanced toward the wracked body and gave a tiny shrug. "He is well-served now." She started forward.

"I know something else as well," Euthalia said. "I know Odur left you."

Freyja went rigid and cold, an icy frost in the shape of a goddess. "What?" It was not a question.

"I know your husband Odur left you, and you go out at times to seek him," Euthalia said. She kept her voice soft, not sharing her knowledge with the valkyrjur. "I have heard you crying through the worlds."

Freyja opened her mouth but said nothing, torn between shock and shame and fury, unable to react lest she betray her shame to her proud shield-maidens.

Euthalia held her eyes. "I hope you find him," she said evenly. "And I hope you are reunited with him."

Freyja stared at her, lips shaping a word which never quite came, and then she strode back to her low wagon and called to her cats. They turned and leapt forward, and the goddess swept out of the cave.

The valkyrjur followed, but for Hildr. She watched Euthalia, waiting.

Euthalia raised a finger to her, requesting a moment. Then, taking a breath, she went to stand beside Loki and Sigyn.

Loki spat at her and launched into a stream of accusatory invective as acidic as the venom dripping over him.

Euthalia ignored him. It was lies; it did not hurt her. She looked at Sigyn. "Will you come?"

Sigyn looked at the bowl and at Loki, and she shook her head.

"But..." He had shoved her away, had been willing to kill her with the others in Ragnarok. He had hesitated only for his children.

Sigyn shook her head again. "I stayed with him," she said. "I will stay with him now." She looked at him. "I love him."

Loki smiled at her, tenderness creasing the scars. And Euthalia's blood chilled as she watched them. He needed Sigyn, needed her desperately, and he gave her that tender smile, that dangling tidbit to lure her to stay. Was it a lie? Did he even know himself if it were a lie? And when he was released again, when Ragnarok could not be stayed any longer....

She touched Sigyn's shoulder. "Come with me."

Sigyn shook her head. "I'm sure." She hesitated, and then she met Euthalia's eyes. "I know. But I will stay."

Euthala nodded slowly. She turned away.

Sigyn stopped her with a word. "Wait—take care of Narfi for me?"

Euthalia followed her eyes to the wolf, watching them from the edge of the lamplight. But his wide eyes were less intelligent, less understanding than they had been. He was slipping.

Sigyn understood. Tears slipped down her cheeks, and she rubbed her cheek against her shoulder as she held the bowl steady. "He may not be himself," she said, her voice cracking. "Maybe never. But please, just make sure he's safe."

Euthalia embraced her, careful not to jostle the bowl. "Of course I will."

"Tell Vidar I'll see him in the end," Loki said. "But oh, you won't see him, will you?"

She looked down at him. "He came to me today," she said evenly. "To pull me from Hel's hall. I will see him tonight in our home."

Her answer frustrated Loki. He managed a sneering grimace. "How you must hate me now."

She shook her head. "I pity you."

It was the worst truth she could have said. Loki screamed obscenities after her until she had followed Hildr all the way to the mouth of the cave, where they mounted and rode away.

CHAPTER 39

Euthalia sat in her wooden house, wrapped in the bearskin she had been given on the boat so long ago. She faced the door and waited, watching the light fade from the chinks in the walls and the rawhide-covered windows.

He came in the dark.

He knocked at the door, asking permission to enter. She called, "Come." There was no one else in her empty village, and no one who would be coming so late.

He opened the door and stood silhouetted in the frame, a blacker mass against the starry night behind him. "May I enter?"

"I have just said so," Euthalia said. "And besides, it is your house." His hesitation worried her.

He stepped inside, closing the door behind him and working the wooden latch more thoroughly than it needed. "I was glad—today—Euthalia, love, I should have told you. From the beginning. I should have asked for your patience and understanding rather than your obedience."

"I should have respected your wish even when I didn't understand it," she said, "as I could see it was so important to you. I should have asked you again rather than believing another."

He crossed the room and knelt beside her trunk-seat. "Forgive me for not trusting you?"

"Of course I do." She kissed him, and when he lingered she pulled away. "And you—do you forgive me for not trusting you?"

"You know I—"

"And for freeing Loki and opening Ragnarok and nearly bringing about the end of all things?"

He hesitated. "You sound as if you do not want my forgiveness."

"That's not true," Euthalia said, and her voice grew tight with her stomach. "I do want it. I want it badly. But I need to know that you forgive me for everything, because—because it's a lot. And I couldn't bear to think that you might kiss me now and later, in months or years to come when you are angry, you might hold it against me. That you might secretly resent me for what I have done. And it would not be without reason, I know, but I—but I want to know if you forgive me."

Vidar remained silent a moment, and Euthalia's heart sank. Her throat closed and tears stung her eyes, despite her best admonitions that she could understand perfectly well, that she had no right to expect forgiveness for an error which had nearly cost the world itself.

"It is a fair question," he said, and she caught her breath. "I think it is one which deserves consideration, as when I think on it, I see I too would want to be certain of my lover's forgiveness and love."

Euthalia nodded, even knowing he couldn't see her in the dark.

"But Euthalia, I cannot blame you any more than I can blame Loki, or Baldr, or my father Odin, or any other of them. You never acted in malice, and often you acted in kindness, thinking to do good by your actions, and it was others who twisted them. So even if I wished to blame you, I could not."

Her heart began to beat again. "Then you forgive me for all of it?"

"I forgive you as wholly as you forgive me," he said, and she could hear the smile in his voice. "Is that enough?"

"It is more than enough!" she answered.

He leaned toward her, but she placed a hand on his chest to stop him. Then she caught his hands and guided them toward the wooden piece in her lap. "I was not sure I could break this myself," she said. "I would prefer it we tried it together."

Vidar's fingers wrapped around the slat, felt across the runes carved into its surface. His fingers tightened about the wooden piece and Euthalia's hands on it. "Yes," he said. "Let's."

He lifted the wooden slat, his hands against hers, and snapped it down sharply over his bent knee. It splintered and came apart, dropping from their hands to the floor.

Euthalia thought she might taste the heart pounding high in her throat. "Did it—"

Vidar placed a finger against her lips, signaling her to wait. And then she heard the scrape of flint and saw a spark jump. She caught her breath and could not release it.

After a few tries the light caught, and Vidar lifted the filtered lamp and set it to one side, illuminating both of them. The yellow light fell over his broad-planed face, shadowing beneath his beard, sparkling in his eyes.

He was handsome.

She grasped his face in her hands, feeling, savoring, claiming him. She pressed the smooth, healthy flesh, the firm bones, the thick eyebrows. She ran her hands through his dark hair and kissed his light eyes and devoured him in love.

"I would love you even if I could not see you," she breathed. "I went to the end of the world for you."

He chuckled, embarrassed. "And I would love you if I could never look upon you," he answered. "But I will confess that I do greatly enjoy looking upon you."

She wrapped the bearskin about the two of them, and in the lamplight they kissed and touched and loved, gazing upon one another as if afraid they would disappear in an eye-blink. Outside, an owl called over their wooden house, and the unbroken moon passed overhead with cool, uninterrupted light.

THE MYTHS

There is a great deal of knowledge we simply don't have about Norse mythology, due to the fragmented and filtered versions we have recorded. (See my blog posts on the subject at www.LauraVAB.com.) In several places I have chosen to be somewhat flexible in interpretation or have opted to use a later (and thus better-known) version rather than an earlier (and probably more accurate) telling of a particular scene or story, as in the death of Baldr. I have done this mostly where the accounts we have are in conflict, and I have tried to remain more true to the aspects which are more generally agreed upon.

Áss is the word for a single god of the Æsir, and so should be the correct singular noun. While it is certain that Loki would embrace its usage were he aware of modern cultural connotations, I have elected not to use it to avoid its homophonic and visual disruption to the modern reader. As a writer, one doesn't want a dramatic scene interrupted by a prurient giggle-snort.

What has survived of Norse mythology is not clear on the sorting of the human dead to Valhöll, Folkvang (another of Freyja's halls), or Helheim, and indeed the punishment of the wicked in Helheim appears only in later sources. It appears in the older sources that they were all closely related or perhaps even synonymous at times. In this story, I have kept Valhöll in Asgard and used a later and less pleasant version of Helheim.

The story Bragi tells on Euthalia's first night in Valhöll, of the *seið-kona* magically concealing her son, is the story of Katla and Odd in the *Eyrbyggja saga*.

LOKI'S FAMILY

Narfi and Nari are the names given to Loki's unfortunate sons in the *Lokasenna*. In the *Prose Edda*, the names are generally translated "Váli and Nari or Narfi." There may also be some source or translation confusion with Odin's son Váli, conceived especially for the purpose of avenging Baldr's death by killing Hodr, so I have opted to use Narfi and Nari, to make them distinctly Loki's offspring. Likewise, sources differ on which brother became a wolf and which died; I have chosen to make Narfi the wolf, per the *Lokasenna*.

Almost nothing is known of Sigyn, other than that she held the bowl over bound Loki's head. I have elected to make her human in this story, and to give her an opinion on her obscurity.

Eisa and Einmyria are sometimes listed as additional children of Loki, daughters by another wife called Glut. However, this seems to be based on a confusion of Loki with another entity called Logi or Loge. A fourth child with Angrboda, devoured by the mother, is my own invention.

Garm is the hound of Hel, sometimes suggested to be an equivalent figure with Fenrir, though I have kept them separate in this story and instead opted to make him another of Hel's siblings.

THE OLD NORSE

Many of the names we know these entities by today are not original to their time and place. While they have largely been adapted to modern English alphabet and pronunciation, I have tried to preserve the original flavor where I thought it would not prove too disruptive to the reader (Baldr in place of Baldur, and Valhöll for Valhalla, for example).

I have listed here the original Old Norse (transliterated) and the most common modern adaptations. Definitions or explanations are included.

Ásgarðr – Asgard, the world of the Æsir

Baldr—Baldur, a son of Odin and Frigg

Bifröst—Bifrost, the rainbow road guarded by Heimdallr

einherjar—the dead chosen by Odin and the valkyries for Valhalla and the fight at Ragnarok

Folkvang—another hall belonging to Freyja

Gefjon—Gefion, an Æsir goddess

Glaðsheimr— Gladsheim

Heimdallr—Heimdal, a sharp-eyed Æsir god who guards the Bifröst

Höðr—Hodur or Hodr, a son of Odin and Frigg

Jörmungandr—Jormungand, also called the Midgard Serpent

Jötnar—plural of Jötunn

Jötunn—literally "devourers," often translated "giant" though the source material does not specify general unusual size and this may be conflation with the Greek Titans

Mjöllnir—Thor's magical hammer, forged by the dwarfs

Naglfar—Ship of the Dead

Nágrindr—Corpse-Fence

Niðavellir—Nildavellir, the dark dwelling place of the dwarfs

Óðinn—Odin, in later sources the chief god or "Allfather" of the Norse pantheon

seiðr—seidr, a form of magic associated strongly with weaving and women, used particularly for illusion, delusion, or other mental effects

Sessrúmnir—Freyja's hall

Skaði—Skathi or Skaldi, a Jötunn who married into the Æsir
Skíðblaðnir—Skithblathnir or Skidbladnir
Þórr—Thor, a son of Odin (and half-Jötunn)
þræll—thrall (slave)
Urðarbrunnr—Urdarbrunnr, the Well of Destiny (urðr, wyrd)
Urðr—Urd
Valhöll—Valhalla, the Hall of the Slain
Váli—Vali
Valkyrja, valkyrjur—Valkyrie, Valkyries
Verðandi—Verdandi
Víðarr—Vidar
Yggdrasill—Yggdrasil, the World Tree which holds all the
    worlds in its branches and Urdarbrunnr in its roots

Ευθαλία—Euthalia, a Greek name carrying the meaning of
    "well-blooming" or "flourishing." It is also the name of a
    genus of butterflies. The butterfly is the symbol of Psyche
    in Greek mythology, and thus a symbol for the soul in
    Western art. Psyche married the god Eros who forbade
    her to look upon him, and her midnight peek opened
    many tribulations for her before they were reunited.
Ῥαψῳδός—rhapsōidos or rhapsode, a stitcher of songs in
    ancient Greek

DISCUSSION GUIDE

Download a free guide for book club or discussion groups
at **http://bit.ly/2lA9ox5** with discussion prompts, reader
questions, and additional insights.

GET A FREE STORY

Go to **http://bit.ly/LauraVAB** to receive a free story as
well as sneak peeks, special discounts or advance offers, and
more.

And thank you for reading, and **please leave a review** for
The Songweaver's Vow. I read every one! and I'd love to hear
from you.

ABOUT THE AUTHOR

Laura VanArendonk Baugh is an award-winning writer of speculative fiction, mystery, and non-fiction. She lives in Indiana with two dogs and a prepper stash of emergency dark chocolate. Her works have earned numerous accolades, including 3-star ratings (the highest possible) on *Tangent*'s "Recommended Reading" list. Laura speaks professionally on a variety of topics, from animal behavior to folklore to writing to cosplay. Find her, get a free story, and read more about the research and background of this book and others at www.LauraVAB.com.

Made in the USA
Lexington, KY
07 August 2017